Give Me Str

A Story From The Rhymney Valley

Give Me Strength

A Story From The Rhymney Valley

Cari Glyn

Publish & Print
www.publishandprint.co.uk

"Dedicated to those men and women of an
ever distant past and an ever present place"

Funeral procession of Evan Thomas 1909

Prologue

A sonnet

Masters and men – bretheren – come gather round
Respectful homage to him pay this day
Who was our friend. He knew the 'better way'
And loved and lived it, heeding not the sound
Of petty human strife, but aye was found
In duty's path. Calm judgement, wisdom's way
He followed – love nor hate could make him stray.
(Oh! that such leaders may not more abound)
The scholar found him a trusty friend;
The collier with his grievance to him ran;
The worker and the workless to defend
He spent his strength – what more could mortal man?
Yonder – I see the valiant leader bend
And he who crowns him is the Son on Man

*Rev. T. Goshen Evans, Bargoed on the death of
Mr Evan Thomas CC miners' agent March 1909.*

This eulogy, written by the Anglican clergyman and printed in the Merthyr Express, gives a flavour of the times and represents the great esteem and respect given to the miners' agent by all sections of the community. The funeral of the late Mr Evan Thomas was reported in the newspapers in detail.

The thousands of mourners lining the streets included the mine workers he represented, waiting their turn to relay the coffin, carrying it on their shoulders over the rough terrain for the 3 mile journey. It was their opportunity to show their respect to the man they considered their leader.

A procession behind the coffin set out from the Federation offices in Bargoed via his family home to the cemetery of the historic Baptist chapel in Cefn Hengoed. It numbered 3000 and extended ¾ of a mile arranged as follows: the police force, fire brigade, MPs and church ministers, County Councillors, representatives of the Education Authorities, local bodies, district officers, executive of South Wales Miners' Federation (the Fed), delegates from the conference at Cardiff, the Sunday school class of the deceased with the bereaved family following behind in coaches. Crowds lined the streets and on passing the local boys' school in Pengam the school choir sang 'Lead kindly light'. Mr Evans had been ill for some time and had gone on a Nile cruise in an attempt to convalesce. During his long absence his deputy acted as the miners' agent and was elected to the post the following month. That man was Walter Lewis and this is where our story begins.

Chapter 1

Walter Lewis was about to close the front door behind him when he heard his wife, Elizabeth, call out from the back kitchen. He opened the door and watched as she bustled down the passage towards him, almost filling the whole width of it and holding out before her a small and neatly packed basket.

"You'd forget your own head," she said leaning forward to hand him the basket and was quite flustered when he gave her a quick peck on the cheek. "Get on with you." She flapped her hands and shooed him towards the door. "Now, you don't want to be late to meet that train. Every other person down the road will want to stop and bend your ear... even more so when they see you with that basket," she laughed. Walter noticed the added colour to her cheeks. She could still blush at any small sign of affection from him after fifteen years of marriage and six children.

"And what have we got here?" he asked poking a finger beneath the tea cloth covering the contents of the basket.

"Just a little light refreshment to offer the gentlemen and our visitor during your meeting at chapel this afternoon," she replied.

"Caviar and champagne?" he asked amused and in English - there being no Welsh equivalent he could think of.

"As if, the very shock of it. No, just some oatmeal biscuits and cordial. Although I did use the last stem ginger left over from Christmas for the biscuits and the cordial is homemade. It's this year's elderflower Dan picked. I hope it will do although I am sure Mrs Joby Jones will be by to put the kettle on for a cup of tea later. Now get going. I'll see you and Miah Thomas in time for supper. No later, mind you. And for goodness sake don't forget to tell Mrs Joby

5

Jones to dilute the cordial or it will be too sickly sweet," she said and closed the front door behind him.

Walter chuckled at the mild rebuke from his wife. The warm summer weather after several days of heavy showers and Lizzie's blushes all helped to make Walt feel truly blessed. The Lord was in his heaven and life was good he though, offering a silent prayer of thanks. There was a definite spring in his step, despite his heavy boots, as he set off across the road on his way through town to the railway station.

He had left the office early that Friday to meet Mr Nehemiah Thomas, Welsh Baptist minister and an old friend of the family. There was to be a meeting of local ministers and deacons representing the Rhymney Valley Baptist Union later that afternoon at the school room of the Hanbury Road English Baptist church in Bargoed. It was the newest and biggest Baptist chapel in the town seating over 1000.

Their purpose was to discuss the calendar of forthcoming events in the district after the very successful singing festival for Sunday schools in Hengoed last month; that and the inevitable, on-going problem of empty pulpits in the area. This latter issue had arisen in the aftermath of the religious revival in 1904/5 creating huge gains in the local congregations. Thus, in turn, began a frenzy of building work to accommodate expanding numbers. Three new chapels had opened all within a one-mile radius of their mother church which now occupied its permanent home in Hanbury Road. One of these new places of worship was in Pengam, another in Aberbargoed and the third a Welsh chapel in Bargoed for those who, like Walt, preferred to conduct their worship in the mother tongue.

Walt was to fulfil his usual role of secretary at the meeting and Miah Thomas had been invited to attend as a representative of the Baptist Union of Wales and to offer his specialised input on matters financial. This included new bursaries available for the training of married men for the ministry, fire insurance for chapels through the new Baptist insurance company and any other advice he may be called upon to offer. He had been kept especially busy over the past few years arranging loans through the Baptist Union of Wales for the construction of new chapel buildings.

Walt had seized on the opportunity of his old friend's visit to invite Miah to present the first ever certificates for Bible Knowledge to the senior scholars at the Sunday school at his chapel, the new Welsh Baptist Noddfa, the following day. This meant Miah Thomas was staying the night as a guest at his home, just like old times.

He had barely crossed the street in front of the house when, just to prove Elizabeth right, he heard his name called out. "Gwallt, how be bach?" It was old John Thomas, 80 if he was a day and one of the first applicants of the old age pension brought in by Lloyd George that year. Welsh is spoken by many in the town and old miners like John spoke little else. Walt loved his native language. It was spoken in the home and at chapel but, like many of his generation, he was fluent in English.

"Well, I see those builders are finished at last. Look as if they made a right mess of your place the last few weeks," said Old John. "I can't see the need of it myself, putting an extension on a grand new house like that for just one family" added the old man. Walt smiled at this rather blunt observation. As long as miners like John survived they would never let him forget his humble origins and get away with too many airs and graces.

Old John lived with his widowed daughter-in-law in a 3-storey house down the street opposite. There was also his grand-daughter and her husband, their three grown up children and they took in two lodgers besides. The improvement in the quality of new housing did not mean that wages for a mining family could still cover the rent and leave enough over for food and clothing, never mind support dependants such as the elderly. Besides, old habits die hard and many families like John's were still crowded into houses not intended for so many inhabitants to live in comfort.

"It made more sense than moving house again," replied Walt, "and we need the room so I don't get under Elizabeth's feet. We've had a gas stove and a geyser for the hot water put in too."

"Aye, 'spose we must keep the women happy. No more boiling kettles on the fire for Mrs Walter Lewis," said John. "Now then, I've been thinking, see boy, and I cannot for the life of me understand why you have decided to give a house a name. What's wrong with a number like all the others in the street? The post would arrive at 47 as readily as Ty Gwent or do you think it will look more fancy on the letterheads?" he added.

"Well, strange you should mention that. I'm just on my way now… heading to the printers… to put in my order for some personal headed stationery for Ty Gwent," said Walt. The old man looked a bit bemused by this reply, not sure if his leg was being gently tugged. "We must all try our best to improve our lot," added Walt, "with the help of the good Lord above."

"Pity the good Lord don't do a bit more like Mr Lloyd George has done with this old age pension," replied the old man rather sharply. "Aye well I can see you're on some important errand for the missus with that basket and won't keep you chopsing," he added, hoping to avoid a sermon after his elevation of the Liberal chancellor to the saviour of the elderly.

They both knew that John was heading for the public bar at the Capel Hotel for his usual pint and that Walt did not approve being teetotal and a staunch Baptist. Good Rhymney bitter was hardly what the five shillings a week old age pension was intended for. Inebriation automatically disqualified applicants for the state pension and it occurred to Old John that perhaps Mr Walter Lewis off the council Pension committee had the authority to revoke his pension application as readily as Mr Lloyd George had given him the right to apply in the first place. With a curt but polite good day, they went their separate ways at the crossroads; both intent on their disparate business.

Walt walked with purpose through the main street, staying to the pavement where possible to avoid the mud churned road after the recent rain. With busy shops on both sides with their awnings out wide, he negotiated the many shoppers and nodded and smiled good day while touching his cap to the ladies. By hurrying purposefully along he succeeded in not getting held up in conversation.

The town was always busy these days, the sign of new prosperity since the sinking of the mine. The attraction was the work and business opportunities that had brought many families to the area from near and far. Bargoed had become the centre for commerce and enterprise in the valley as well boasting the largest and most advanced deep mine in the area. Earlier that year Bargoed colliery had set a world record for the amount of coal raised in a 10 hour shift – more than four thousand tons.

Over the past decade Bargoed and its surrounding villages had expanded at a rate faster than the local services could adequately provide. Walt understood the problems far better than most. He had spent the last three years since moving to his new house in the town sitting on the local council for the parish of Gelligaer. Before that he had been councillor for Bedwellty parish across the river in Monmouthshire and had already given many years of faithful service to his local community, a role in which he took great pride.

Improvements in water supply, drainage and roads to keep up with the building of homes, shops and offices still occupied the greater part of the Gelligaer parish council's fortnightly evening meetings. But what progress had been made in providing new services had sadly lagged behind the building of new properties and this left the residents coping with floods after heavy rain due to the poor drainage. The roads were often impassable owing to the quantity of mud churned up by the passage of heavy goods wagons. The town wallowed in very insanitary conditions because of this in combination with the unsatisfactory collection of household waste by the scavenger. And the warm weather certainly did not help on that point even if it dried the roadways somewhat. The new steamroller, the council's latest investment, helped by compacting the road surfaces. At least it did when it was not sitting idle parked up in some side street.

The efforts of the local council still did not have the situation fully in hand. Every week the vociferous criticisms of the town's chamber of trade, often referred to locally as the 'House of Lords', were printed with malicious glee by the local newspaper reporters. They did not hold back with their vitriol, neither the members of the chamber of trade nor the newsmen. Matters were not being helped by a pending high court case against several ex-employees of the Gelligaer parish for misappropriation of funds over the preceding years. The community did indeed have just cause to complain thought Walt as he stepped gingerly over the muddy ruts when crossing the road. It could well be some time before he might abandon his working boots for something less cumbersome to walk to his office in the Bank Chambers he had just passed on the High Street.

Walt stopped briefly at the news stand outside one of the many new grocery stores to buy this week's edition of the local Journal. It kept him up to date with public opinion on council matters and the outpourings of the 'House of Lords' which was one of the few influential bodies in the town to which he had no direct access. He put the newspaper on top of Elizabeth's basket. His last chore on the way to the railway station was to pick up the printed Bible Knowledge certificates he had ordered. He headed into Percy Phillips Printers on upper High Street, proprietor and printer of the Journal and supplier of various items of stationery.

Walt was very pleased with the certificates having chosen a very elaborate embossed design on the highest quality card. Mr Phillips had done an excellent job knowing full well that Mr Walter Lewis was one of his best customers and he would get many more orders from him in future; personalised stationery perhaps?

"I doubt very much if the students of the University are presented with a more beautiful diploma on their graduation," said Mr Phillips. The printer himself wrapped the small bundle into a parcel with brown paper and string which Walt carefully placed underneath the newspaper on top of the basket. It was proving most useful on his errands.

Walt took his battered old tin watch from his waistcoat pocket to check the time as he hurried out of the printers. He noticed a new window display in the Emporium, a full set of brightly polished instruments for the Bargoed Silver Band. Unfortunately he did not have the leisure to stop and admire them today. He passed the New Hall theatre and Berni's temperance bar and much regretted that the proprietor of the New Hall, Mr Withers, had chosen to apply to the council for a licence to sell intoxicating liquor on the premises. As if there were not enough hotels and public bars in the town already. His next call was the railway station and he arrived along with the train down the valley on the Merthyr Brecon line. Before he could put his coin in the slot of the platform ticket machine he saw the unmistakeable figure of Mr Miah Thomas already ascending the steps two at a time.

Over 6 foot tall and dressed entirely in black, Miah stood out in any crowd; a gaunt and forbidding figure with an old fashioned frock coat, immense bushy beard and tall hat. He was the epitome of a nonconformist minister. Grey hair now heavily streaked his over abundant whiskers. Walt in contrast was below average height, had no beard only a very full moustache and was the picture of neatness and pink rude health. He always left the house each day with a clean collar or he'd never hear the end of it from his wife. He had undoubtedly benefitted from his work above ground for the past few years, that and Elizabeth's good cooking.

Walt smiled as he observed his old friend with his somewhat distracted air. Miah was a respected intellectual and scholar of the Bible and one with a heartfelt calling to the Lord's work. Perhaps he cultivated his austere image to add gravitas to his position. Walt remembered the more light-hearted young man with a sense of humour that often saw him on the wrong side of the deacons at the chapel when he first started his ministry. That was many years ago now in Argoed near Hollybush, Walt's childhood home just a few miles distant across the river in Bedwellty. Miah was a man of independent means and it was rumoured that he had inherited considerable personal wealth. Although, if that was the case, Walt thought he could at least afford to buy himself a new hat and coat to replace his worn and outmoded attire.

As the passengers left the station Miah finally looked about from the top of the stairs into the ticket office and noticed his old friend across the vast hall. He raised his tall hat in greeting and, as he approached, looked down at Walt's mud splattered boots and trousers with a broad smile.

"It's been a few years since I shook the mud of Bargoed off my shoes and it seems I've arrived back to find it more stick fast than ever," he said.

"We are still working on the problem," said Walt and with a hearty laugh both men instantly resumed the easy friendship of their younger days.

"I must extend my belated congratulations to Mr Walter Lewis miners' agent," said Miah shaking Walt's extended hand enthusiastically. "I read of your successful election and it was remiss of me not to write to congratulate you at the time."

"We are both busy men although we represent unions of a different nature," replied Walt brushing aside his apology. They left the station side by side, deep in conversation and both looking forward to the pleasure of rekindled familiarity undiminished by time.

*

Back at Ty Gwent Elizabeth was buttering some bara brith ready for the children hungry from school. In her mind she was going through the contents of the larder, concerned in case she had forgotten anything for their meal this evening but reassured that the shops would still be open later, some

13

until at least 10 o'clock at night. She had been busy cleaning all day still convinced the house was dirty dusty from the building work. Even little Gwladys had gone 'round with a duster copying her mother's example. Elizabeth did appreciate the extra space in the kitchen the extension had provided which she grudgingly admitted made the inconvenience of the building work worthwhile. It also meant Walt could have the exclusive use of the small sitting room as a study for the work he did at home in addition to his responsibilities at the Fed offices as the newly elected miners' agent.

Across the well-worn table Esau, her younger unmarried brother and lodger, was reading an old copy of the Merthyr Express at arm's length, his long legs fully extended and enjoying an idle cigarette. Gwladys, the baby of the family at only four, was chewing contentedly on the tasty crust to keep her quiet while watching her mother's dextrous hands with the butter knife.

"Dew, dew, dew. Who would believe it? Have you read this in the paper, Elizabeth?" he asked.

"Now when do I ever get a chance to put my feet up and read the newspaper?" asked Elizabeth.

"Well you should read this. A builder from Bargoed has been up before the magistrates. He's accused of using all sorts of rubbish in his mortar, even small coal and horse dung. A lack of available lime because of all the ongoing building work apparently. Here, read it for yourself," he added passing the newspaper to an astonished Elizabeth. "I hope he did not build this fancy new extension or it will be falling about our heads all too soon." He looked up at the ceiling while Elizabeth cast her eye over the article. "Is that a crack I can see up b'there?" he asked pointing at the corner.

"Get on with you, trying to scare me," she said and swiped him on the shoulder with the folded paper. "No, it's not our builder thankfully. But I'll mention it to Walter to make sure he avoids giving any public contracts to the charlatan. But I expect he knows all about it already and has more sense than to worry me with the nonsense. Unlike you," she added tossing the paper on the table in front of him.

"So, am I eating with the family later," asked Esau changing the subject "or does my banishment to little England begin as soon as Mr Miah Thomas steps over the threshold?"

"You are teasing again I hope," replied his sister. "It is good of next door to offer to put you up tonight. You are fortunate they have a spare room so you and Miah will not have to share the bed. It's not every day we host a representative from the Welsh Baptist Union in our home, even if he is an old friend of the family. Anyway, you like Mr and Mrs Braithwaite and we couldn't ask for kinder neighbours."

"That's true," said Esau "although I doubt Mrs B will tolerate tobacco smoke in her kitchen even with the back door open. Your father doesn't approve of the evil weed either," he said addressing the last remark to little Gwladys who was staring at him with huge, round blue eyes agog. "Indeed, there's a great deal your father disapproves of – especially me."

"Don't speak like that in front of the child. You know she repeats everything she hears which in this case is far from true," said Elizabeth. She pointed the buttery knife at him in mock remand. "Any more talk like that and you will be banished - for good." Esau held up his hands in surrender.

15

"It's a good job I know you love me sister," he replied getting to his feet. He plonked a big kiss on her cheek. "I'm out for a stroll to make the most of this sunshine," he said as he put his hat on and pocketed his tobacco tin before taking a piece of the buttery bara brith intended for the children.

"Well don't be late back. There's a roast tonight and we don't get that often. And if you see Dan about the place send him home. I need him to pick some rhubarb from the garden," she added as an afterthought. Dan would run any last minute errand she might need.

Esau left out the back way and Elizabeth smiled across at her little girl. "Something's got into the men in this family today, Gwladys. I'm not used to all this lovey-dovey nonsense. Must be the fine weather," she said.

Gwladys looked at her mother quizzically. "When's Criddy home?"

"Go look at the mantle clock and tell me the time. I haven't heard the second post yet," said Elizabeth as she helped Gwladys off her cushion on the wooden chair safely to the floor.

"Five and twenty to four o'clock," said the little girl confidently.

"I really must get a start on with this dinner if we are going to eat before midnight," said her mother as the letterbox rattled distantly in the passage. "Go fetch the post, there's a good girl."

Chapter 2

Higher up the valley over in Graig Fargoed, some children were outside enjoying the fine weather after school. The long summer evenings this time of year made it difficult to tell when it was time to go home. Edith was starting to feel a little anxious as her tummy rumbled, a sure sign it must be nearly time for supper. Then it would soon be bed for the little ones she thought as she listened to the familiar sound of the children playing.

The younger children from Club Row were down by the brook at the bottom of the field in front of the row of cottages where they lived. Edith had been charged by her mother to keep a watch over them as some were barely toddlers. There were the three older Prosser boys from number 3, her own 'baby' sister May aged five and the little boy, Robbie, just a dwt, who was the son of the new tenants at number 6. The village children had dammed the fast flowing mountain stream to create their own paddling pool and the boys were trying to repair the dam after the heavy rain of the past few days. At 13 years of age and the eldest, Edith had long been expected to help with the children at home and was used to such responsibilities.

She decided they could have a few more minutes to play as she lay back on the short, springy turf and closed her eyes to better enjoy the welcome warmth of the sun. May and Robbie, wearing the daisy chains Edith had helped to make, wandered off together down towards the stream where the boys were paddling up to their knees in the cold water. It was easy to forget that hidden over the hill just a few hundred yards across the valley, the hewers and hauliers of Bedlinog pits were raising tons of coal to the surface using naked flames in that dirty dank old hell-hole called a mine.

17

Suddenly Edith heard a scream and a wail. "He's throwing stones," shouted little May. Edith got up quickly and rushed down to the children.

"Who is?" asked Edith putting a protective arm around her little sister. "That stuck up Albert Waters. Look you, he's hiding in the bracken over b' there," said May pointing.

"Come out you coward," shouted little Billy Prosser in English. "I'll give you what for, you nasty bugger... He's got a catapult."

"That's enough Billy," said Edith, "leave him be or there'll be more trouble than you bargained for with your Mam. And mind your language in front of me and the little ones. You're not too old for a clout 'round the ear."

"Look, Edie, Robbie's bleeding," said May. Edith bent over the little boy who had his hand to his head. Large tears pooled in his eyes threatening to spill over onto his cheeks. She saw a trail of dark blood ooze from the blond curls behind his ear.

"Oh Dew," said Edith picking up the toddler, "let's get home to Mam quick before there's more trouble." Little May ran behind her back up the hill towards their home at number 4 abandoning the Prosser children to their own devices in their urgency to get home to Mam with the little boy.

"It was bully Bertie Waters throwing stones again," said May as the girls ran into the kitchen where their mother was preparing vegetables for the pot. Their sister Cath aged 12 was bouncing baby Henry on her lap, the only boy in the family and not yet one year old while Nell, their 11 year old sister, was playing cat's cradle to entertain him.

"Now let's not tell tales, May," said her Mam. "Is he badly hurt?" Rachel Jones reached out to take little Robbie from Edith. She was used to the scrapes and bruises of childhood after 5 surviving children and much worse from the all too frequent and far more serious injuries she had tended from incidents in the mine.

"I don't think so," said Edith as she handed over her burden to her mother. "But he is bleeding look here, behind his ear."

"Go up to number 6 and fetch his Mam, Edie. Tell her not to worry. It's not bad, these scalp wounds bleed much worse than they are," said her mother. "Now fetch some water and put the kettle on to boil Nell. We'll all need some tea in a minute. May, go help Nell while I have a look at this little man." She sat Robbie on her knee and gently parted his hair. "I'll just fetch some clean rags and my sewing box. There's a brave boy, no tears," she said as she gave the little boy a comforting cwtsh before putting young Robbie down on the hard chair. He clutched onto the edge of the table for balance as his little barefoot legs dangled in mid-air.

"Oh Mam," said Cath "you're not going to sew up his head are you?"

"Don't be silly love, you'll scare the child. But I will need the scissors to cut a few curls. Then I can clean the graze and get some iodine on it," her mother replied.

Robbie's mother hurried into the kitchen behind Edie anxiously wiping her reddened hands on her apron. When the little boy saw his Mam he started to wail and held out his chubby arms to be picked up. His young mother was no bigger than Edie and would not have looked much older if not for her pale-drawn and anxious features. A handsome girl nonetheless, Rae had always though, with that stunning red-blonde hair but far too thin. She returned to her task and it took only a few minutes of attention from both mothers to clean and dress the wound.

"I'll cover it up for now as head wounds take some time to stop bleeding," said Rae. "But don't leave the dressing in place too long. It's best to let the air get at it."

After improvising a strip of cloth around Robbie's head to hold the dressing in place, Rae wiped his grubby face with a cold wet flannel. She told him he looked like a wounded soldier and was just as brave which almost raised a smile on his pudgy little face. Meanwhile the kettle had boiled on the range and Edie poured the hot water on the leaves in the pot.

"Stay for a cup Mrs Brown," said Rae to the young mother.

"Thank you, Mrs Jones, but I've already caused you too much fuss for one day," she said looking around the room at the curious faces of the girls.

"Now I won't take no for an answer. You've had a shock and the tea's already brewing in the pot, just what we need. Put an extra spoonful of sugar in for Mrs Brown, Edie. It's good for the shock and upset. Go fetch the milk from the stone jar out the back, Nell. Or do you take it black?"

When the tea was poured the four Jones girls sat in their places in order of age on the bench opposite listening as their Mam's gentle chatter began to put the young woman at her ease. She kept the conversation on safe ground as, although they had been neighbours for several months already, the young couple at number 6 had kept themselves very much to themselves. This was the first time Rae had any opportunity to chat properly with young Mary Brown in her kitchen over a nice cup of tea.

She talked about this and that, the weather and the May Day show everyone in the area had attended at Bargoed. Baby Henry was much admired and passed to

Mary to hold. But, as polite as Mary was, she was no chatterbox and the exchange of information seemed very one-sided Rae thought during a prolonged lull in the conversation.

"Mam, are you not going to tell Robbie's mam that it was stuck up Albert Waters what threw the stone and hit poor Robbie?" said little May.

"Heisht, we don't know that dear," replied her mother "perhaps Robbie slipped and hit his head."

"No he didn't. I saw Albert. And Billy Prosser reckons Albert's got a catapult and then Billy said a rude word and wanted to hit him. And he would have if Edie hadn't stopped him," May added in a fluster and looked to her big sister for support knowing full well her mother was not pleased with her outburst.

"Is this true Edith?" said her Mam.

"Honestly? I do not know how Robbie got hurt Mam," said Edith going red. "I was not watching when it happened," she said hanging her head in shame. Mary stood up holding her little boy drowsy in her arms.

"Well thank you very much for your help Mrs Jones," she said "and for being so kind. But I'd be grateful if you'd forget this whole thing with the stone throwing. Please don't mention it to your husband. I don't want Hugh to get to hear about it, just in case you know. He can get a bit too concerned over me and my boy and I don't want any trouble with the neighbours." The young woman looked pleadingly at Rae. "It's not like Robbie is badly hurt. He's still too young to be out with the other children. Wandered off outside on his own he did while I was busy with the housework. I'll keep him close to home in future."

"Well, if you insist, we won't mention anything to anyone, will we girls?" said Rae to the curious children looking on.

"Thank you, you are very kind and understanding. But I must go now. Hugh will be getting up for his shift soon and wanting his food. And I am sorry for the fuss and bother we have caused." After that little speech she looked very flustered and left the room carrying her little boy. She could be seen hurrying down the path at the front of the Row to her home.

"Oh dear," said Rae wondering what the young woman meant by keeping it from Hugh. He was her husband after all and Mary's concern he should not find out about the matter seemed out of proportion to the incident itself. "Well, she was upset, hasn't even finished her tea. Now, you all heard that girls, let's not stir up more trouble on the Row. There's no need to tell your father when he gets in from work and no gossiping with the neighbours. Can you remember that May?" The little girl stuck out her lower lip.

"Yes, if you say so Mam," she said.

"Now let's clear away these tea things and get food on for your father. It won't be long before he's back and your uncles could be in any time now," said Rae to relieve the atmosphere in the room.

"You sit there and finish your cup. We can clear up and get the supper done, can't we?" said Edie looking at her two older sisters. "That's if you tell us what needs doing, Mam."

"There's good girls you are," said their mother glad of their help after another busy day indoors. It was a relief to take the weight off her feet while she fed little Henry. Edie topped up her mother's tea cup from the pot while Rae moved a chair outside the front door in the sunlight. She would enjoy a bit of fresh air as she nursed her best boy.

*

Back in her own small kitchen Mary sat on the chair and rocked little Robbie to comfort them both. She hummed a little tune to him, her lips brushing his soft cheek. Then she spoke in a whisper as she quietly gave voice to her concerns; no matter that he was too young to understand.

"Oh, dear Lord, what must she think of me? Have I said too much? I know I said something amiss, something she thought strange but was too polite to ask. They are such kind folk. Hugh must be mad, quite mad to think we can live in this village, among these good people, but keep ourselves apart. With this warm weather and you, bachgen, walking and so eager to be outdoors in the sunshine. I cannot keep an eye on you every minute of the long day. Hugh will be angry if he hears any of this. He will want to move on again now the bad weather is over.

"Oh Lord, I am so tired. Tired of running and hiding, tired of his suspicions, so tired of this burden of guilt. I know his money pays the rent and puts good food on the table. He keeps us both from the workhouse or worse, for which I am truly thankful. I have been weak and sinful, Lord. Give me strength to carry on for the sake of my beautiful child. If only I had the courage to get away from him. But with no money and nowhere to go... Please Lord, show me the way."

Mary heard the floorboards creak upstairs. It was time for the late shift and Hugh would be wanting his food. "I c-c-could hear talking just now," he said, his large frame filling the doorway. "Who were you t-t-t-talking too? Has anybody else b-been here?"

"Just me, comforting the child. No need to fret. Robbie's had a little bump to the head falling over and in the wars again," she said rising from the only chair so Hugh could sit at the table to eat.

Chapter 3

Rae felt sleepy sitting at her ease in the sunshine and found her mind wandering. Number 4 Club Row had been Rae's home for many years since, as a young girl, she and her two older brothers had moved in with their widowed grandmother. The boys' wages supported the household while Rae did the lion's share of the housework. Between them the grandchildren kept their Grandma Rachel out of the workhouse. Rae's own parents had moved on to find work in Merthyr taking her baby brother with them. Seth had been barely a year old then, about the age of her little Henry now. Her mam was still nursing him she remembered as she fondly stroked the downy head of her own infant son.

Rae had first known her husband Sam back then, when he was apprentice blacksmith in the mine. He was a strong handsome lad, still was despite the passage of time she thought. He had lived with his own family a few doors along the row. When he eventually finished his apprenticeship, they married and Sam had moved in with her family at number 4. Grandma Rachel was now long since buried and Sam's family had moved on to find work eventually settling back in Merthyr. They had seen many, many people pass through the area while others, like her and Sam, had settled in the village to raise their children. He was lucky to have steady work at the pit.

Originally funded by a miners' Building Club back in the '70s most of the houses in the row had now been bought up by the colliery company and rented out to new people coming to work in the pits. There had been a lot of trouble since the Waters family had moved into number 5 last year which would account for, but did not excuse, the stone throwing incident according to May's version of the event.

The Waters were English and spoke no Welsh. Maggie Prosser at number 3 had taken against them for no other reason than her stuck up foreign ways. Lydia Waters, not to be out done, disliked the Prossers in turn for what she described as their slovenly, heathen ways. Rae had to admit that Maggie had struggled with four children under six and a husband far too fond of the beer at the end of his shift. Bert Prosser was always boasting of his boxing prowess when drunk but Rae suspected he now used poor Maggie as his punch bag and probably the children too.

The other mothers in the village looked out for the Prosser children as they were growing up but felt limited by the often hostile response to any small act of charity by both the parents. Bert was aggressive in drink and Maggie had a quick temper and foul mouth on her when riled but everyone had their pride as Rae well knew. Old Nan Evans at number 2 was the only one that Maggie readily accepted any practical help from.

Nan's husband had been fatally injured in a roof fall in the mine almost a decade ago now. Rae had helped Nan nurse him at home the last few days he lingered on. It had been a bad time Rae remembered and, as if on cue, a cloud passed in front of the sun taking away the heat and making her shudder. But Nan had been allowed to keep the house by the colliery managers on the understanding she would take in any single men needing lodgings in the pits; a rare example of charity on the part of the managers. Now well into her seventies Nan was a well-known and much loved character in the village. She reminded Rae so much of her own grandmother. Nan even had her own side line in confectionary, just like Grandma Rachel, and readily sold, or more often gave away, her home-made boiled sweets to the village children who called them 'black bullets'.

Rae remembered how matters between their warring neighbours had come to a head last autumn. It was when the NSPCC inspectors turned up at the Prosser's home and found Maggie in bed during the middle of the day. The fire was unlit, no food in the house, the baby soiled, the other children barefoot and only partly clothed and the eldest not in school. Both parents were prosecuted for child neglect. Rae, along with the rest of the valley, knew every detail from the magistrate court proceedings reported in the Merthyr Express. Maggie Prosser decided it must have been that stuck up Lydia Waters' interfering that had resulted in the public shame she had to endure at court. Everyone knew of families where the mother was struggling to cope under similar circumstances to poor Maggie Prosser and the NSPCC did not call on all of them.

After the court hearing last November Maggie could be heard screaming abuse on the threshold of number 5 aimed at her imagined protagonist inside. Even Maggie's husband Bert seemed embarrassed by his wife's behaviour and bad language and was doing his best to calm her; he was quite sober for once. It brought all the neighbours out on their doorsteps hoping to witness the fracas escalate into a fight between the two women but they were to be disappointed. Alf Waters physically restrained his wife and got between the two women to prevent the situation ending in an exchange of blows. To aggravate matters the eldest Waters boy, Albert, had run out the back to fetch the police constable from the village police house.

Lydia, against all advice including her husband's, insisted on prosecuting. When the police constable arrived on the scene, Lydia insisted that Maggie Prosser be charged with assault and permitting bad language in public. The neighbours were asked to give statements to the constable about the incident. This saw the Prossers in court twice now in almost as many weeks. Based on the evidence presented to the magistrate, including a statement Rae had given the police constable on the day in question, the magistrate dismissed the charges against the Prossers. Instead Lydia found herself bound over to keep the peace after a vitriolic outburst against the defendant in court.

When her Sam read the account of the case at Merthyr magistrate's court in the paper he could not help but laugh out loud at the comeuppance of it all. It had all been a storm in a tea cup he said, and the silly woman had deserved the magistrate's censure given her outburst in court. Rae had to admit there was no proof that Lydia had ever called in the NSPCC but she would neither admit nor deny it now after all this fuss. Rae thought it more likely it was someone in authority that reported conditions in the family, the school perhaps or more likely the local curate.

Determined not to take sides, despite living between the two families, Rae kept her own council on the matter. She had seen the Waters family at church on Sundays and saw no harm in them simply because they, like thousands of other families, had moved far from their birthplace to find work. Sam's own father Henry, who the new baby was named for, had moved off the land near Wrexham to find work in Staffordshire before settling in Merthyr where Sam was born. There were few families like Rachel's who were born in the parish since the expansion of the mines.

It's not as if poor Maggie Prosser was alone in having a husband too fond of the beer and struggling to cope under the burden of a baby a year. Rae's three eldest girls were barely a year apart and, if not for several miscarriages and a still birth until May then Henry came along, she herself would have had several more mouths to feed and feet to shoe. Even with a kind and caring husband like Sam their start to married life had not been easy.

Over the winter Rae noticed things had settled down in the row as the cold weather and pitch black kept most indoors or in bed to save coal and lamp oil. With the return of fine weather allowing the children out to play after school, hostilities between the two families now surfaced in aggression between the younger members, particularly the boys Albert Waters and Billy Prosser who were of an age. Rae personally thought Albert was a bully and Billy a budding pugilist like his father and there would have been problems between those two boys regardless. Both lads though seemed more than usually intent on causing trouble despite the fact the Prosser children could be taken into care and Lydia Waters be back in court if there were any more problems reported to Police Constable Evans in Bedlinog.

Mary and Hugh Brown had only lived in the row since the New Year. She remembered them arriving in the snow, Mary carrying the baby Robbie wrapped in a blanket while Hugh pushed their few belongings along in an old hand cart. They rented the small cottage from the colliery on the end of the row after Hugh had found work in the pits. Rae had called in that first day to offer help but whenever she made a friendly approach Mary politely but firmly rebuffed her neighbourly overtures. The baby was teething, he had a chill, had kept her awake all night; any excuse.

It was nigh on impossible to keep your business from the neighbours in these older mining communities clustered around the pits at the north end of the valley but the young couple were doing a better job than most. Rae had long ago realised that people would invent their own version of events based on the scantest information and often took great delight in spreading unwarranted rumour. She always spoke out against idle gossip as a matter of principle and never joined in the village rumour mill.

It was not her place to tell Mary about the ongoing battles between the Prosser family and the Waters which happened before she had moved into the Row, not without appearing to be indulging in gossip herself. Mary Brown had been most insistent they did not mention anything to Sam about the stone throwing should it get back to Hugh. Perhaps Mary worried Hugh would have a go at the Waters over Albert having a catapult and hurling stones about the place. That is until he broke a window or two.

Now what was it Mary had said about Hugh being over concerned? It seemed odd now that Rae thought about it. She'd said "me and my boy" as if Hugh was not the child's father. Here she was speculating over a little slip of the tongue, no doubt. "I am getting as bad as any of the local gossip mongers," she said aloud, chastising herself with a wry smile. While it might be human nature to be curious about others Rae could reassure herself that at least she would not give voice to her silly suspicion. After all, it was not unusual for a man to take on a young widow and her child - especially if the young widow happened to be as pretty as Mary.

Ray heard the hooter sounding from the colliery for the change of shift. All the men in Club Row worked in the Bedlinog pits except Rae's unmarried brothers and lodgers Seth and Lewis Lewis. They still worked the land as hired labour and did road repairs in winter. Seth swore nothing would ever induce him down that "hell hole they call a colliery". Lewis had worked as a door boy from the age of 8 when their grandmother had been alive. He and their elder brother George had been one of 161 men and boys trapped underground for over 24 hours in 1884. Since then Lewis

29

feared the confinement of working underground and left the colliery never to return.

Rae's husband Sam was now the head ostler underground and was responsible for the welfare of the pit ponies that hauled the coal drams. He had told his wife that Hugh Brown had been taken on nights as ostler and had a rare way with the horses. Sam had described him as a gentle giant and she knew her older girls blushed when they saw him passing. He would touch his cap to them which made them giggle and colour up even more. He is a handsome, well built young man, thought Rae and he and his young wife were well matched for looks.

Sam was glad to have someone working with him who knew about the care of the animals for once and who took the trouble to get to know each of their charges. One of their colliery pit mares had won a prize at the Bargoed May Fair last month and, proud as he was, Sam swore it was down to the knowledge Hugh had of horses. It was obvious to him that Hugh had been brought up with the animals from a young age and probably in the countryside. Sam had warned his wife that Hugh had a bad stammer and rarely spoke more than a few words together. When he did, he sometimes shook with the effort to get his words out the stutter could be so bad. Sam did not want her to think Hugh was ill mannered if he did not stop to speak in passing.

"You can understand him well enough," Sam had said "but it's uncomfortable to watch a fine strapping young man struggling to speak more than a few words together. But he whistles like the skylarks over Graig Fargoed. Strange it is until you get to know him a while."

While Rae had been busy with her thoughts, the girls had finished their chores inside. The table was laid, the food cooked and the kettle hummed on the range. Rae rose wearily from her seat in the sunshine. Henry was getting heavy and every bone in her body seemed to ache again today. Age must be catching up with me, she thought. She was 35.

"Dada's on his way," she called out to the girls when she saw her Sam come striding along the lane with his billy can under his arm and chewing on the stem of his empty pipe.

Chapter 4

That evening in the kitchen at Ty Gwent, the Lewis family were entertaining their visitor to an early and somewhat lavish supper for a Friday night. Although the family referred to the room as the kitchen, their new house also boasted a 'back kitchen' or scullery through a low door to one side of the black lead fire range which housed the sink and mangle. Most of the linen and shirts now went out to the Hop Woo laundry in town each week; only delicate hand washing and woollens were done at home.

Elizabeth was getting used to her new gas stove out the back kitchen for cooking after a lifetime of using the box oven and hob on the range. There was a door into a walk-in pantry on the other side of the range. It boasted a large marble slab to keep fresh food cool and mesh covered vents in the external wall to ventilate the space without flying insects invading. The remaining space in the scullery was taken up with an over-sized plumbed in roll top bath with the new gas geyser on the wall above for running hot water. Food preparation Elizabeth did on the kitchen table.

Although the flushing water closet was accessed from outside the house, Walt had the builders install a glass roof to cover the first back yard so at least they had some protection from the elements on their journey to and fro. It was a great improvement on the earth closet at the bottom of the yard in their previous home in Cwmsyfiog. With all these modern conveniences, Elizabeth coped without any additional help in the house and much preferred it that way. She took great pride in keeping a tidy house.

Mother and children spent most of their time in the kitchen around the large, well-scrubbed pine table which was used for all manner of activities but tonight had been transformed for dining with a starched white table cloth clean from the laundry. Elizabeth was using her 'best' crockery for the adults and it all looked quite posh she thought to herself. After Miah Thomas had said grace, conversation was limited to compliments to the cook as she supervised the progress of the meal, unnecessarily urging everyone to eat up and offering second helpings before their plates were clear.

"Will you cut that meat for your sister?" she said to her son Trefor. The eldest in the family at 14, Trefor wore the blue uniform with the badge of a Pengam Lewis Boys' scholar on his worsted jacket. His mother always insisted he wore his school uniform on any formal occasion which made him feel rather foolish. But at least this evening it was only at home and Miah Thomas who, he remembered vaguely from before, was a decent sort for a Baptist minister despite that rather disgusting beard. He dutifully leaned over to help Gwladys who was eating with a bowl and a spoon and a large tea cloth around her neck and looked mystified at the slice of meat left at the bottom of her dish.

When Miah politely refused the offer of seconds yet again he placed his cutlery carefully to the centre of the empty plate. Young Ceridwen copied his example and quickly replaced her knife and fork together on her plate. Two years older than her little sister she wanted to impress their guest with her best table manners with a knife and fork.

It was rare in this busy household for the whole family to sit down together and there wasn't quite room for all of them all around the table with two extra adults to feed. Miah turned to speak to Dan, the Lewis' ten-year old boy, who sat on a stool by the immaculately clean but unlit range eating his supper form a dish on his lap. It was too warm for a fire this evening now that Elizabeth was no longer reliant on the range for cooking or hot water.

"Have I taken your seat at table young man?" he asked. Dan waved his greasy spoon in the air and grinned happily while chewing noisily on the last mouthful of his meal. Walt looked over at his second son and replied for him.

"Dan is happy to accommodate you," he said placing his cutlery carefully on his plate. "Dan is always happy, thank the Lord," he added as his son continued to chuckle merrily as if to confirm his father's statement.

Dan had been a very contented baby but as time went on it became apparent to his parents he was not developing as a baby should despite being in otherwise excellent health. His parents were resigned to the fact he was as the Lord had made him and were thankful he was blessed with a cheerful nature. The school would not take him on so he spent his days at home but Dan had made it his purpose in life to be useful and did many errands for his mother around the town.

His mother did worry when Dan disappeared, often for hours on end some days, but he came to no harm other than the odd graze or drenching in the rain. He had also taken to sleeping in the kitchen chair since his brother William had succumbed to diphtheria during the first year they had moved into their new house. Will and Dan were only a year apart in age and had been inseparable playmates growing up. His older brother encouraged Dan through play and patience and, much to their parents' amazement, Dan had learned to run and talk in his own lop-sided manner. He understood far more than anyone outside the family appreciated.

The tragedy of Will's death at the age of only eight had been the start of a very dark time for the family during the first months in their new home. Tragedy was heaped on tragedy when, only a few weeks later their youngest son, Goronwr, had been taken from them aged just 20 months. It had been a time to test the faith of even the staunchest but they had come through it stronger as a family. Elizabeth now worried that during Dan's frequent disappearances he was looking for his lost playmate Will and could no longer bear to sleep in their bed alone without him.

Miah turned his attention to Esau who was subdued as ever in the presence of Walt, his brother-in-law.

"I am surprised but pleased to see you Esau after all this time. What brings you this way, visiting the family are you?" he asked. Esau looked at his sister as if seeking permission to reply and she smiled encouragingly.

"Orphaned at 30 I'm afraid. Our mother passed away this winter just gone," he said glancing again at Elizabeth "and I would have been without a home if not for my brother-in-law's generosity to waifs and strays. But it's only a temporary arrangement I hope" he added looking to Walt at the head of the table.

"I am indeed saddened to hear that, although your mother must have reached a good age," said Miah. "I remember your parents well from my time in Argoed and will always be indebted to your father for the example and wise counsel he gave to the inexperienced young minister I was then. But so much has changed. Last time I stayed with this family it was in very different circumstances," he said smiling and focussed on the two round-eyed little girls opposite who took in every word of the adults' conversation. "It's all a far cry from that dark old cottage in

Cwmsyfiog where you started married life Gwallt and where these two little ones were born."

"That row of cottages has now been demolished I'm glad to say," said Walt "and not before time... All the workers deserve dry, bright homes with a few basic comforts. If everyone in this valley had running water and sewerage... we might see an end to the dreadful child mortality and disease." He stopped embarrassed at himself for momentarily forgetting his own family's losses. "Not suitable conversation for the table I apologise, Elizabeth... I must remember to step down from my soap box occasionally," he said looking at his wife. "But there is a need to make sure the whole population benefits from advances in the twentieth century... not just the lucky few."

"Dadda's getting a tephalone," piped in Gwladys.

"An elephant you say?" said Miah which made her giggle.

"She means a telephone," said Ceridwen, pleased to be able to correct her little sister. "We're having one put in here, at the house next week."

"Well that shows what an important man your Dadda is now my dear," said Miah and tried not to show how surprised he was by this latest revelation from the Lewis family. How times were changing indeed, he thought.

"Afters everyone?" asked Elizabeth as she gestured to those around the table to pass their now empty plates.

*

High above the valley town on Graig Fargoed at 4, Club Row the Jones family were clearing away their bowls after a hearty supper of the stew and bread that fuelled all working families in the area during the week. The baby also got to munch on a crust his mother soaked in the juice from the pot and try out his new teeth.

Seth and Lewis, Rae's brothers, rose in silence and left the warm crowded kitchen. Conversation was not their strong point and they left the rest of the family to catch up on their day. Outside the back of the house the brothers tended a large vegetable patch and an assortment of animals and fowl. They had made a pigsty using the local tradition of dry stone walling on the slope of mountain land beyond the garden boundary and kept all kinds of birds in a large wood and wire enclosure with a wooden hen coop.

There were many advantages in having men who retained their connection to the land in the family. Not only did the eggs and vegetables supplement the family's diet but their cured bacon and fresh ducks and geese were a good source of income at Christmas. Rae always carried the family's contribution to the harvest festival at the church each year with great pride knowing full well that few other families could match the range and quality of produce her brothers' efforts displayed. The long summer evenings allowed them more time to maintain their patch, as they called it, and tend the livestock. The family would not see them again until morning as the brothers only seemed to use the house to eat and occasionally sleep in the winter. But it was still their home.

"Are our neighbours behaving themselves? I cannot believe that a truce could last this long between those two women either side" said Sam in general as the girls cleared away the table. He sat in his hard backed chair by the hearth and was filling his pipe idly staring at the low fire in the range which heated the blackened pot and boiled the huge copper plated kettle.

"What makes you ask?" said Rae as she gave little May a stern look of warning. "You know they both have a lot to lose after all that palaver in court last year."

"Nothing really, just wondering. It's been far too quiet round here lately. I could do with some entertainment," he said laughing. "Right who's for the latest instalment of the series?" It had become a family tradition of a Friday night for Sam to read out loud to the girls before they went to bed. With limited reading material in the house they relied on the serialisation of novels published in the weekly edition of the Merthyr Express. It was good for their English vocabulary he thought. He picked up the well-thumbed copy of the paper and started looking for the page.

"Wait a bit, give us a chance to finish the clearing up and we can all sit down and enjoy it," said Rae. She had never been comfortable with her husband's choice of reading matter with the girls at such an impressionable age. Some of those stories were a bit near the knuckle in her opinion but Sam dismissed her concerns. The girls were growing up quickly and could not be kept at home for ever. At the end of the year Edie would leave elementary school and Rae herself was already sounding out her many connections in the nearby town of Treharris for a suitable place for her oldest daughter. It was the lot of many girls to go into service at 14 or younger and they often started in the homes of relatives or friends of the family until, or if, they were lucky enough to find a husband and start their own family.

Sam made his readings of the weekly serial very entertaining by putting on voices and pulling faces and she laughed along with the girls 'til her sides ached at times. And she often overheard the girls acting out some of the scenes from the stories which had fired their imagination during the following week. Her Sam was a hard worker and a good family man. Rae knew how fortunate they were.

"Right then let's hear this week's advice to 'Mother and Daughter' while we wait which is more than apt for this family," he said. "Little Henry and me are outnumbered by our bevy of beauties. Nell, we haven't heard you read for a while. Put that baby down for a few minutes and read aloud to your father." He handed the paper to 11-year old Nell pointing to the relevant column with the stem of his pipe. "Go and sit by her at the table Edie and help her out." Nell was very reluctant to read out loud but knew that there was no point arguing with her father. He had chosen her on purpose she knew as she did not read as fluently as her older sisters and hesitated over the less familiar English words. The print in the paper was so tiny even her father put on his wire rimmed spectacles to read it.

In her clear high voice she started "All praise…" "Doctor Morse's," said Edie…. "Doctor Morse's," echoed Nell "In-di-an root pills".

"That's an advertisement for some quack remedy, girl. The next paragraph down. Here try my glasses," said her father passing them over. She put them on and focussed on the newsprint. Suddenly, for the first time, Nell could see the letters clearly and carried on with more confidence.

"The daughter who has a mother's advice to guide her through her early married life is for-tun-ate indeed," she read more fluently. Sam looked over his daughter's bent head as she continued reading to catch his wife's eye. He tapped his pipe stem on the side of his face, just below his eye. Yes, thought Rae, Nell needs reading glasses like her father. How clever of him to realise and nodded back to her husband to show she understood.

*

With the girls safely tucked up in bed and Elizabeth, Trefor and Dan at their various chores, Walt and Miah had retired to the sanctuary of the small sitting room or 'study' as Walt preferred to call it. There was always something to be done as he filled in the certificates for Bible Knowledge in his wonderfully fluid handwriting before passing them to Miah to sign. They indulged in some fond reminiscing about their first acquaintance as young men at the chapel in Argoed before the conversation eventually turned to Walt's increased responsibilities in his official role as miners' agent.

"There is always a dispute somewhere in the Valley," said Walt. "The Deri pits have been out most of last month... and the owners threatening a lockout of the whole South Wales coalfield. Thankfully that was averted... but the men of Groesfan are still locked out. It's the impact it has on the families... especially the children... when any dispute is not resolved quickly or satisfactorily... It sickens me to see the little ones suffer... the owners resort to starvation to get the men back to work. I remember my father out for 8 months back in the 70's... How we survived as a family... that I'll never know. The owners hold the key to the pantry at the end of the day... But until we get all the men signed up to union we cannot avoid more disputes in future."

"Yes, there is undoubtedly strength in numbers where people are unified in a just cause," said Miah.

"Union membership is to be our main focus in the months ahead... that and keeping members' contributions up to date... Far too many lapse... falling into arrears with their payments which makes my job difficult when it comes to paying out claims. Worryingly there are some factions beginning to speak out strongly against the Fed... and its leaders. Do you follow any of this in the papers?"

"I was aware there was some disunity among the workers and their leaders. But it is ever the case within such a large organisation," said Miah.

"I see you keep abreast of current affairs. Now, would it surprise you to hear that I have been summoned to appear in court next Friday? Obstruction of the highway…. it was during a local rally to encourage union membership… only last week in Groesfan. The newsmen had a field day with that story…"

Miah looked at Walt wide-eyed in surprise. "Oh, don't be alarmed. It is an all too common ploy by some of the owners… to bring legal action against striking miners or their leaders. The Fed will provide legal representation and cover any costs. I assure you… it is likely to come to nothing. The police made a mistake when they rounded me into the police wagon… along with a handful of miners supporting our cause."

"I am most relieved to hear it but it saddens me to see you having to cope with rowdy behaviour and aggressive tactics in carrying out your duties. Large gatherings of workers are quite a different crowd to stand up and address compared to a full congregation of worshippers. It amazes me how you take it in you stride," said Miah.

"It can be daunting at times… but I have the full might of the Fed behind me now… and we are gaining in strength with every passing year I am proud to say. It could get worse… this industrial action… before we get all the men on side. But one day the union's power to negotiate with the owners will be able to avert strike action. Reason will prevail and make lock outs and strike action a thing of the past. That is my belief… and I will continue to strive to achieve it with the good Lord's grace…"

"Let us pray that day comes sooner than later. For the sake of the children of the coalfields if no one else," said Miah.

"Indeed… Mabon himself endorsed my election as miner's leader during a visit to Bargoed earlier this

41

month... It was part of his lecture tour of South Wales," said Walt with a note of satisfaction. "He was to talk about the procedures in the House of Commons... but given the large turnout of miners in the audience he addressed many of their concerns about the coal crisis... and the 8 hour Act... directly from the platform. We took a lot of money that night... which was fortunate since the proceeds from the door went in aid of a non-union man in Greenfield Street... He has been unable to work for the past two years... crippled after an accident underground and cannot leave his bed poor man."

"I imagine that alone would be incentive enough to increase your membership. The union supports its disabled members financially, I understand."

"Yes indeed. We also support the widows and families of men killed at work... along with those miners now too old infirm to graft underground," said Walt. "But with the Liberal Chancellor's Old Age Pension Act coming into force, hopefully... many of our oldest beneficiaries will surely apply for it. The state old age pension... it will be twice the amount the Fed pays out at present. We intend to ballot our members to determine whether aged miners will continue to receive their ten shilling a month from the Fed."

"Lloyd George is a figure of great inspiration to all Welshmen; a man for the people who is true to his principles and much to be admired," said Miah.

"As much as I may agree with your opinion of Lloyd George... we must move with the times. I admit the Liberal Chancellor's budget contains a welcome redistribution of wealth with his increased tax rates for the rich... that is if it gets through the House of Lords... But the Fed is to become affiliated with the Independent Labour Party. It is the workingmen's party... and our aim is to increase representation in parliament. We are following in the footsteps of Keir Hardie here in the south Wales coalfield. The ILP campaigns for improving the conditions of working men… and their families throughout the nation … and I am all for that. There are exciting times ahead I tell you... when real progress can be made in our struggle…" Walt laughed.

"Well listen to me on my soap box again. Politics does that… gets me all fired up. But… enough of me and my concerns. What of your new role in the Baptist Union? I knew you have been on the editorial board of the Baptist Weekly for some years and had some input into the Baptist College, but when did you take on this responsibility for financial matters?" asked Walt.

"I was wondering when you'd get around to asking that. It's a long story which I doubt we have time for this evening. Safe to say that God works in mysterious ways," answered Miah and seemed reluctant to be more forth-coming as Walt looked at him expectantly. "One favourable aspect of the work is that it allows me to travel widely throughout the principality," he added. "But now I offer financial advice in addition to any spiritual guidance I might be called upon to give. It may not be everyone's idea of the role of an ordained minister and sometimes I must admit I feel more like a travelling salesman than an itinerant preacher," he said smiling at his own joke.

"Well I am thankful at least it has brought us old friends together again," said Walt. "I only regret I cannot hear you preach on Sunday at Fochriw... Union business again... there is a rally for the men in Rhymney I must attend that afternoon. I enjoy a good sermon that makes me think... not all just hellfire and damnation."

Miah laughed heartily at that unguarded remark from his old friend. "I am too often criticised for my lack of passion in the pulpit and need more men like you in my congregations."

"The men were very impressed when Mabon addressed us from the pulpit... on the Sunday of his visit at Bethania. He is another great leader and an inspired orator... like your Mr Lloyd George. Both would have made excellent preachers," said Walt.

"Well, I hope the good people of Fochriw are not expecting such great things from me," said Miah with a smile. "I have always preferred my academic studies and writing. But with persistence I have found my niche within the church at last, just as you seem to be thriving in political spheres."

There was a polite knock before Elizabeth poked her head around the study door. "Are you two staying in here all night?" she asked. "Miah will be fed up of talking politics by now" she added knowing her husband's preferred choice of conversation well. "I have made some tea and will serve it in the front parlour if you'd like to join me. The boys are ready for bed and eager to bid you goodnight."

It was still light outside despite the lateness of the hour as Walt lit the gaslight and drew the heavy curtains across the bay window. Miah and Elizabeth settled into the large over stuffed sofa while Walt took his usual seat in the armchair. Their conversation turned back to how much had changed for the better during their lifetime. It was good to reminisce with old friends

Esau stubbed out his cigarette in the backyard before stepping easily over the garden fence into next door's garden. He had found the latest copy of the journal to read which was tucked under his arm as he rapped on the neighbour's open back door. "Here I am" he called out "in need of sanctuary as usual."

Chapter 5

Rae always got up with the men in the house every morning to light the fire, fetch water from the pump in the yard, make up the cans and see them off to work with some hot tea and breakfast and Saturdays were no exception. Sam only did half a shift today and Seth and Lewis never lay abed after dawn even in the summer when the sun rose so early. The girls got up after the men had left the house for work to relieve the crush in the kitchen. Edith would see to them later. Saturday was a busy day for Rae as she also left the house early to make the journey a few miles into Treharris to work once a week.

Rae was a confectioner, a craft she'd learned from her grandmother, and the local baker employed her to ice and decorate the 'fancies' he made for sale at the bakery once a week. Mrs Beynon, the baker's wife, had four children under five and was now far too busy to help her husband with his business. The fancies were a local dainty made just for the Saturday tea table to supplement the muffins, current buns and lardie cakes he sold all week as well as his soda bread and milk bread and white loaves. What made the fancies special was the care and creativity Rae put into the finishing touches. Since the baker had found a wholesale supplier to the trade in Pontypridd, her little enterprise had expanded.

During the week with the girls at school Rae made tiny coloured marzipan and sugar paste decorations for the fancies and large trays of toffee and fudge. She even had moulds to make sugar mice. Last Christmas she had some success with hand-made chocolates but found that too troublesome in the heat of summer when the chocolate would not set. In the autumn she made taffy apples and Mr Beynon the baker was happy to sell everything she produced in his shop during the week for a small commission.

Nan Evans from number 2 called by most days to see what Rae had dreamed up in her kitchen and often stayed to lend a hand but had little patience for the more intricate work. Her eyesight was no longer the best. Rae often thought the old lady's herbal boiled sweets, the black bullets she gave away so freely, could rival Dr Morse's Indian root pills and were probably just as efficacious but would never have dreamed of saying so.

Rae's grandmother had an extensive knowledge of local plants and herbs which she used for colouring and flavouring and even added to the stew pot. She also used plants as an ingredient to make remedies and anointments for common ailments. But Rae preferred to use the convenience of the wholesaler to tramping the woods and mountainside with the children traipsing behind her as she had so often done with her grandmother. Not having bunches of flower and seed heads, leaves, stems and roots to dry, prepare and store in the old way also made life much easier; how times had changed she thought when looking back to her own childhood.

Every Friday afternoon, before the family arrived home, Rae would carefully pack her tin trays and boxes into the cart Sam had specially made for her on an old pram chassis he had salvaged in readiness for the trip into town. After his morning shift Sam would meet her at the bakery and push the cart back home up the hill. This time it would be loaded with block sugar and other basic ingredients she ordered in advance from the Co-op. More often than not these days they took the train.

Rae's little enterprise would never make them rich, especially with the competition from the increasing availability of mass produced sweets, but it made her feel useful to contribute to the family's income. Sam let her keep the money and spend it on the little luxuries women found so irresistible. Last year she had saved up and bought a chaise long for the front parlour from the Pontypridd Furnishing store; very lah-di-dah indeed. She also enjoyed the reputation she had earned for the quality of her handiwork. Mr Beynon the baker always said he could sell more of her confections if she had the time to make them. The Jones girls never hankered for their mother's sweets treats having eaten too many of her mistakes in the past. Her girls' idea of a real treat was to tuck into one of Mr Beynon's satisfying lardies for their Saturday tea.

*

Over breakfast at Ty Gwent Walt and Miah went through their itinerary for the day like a minor military campaign. The service for the presentation of the certificates would take place at two o'clock at Noddfa in Bargoed. Trefor's name was among the list of scholars although Walt thought the boy could have done better as his was not the best result in the class. The presentation was to be followed by a tea for all the chapel members prepared by the ladies of the refreshment committee.

Afterwards the older children and anyone with enough energy were walking up the mountain to meet their counterparts from Noddfa in Fochriw mid-way between the two communities for some informal games organised by the Sunday school teachers. At seven o'clock there was to be a concert in Fochriw where the chapel was much larger and sat 450. Bedlinog United choir were the guests and were widely acclaimed since winning the choir competition at the local Eisteddfod the previous month. Other contributions were to be prepared by the senior scholars of both chapels and were eagerly anticipated.

The Bargoed group were then intending to return home over the mountain by torch light. Walt thought the last idea rather impractical even given the long light evenings at midsummer but, since it had been suggested, it had been taken up with such great enthusiasm by the young people he kept his reservations to himself. Knowing how dangerous the mountain track could be at dusk, however, he had prevailed upon John Baldwin, a fellow deacon and local milk man, to drive his horse and cart with the procession in case anyone was too tired to walk or had a fall. If Walt was expected to take part in this folly he fully intended to ride back alongside Mr Baldwin in his cart.

"I have to go into the Fed offices first thing... just in case anything urgent came in yesterday afternoon while I was out and which might need my attention," said Walt. "Feel free to use the study here if you have anything to prepare for your sermon at Fochriw tomorrow," he said to Miah. "The only question remaining is... do you wish to accompany us across the mountain on foot... or would you prefer to join us later for the concert... by train?" asked Walt.

"Given the weather I think I'd much prefer to see some of the local countryside. A walk over the common would be a very welcome diversion," replied Miah.

"That's settled then. I must then leave you in the capable hands of Mr Leyshon... the minister at Fochriw.... he will arrange lodgings for the rest of your stay. Then I assume you will take the train back to Brecon on Monday morning... It seems your stay here with the family has been all too brief."

"But most enjoyable in spite of that. You have welcomed me into your home and it's been a real pleasure to feel so at ease among old friends," said Miah. "It's not often I have a bed to myself on my visits around the principality never mind an entire room complete with wash stand. And Elizabeth, I will not need to eat for another week," he added as he wiped the egg yolk and grease from his plate with his bread and butter and popped it into his mouth. He took a good swig of his black tea and beamed at the children opposite.

"Where is Esau this morning?" he asked. "I cannot believe he is still abed."

"Banished to England," Gwladys answered too loudly to be ignored. Elizabeth looked at her husband in some alarm.

"Heisht Gwladys and eat your egg like a good girl. The child means he has gone next door to our neighbours - they are English. He stayed there last night because they have plenty of room," she explained. "Mr Braithwaite has a barber shop in town. He does seem to be doing very well out of it. He and his wife have no children sadly but they are a very kind couple. Mrs Braithwaite often has Gwladys for an hour or so each morning. They offered Esau accommodation for the night knowing we had a house full here. Roman Catholic they are."

"We can all show Christian charity I hope regardless of where we worship," said Miah. This remark shocked young Trefor coming from the mouth of a preacher high up in the Baptist Union. It did not surprise his father, however, who knew his friend to show a level of tolerance not shared by many of their religious persuasion. Miah always looked for the good in everything no matter how grim, unlike others he could mention.

"Now Trefor," said Walt changing the subject, "do you have any home studies to complete?"

"Actually, father I do," he said and with enthusiasm he went on to explain that his Welsh master at school was planning to publish a book of Welsh rhymes and folklore written by the boys themselves. "I rather hoped with your permission I could write out your rhyme, the one your grandmother taught you when you were a boy. It might get included in the final book. The girls seem to like it well enough."

"Ah.... but how are you going to get the actions in?" said Walt with a grin. With that he scooped up Ceridwen onto his lap. "You're getting a bit too big for this," he said and started to mimic the clip clop noise and action of a horse rocking the girl up and down and reciting the old Welsh rhyme in his lilting baritone voice.

"*Gee ceffyl bach yn cario ni'n dau. Dros y mynydd i hela cnau. Dwr yn yr afon a cherrig yn slic, Cwympo ni'n dau*," he let the child fall to the floor catching her under the arms before she hit the hard quarry tiles on the floor, "*wel dyna'i chi dric*."

Although Criddy knew full well the drop was coming, it never ceased to surprise her and she laughed as she turned to her father and gave him a hug.

"Me, me, my turn," said Gwladys as she struggled to get off her seat, eager to get onto her father's knee and pushing Ceridwen out of her way in the process.

"Now look what you've started," he said to Trefor repeating the whole exercise again knowing he would get no peace until he did.

"Perhaps I could put the actions in like the stage directions of the play we are rehearsing at school," said Trefor eagerly as Gwladys laughed still sitting on the floor between her father's slippered feet.

"Now there's the solution... We are very fortunate you know," he said addressing Miah "to have such a good... and established school in the valley. And you, young man," he turned to his son "must make the most of your opportunity to get a good education... Excellent teachers they have there." Walt could not help but think of his own limited schooling at the old Board schools at Tredegar Town hall and later in the dark, cramped back room of the inn at Hollybush. "But if you'll all excuse me... I must be off the sooner to be back," he said getting up from his comfortable chair at the table. "Fetch me my boots Dan."

Dan was sitting on his stool by the range and, lined up in front of the hearth, were all the family's boots, including Mr Miah Thomas', polished to a dull gleam. It took him a long time every evening with the boot blacking and brush but was another example of Dan making himself useful.

"And I'd like to take a closer look at this burgeoning metropolis which seems to be becoming the centre of commerce and industry in the Rhymney valley. Perhaps we can give some business to your neighbour at his barber shop in return for giving Esau a room for the night," said Miah stroking his over-abundant beard complete with crumbs. "Do you fancy showing me your home town?" he said addressing young Dan. "That's if your mother can spare you," he said looking to Elizabeth.

The look of sheer pleasure on her son's face at the prospect of such an important task and the kindness of their visitor towards the boy made her heart swell.

"Of course I can," she said. "Off you go, enjoy yourselves. That will give me plenty of time to get these girls ready for the presentation and tea party this afternoon."

Chapter 6

At precisely 1.30 pm, according to Walt's battered but reliable old watch, he and Miah arrived at Noddfa chapel to be greeted by the lay preacher, young David Price who was presiding over the afternoon celebration. Miah was looking very spruce with his neatly trimmed beard and short haircut the effect of which made him look at least a decade younger despite his austere long black coat and winged collar. The grey in his sleek hair was less obvious and the tall hat was noticeable by its absence. Was that a waft of Macassar oil or something similar Walt wondered? His neighbour, Mr Braithwaite the barber, had worked a minor miracle on Miah's appearance with a bit of professional grooming. Perhaps it was time he also paid a visit to the barbers on a more regular basis.

They stood in the porch of the new Welsh Baptist chapel while Walt introduced his old friend to the young man who would lead the service this afternoon. Walt had already singled out David Price as a candidate for one of Miah's bursaries to study for the ministry. He would be interested to find out Miah's opinion of the youngster after he had a chance to see the boy in action.

The chapel building was made of sturdy stone but of very modest proportions compared to the mother church at Hanbury Road. With only 87 signed up to the Welsh cause a larger building could not be justified but no expense had been spared on the quality of the masonry. The scholars who were to receive their prizes today had turned up early as requested and there was an excited hum of conversation inside. The ladies of the refreshment committee had been busy and already laid out at the back of the hall were trestle tables laden with plates and trays covered in waxed paper and tea cloths. All was in readiness for the celebration tea party after the presentation that afternoon.

Putting on refreshments was quite a challenge in the chapel which had no running water, hence the need for the industries of the refreshment committee. Mr Joby Jones the butcher, one of the deacons who lived nearest to the chapel, allowed the ladies to use the kitchen in his house for food preparation, water and tea making facilities under the supervision of his wife, Mrs Joby Jones chair lady of the refreshment committee. A large wooden cupboard at the back of the hall stored the chapel's large enamel tea pots alongside the Welsh Baptist hymnals. Jugs and kettles of boiling water had to be ferried across from the kitchen by a small army of willing helpers to make the tea in the quantity needed. Chapel members provided their own crockery and cutlery. Experience meant the ladies had honed the logistics down to a fine art and tea and refreshments were often provided at special events such as the Sunday school presentation today.

Walt worried that the ladies of the chapel competed to provide excessive amounts of food for these occasions and for some, who could ill afford it, that would mean the family went without during the week. As a consequence, in his capacity as treasurer for the new chapel, he provided a small budget from the chapel funds for these events to pay for some basic necessities for the refreshment committee; tea, sugar, bread and butter and whatever else was deemed essential. The chapel had its own account at the Co-op grocery in town.

The solution had been Elizabeth's but was none the less a good idea he was happy to adopt and pass before the deacons of the chapel. This only partially relieved the problem since the ladies would still bake pies, biscuits and cakes to supplement the basic fare on offer. But Elizabeth told him not to fret, they enjoyed doing it and he should be content the chapel-goers were happy to feed the body as well as the soul.

Mr Price called the scholars to order and set about arranging them on the front bench. There were no fixed pews in this humble building which proved useful. It made the limited space more versatile and they could be stacked out of the way later for the tea party.

"Now then," said the Mr Price "shall we have them up in order of merit saving the best 'til last?" He looked indulgently at a bespectacled youth, the son of a local undertaker and carpenter, called John Williams who had scored top marks in Bible Knowledge that year. He was a favourite of Mr Price because he played the organ exceptionally well for his age and accompanied the singing at the children's services before Sunday school.

"I think it would be fairer to have them alphabetically... by surname if you agree Miah?" replied Walt. Miah nodded his approval. "Although you might make a point of mentioning that young John Williams has excelled in his Bible Knowledge and has one of the highest scores in the district," Walt added smiling at the boy. "That should earn an extra round of applause from our congregation today."

Trefor, who was also to be presented with his prize today, was visibly relieved. He knew his father would be disappointed to see his son well down the placing in order of merit. Walt passed the certificates to his son with instructions to arrange them alphabetically. Mr Price then called out each child's name and sat them in the appropriate place. They then practiced getting up, walking to the front, shaking hands with the minister and returning to their seats without unnecessary incident. There were a few giggles and exaggerated trips but the four boys and six girls who were to receive their senior prizes today were very much aware of the importance of good behaviour during the formal part of today's proceedings. They could console themselves with the fact there would be lots of opportunity for fun later.

During the preparations for the presentation, those family members who were able to attend to see their young people receive their prizes had started to arrive and take up their places on the remaining benches. The congregation was made up mainly of mothers and younger members of the Sunday school. Some of the men would be at work on a Saturday. It was unheard of to serve food and applaud in chapel on a Sunday, however, which explained why the Saturday had been chosen for this celebration; the first of many it was hoped.

Walt noticed his wife Elizabeth and young daughters arrive. Everyone was wearing their Sunday best and Elizabeth looked formidable in her tailored outfit and matching hat. She came from a long line of dressmakers and still made most of her own clothes as well as those of the children on her treadle Singer sewing machine. Little Gwladys and Ceridwen wore immaculate white pinafores over their pretty cotton dresses with delicate white embroidery on the yoke. Walt never ceased to be amazed at the range of skills his wife could put her hand to. You would not believe that they had spent a large part of the morning preparing the food for the Sunday school tea with no time to return home to change.

There was no sign of Dan but Walt suspected he would not be far away when there was tea to organise for the chapel members. Several of the younger children handed out copies of the Baptist hymnal to the gathering congregation in anticipation of the singing to come. The chapel was filling up and Walt took a seat by Elizabeth and the girls foregoing his place as deacon in the carved wooden chairs ranged at the side. He felt it more appropriated today to sit as a family since his eldest boy was to receive his prize along with his peers.

A hush descended on the gathering as Mr Price welcomed everyone precisely at two o'clock. After introducing their guest, Mr Nehemiah Thomas representing the Baptist Union of Wales and noted scholar of the Bible, those gathered bowed their heads in prayer lead by the minister. The congregation then sang the first hymn accompanied by Miss Price, sister to David Price, on the harmonium, a small wooden reed organ pumped with foot bellows. It was a Sunday school favourite which everyone, including the children, joined in with gusto.

Despite his fine speaking voice Walt was no singer preferring to mouth along with the words. Somehow he never managed to sing in the same pitch as everyone else although he could hold a tune on his own. His wife and youngest daughter Gwladys more than made up for his lack of volume with their fine strong soprano voices. Ceridwen was a poor singer like her father and mumbled into her hymnal to try to cover up this failing in the hope that no-one noticed.

Miss Thomas, the senior Sunday school teacher, read a passage from the scriptures; Mark 10:14 *'suffer the little children to come unto me'*. Mr Price took up this theme for his, mercifully brief if appropriate, address which the children sat through respectfully. Trefor, for one, no longer regarded himself as a 'little child' and wondered how old he had to be before he was regarded as an adult. It did not help that he was dressed again in his school uniform. With another hymn, the formalities were dispensed with and

Miah, taking his lead from David Price, took over for the presentations.

In a more entertaining manner he told the story of Mary Jones and her Bible, a favourite with them all. They could take example from Mary's love of the scriptures as an incentive to study the Bible. He told how Mary's trek over the hills to Bala had inspired the local minister, Rev Charles, to set up a society to supply Wales with Bibles in Welsh. Did they know that Mary's original bible was now held in the library of the University of Cambridge no less? And he had been there to the library and seen it.

Walt realised that Miah had probably told this story to many similar gatherings throughout the principality but today his eager audience hung on every word. Miah was obviously enjoying the occasion and gave the congregation permission to applaud each scholar on their achievement as they were presented with their certificates for Bible Knowledge. Each scholar was surprised when they were also given their own copy of the bible in Welsh provided by the Religious Tract Society and a paper bookmark with a picture illustrating the text from the scriptures; a fine memento to cherish and an appropriate reward to mark the occasion along with their beautifully embellished certificates.

Finally, when the last scholar took their seat, Miah concluded the presentation with a fine blessing on the young people present. The gathering drew to a close with another hymn and a concluding prayer from Mr Price who also announced, to everyone's delighted anticipation, that tea is served.

The noise of happy chatter in the hall reflected the mood of the congregation on this fine summer's day. The scholars beamed with pride as they showed those of their family present the certificates and prizes and felt well rewarded for their hard work. Walt shook Miah's hand and congratulated him on his contribution to the events of the day so far. Meanwhile benches were pushed to the sides and the wrappings removed from the plates of food as the first kettles of hot water arrived carried by Mrs Joby Jones and Dan. He had been making himself useful as usual thought Walt as he saw his boy holding the door open for Mrs Joby Jones carrying large kettle of hot water to pour into the first of many pots of tea.

Removing her jacket and hat, Elizabeth joined in with other ladies of the refreshment committee to organise the children in distributing bread and butter. Tea was poured for the adults and Gwladys carried the sugar bowl with an important air for those seated informally around the hall balancing their plates and cups and saucers on any available level surface. Elizabeth brought a tray with three cups of black tea across to her husband, Miah and Mr Price followed by Gwladys and the sugar bowl.

"Do go and help yourselves to some food before it all goes," she said as they took their tea cups. "Don't forget it may be your last chance to eat today for a while."

"The ladies have done a sterling job yet again," said Mr Price putting three large spoonfuls of sugar in his tea and stirring vigorously. "I must remember to thank Mrs Joby Jones before the afternoon is over. I know you still have a lot to do in clearing this away ready for morning service tomorrow but it does help to make it a special occasion for our senior scholars."

"The best treat is yet to come," said Elizabeth.

"What might that be then?" asked Miah surprised.

"Wait and see, but I do wish they'd hurry up before people start thinking of leaving," said Elizabeth. As if on command the chapel door opened and in came the Italian errand boy from Luigi Massari the ice cream manufacturer in town with Dan and his friend Jack carrying between them three large pails of ice cream. The children were delighted with this special treat and queued up to get their ice cream served between two Italian wafer biscuits.

"So, is this regarded as an essential for the tea party and covered by chapel funds?" Walt asked aside to Elizabeth.

"As essential to a midsummer tea party as plum pudding is to Christmas," she replied uncharacteristically. Walt could only smile as he looked on the faces of the delighted children. "Well I'm having my ice cream with a piece of that lovely rhubarb tart I smelled baking this morning," he announced. "Will you join me gentlemen?"

Chapter 7

"Come on ol' fellow, keep up!" said Miah Thomas as he stood and waited. Walt looked red in the face and decidedly uncomfortable as he tramped along the mountain road following some distance behind the large excited group of children and young people from the chapel.

"This heat doesn't help," Walt answered mopping his brow with a large white handkerchief. He had already taken off his jacket, unbuttoned his waistcoat and rolled up the sleeves of his shirt.

"It's a glorious afternoon," said Miah, "ideal for an outing." The Noddfa chapel group included some of the Sunday school teachers and their young charges on the tramp to meet their counterparts from Fochriw for some friendly games on the top of the mountain mid-way between the two communities. As well as the scholars performing at the concert that evening it included most of the children from the Sunday school who had not wanted to miss out on the fun and games.

"At least we haven't far to go now," said Miah. "I think I can see our opponents already waiting on the ridge," he added pointing further up the slope. "Hurry along, we must be late."

Many of the children had already broken into a run to see who could be the first to reach the top. Walt sighed and continued his trudge up the hill. He would definitely be riding back in John Baldwin's cart he thought to himself. All this easy living of the past few years sitting behind a desk, taking the train everywhere and Elizabeth's good cooking was taking its toll on him. He rarely walked far these days unlike his youth when everyone relied on shank's pony to get between the villages. Wisely most of the older members from the chapel in Bargoed who would be joining them this evening at the concert were taking the train up the valley. At last he reached the level open space and was able to sink with relief onto the springy warm turf.

"What a view," said Miah looking down the valley with its steep wooded sides in contrast to the close-cropped turf of the upland. Ponies and sheep grazed the common and there was a lazy buzz to the heat of the afternoon.

"I need a whiff for a few minutes," said Walt. Miah twtied down beside him listening to his knees crack in loud complaint. He lost his balance and his dignity as he rolled onto his back on the turf. Miah laughed quietly and sat up next to Walt.

"No harm done," he commented on his tumble "but I don't know what your young people are thinking. I was asked to referee the 5-a-side football match. And I would have been delighted to oblige if I knew the first thing about the game. Anything more complicated than bat and catti is beyond me I'm afraid," said Miah.

"Football has become a very popular pastime with the miners… Bargoed has at least five teams that I know of," said Walt. "The local paper is full of their exploits…. They are organised into Sunday leagues during the winter months… which affects morning chapel attendance among the younger men… Some play cricket in the summer of course."

"And they have you earmarked as starter for the relay races. Think you can manage old friend?" asked Miah teasingly.

"Just about... it's my usual office on these occasions," said Walt taking a large shiny whistle from his waistcoat pocket. All older miners kept a whistle about them and Walt as an ex-miner knew the advantages underground. The shrill sound carried far and could raise the alarm or summon a rescue party. It was far more effective than shouting and a lot less effort. "But I may need some assistance getting up off the ground… if you do not mind old friend… can you give me a hand up?"

The Sunday school teachers from both chapels had already organised the children into teams for each event. Trefor was playing in the football with the three other boys in his Sunday school class. They had co-opted young Jack Williams to make up the numbers. Jack was a very good footballer. He was 11 and small and wiry for his age but had the agility and turn of speed of a mountain hare. Tref knew Jack through his unlikely friendship with Dan. He had chosen him intentionally since he hoped he might make up for the shortcomings of some of the other players on the team. He particularly had Jack's namesake, John Williams scholar, in mind who would much rather be at home practising the piano regardless of the fine weather. That was much more to the boy's liking than running around after a ball on the mountain. Tref had to use a great deal of persuasion to get him to agree or they would have struggled to field a team.

   The referee for the football was one of the young men from Fochriw. He removed his jacket and tie and, stop watch in hand, started off the game. "Ten minutes each way," he shouted and blew the whistle for the kick off. The few onlookers, mostly boys, called out support to their respective teams as the match began.

   Walt meanwhile had found a very convenient large boulder to sit on and, spreading his jacket over the top, decided it made a good vantage point to oversee events. All the other children, girls included, were organised into two teams for bat and catti.

When the referee blew his whistle for the teams to change ends in the football, the Bargoed senior boys were trailing one-nil to Fochriw. Jack Williams had played well making up for the shortcomings of others on the team. It had been embarrassing for John Williams scholar who had been put in goal but stood frozen to the spot every time the ball came near him. Between the two of them Tref and Jack had put up a good show against a better side and were lucky not to have concede several more goals to the opposition.

At the kick-off Jack started encouraging his team shouting for the ball and trying to organise some defence under attack. He obviously had a good understanding of the tactics of the game, thought Miah watching on, and a bit of flair on the ball. The game had re-started with more urgency in the second half. The Fochriw team scored first and had now extended their lead to two-nil. Miah knew very little about the rules of the game and shouts of "off side ref" from some of the more knowledgeable on-lookers simply baffled him. But he was enjoying the spectacle and could understand the attraction it held to miners working underground all week to spend a few hours running around in the fresh air. Bargoed now had the ball and Jack's pass to his team mate, Tref, resulted in a goal after barely a further minute of play.

"Well done lads!" shouted Miah surprising himself. Tref waved in acknowledgement and they continued to battle through towards the final minutes of the game. After fending off a concerted attack from Fochriw, Jack intercepted a poor pass and, with a clear run down the wing to the open goal, looked like scoring the equaliser. Suddenly he went flying and sprawled on the ground, falling almost at Miah's feet. He had been tripped up from behind by a very large Fochriw boy.

"Foul!" cried the on-lookers. "A penalty I think," someone suggested since Jack would most likely have scored if not for the brutal tackle.

"Are you alright?" Miah asked striding over to Jack and giving the lad a hand to his feet.

"Yes, I think so," he replied getting up and rubbing his shin. Miah ruffled his hair in encouragement and Jack went hobbling off for the ball. He placed it on the imaginary spot in front of the opposition goal as the big lad from Fochriw took his place in the goal mouth between two piles of discarded clothing in lieu of goal posts. Jack ran his fingers through his untidy hair where the tall gent had messed it up. He took a few deep breaths knowing this shot would probably be the last chance in the game to salvage a draw. Jack took a few paces back, wiped his hands on his grubby trousers and made his approach aiming low.

"Goal!" shouted Miah and punched the air enthusiastically. Tref ran over to pat Jack on the back. The boy had the biggest grin on his face Miah had ever seen given the mouthful of rotten blackened stumps that were all remained of the lad's teeth.

"Well played," said Miah, "a well-deserved draw," as the ref's whistle blew to end the match.

Miah joined Walt perched on his boulder. "How is the bat and catti going?" he asked.

"No idea," replied Walt, "I'm not even sure anyone is keeping score... but they are enjoying themselves... that's the main thing."

"Well the boys drew in the football, two goals apiece thanks to your boy and that young lad Jack Williams. They played well considering the superior size of their opponents. A David and Goliath contest," Miah said. "The result was quite a credit to the Bargoed team."

It was a good point to have a break from the activities. Everyone gathered together and sat or lay around on the grass enjoying the late afternoon sun. There was plenty of chatter with the excitement of the concert still to come in the evening. Some, like John Williams scholar, were feeling a little apprehensive about their performances that evening. He was accompanying pretty Celia Baldwin's vocal solo on the pianoforte and they'd only ever had a chance to rehearse together once earlier in the week. He knew his own piano part very well having practiced it relentlessly and hoped Celia would not let him down.

Trefor who, like his father, had little talent for music was hoping he would not forget his lines. Like many who could not sing or play an instrument Trefor had, from an early age, been encouraged by his parents to perform recitations and narrative poems from memory. He did not find it got any easier to overcome his nerves the older he got but he had a good memory which had not let him down yet. He knew that he could have done much better in his bible knowledge test with a memory for rote learning like his. But it wasn't school work and now he felt ashamed he had not made more effort. He felt he had let his father down in front of his old friend Miah Thomas who was well regarded as a theologian; but he realised he had let himself down too.

With the teams finally sorted to include any and all who wanted to take part, the participants took up their places for the relay race. Walt stood on the start line ready to set them off with a blow on his whistle and a wave of his handkerchief. Miah strode over to the finish line to oversee fair play. He had just witnessed how competitiveness could fuel the urge to cheat even on a Sunday school outing.

The girls were as competitive as the boys and, with skirts hiked up between their legs and braids flying they hopped, skipped and sprinted across the short course. Individuals had been carefully selected for each leg of the relay according to their specific skills with the best runners left for the final sprint. Jack was chosen for the last leg on his team but they had left him too much ground to make up. He could not catch the girl in the lead and 14 year old Sian Jones was delighted when she brought her team home first.

"Another 10 yards and I would have caught her," Jack said to Miah as he bent over to catch his breath on the finish line.

Looking briefly at his watch Walt wondered if it was time to move on to the chapel at Fochriw when one of the Sunday school teachers approached him and beckoned Miah to join them.

"We were hoping you'd take part in a final event with us for the children's entertainment," he said. "We were thinking a three-legged race for the adults. It would be a nice way to end the afternoon."

"A grand idea," said Walt "but I'll stick to my role as starter if you don't mind." He patted his rounded paunch as if to suggest that anything faster than a brisk walk was quite out of the question.

"And I'll stand on the finish line again in case there is any dispute over the winner," added Miah who thought he ought to retain some dignity if he was preaching at Noddfa chapel in Fochriw the following day. Both gentlemen knew this would prove be a great treat for the children and it was very sporting of the younger teachers to volunteer to share in the spirit of the occasion.

Those taking part chose their partners and used the men's ties or girl's hair ribbons to attach themselves at the ankle. There was a lot of hilarity and a few tumbles as they practiced the unfamiliar manoeuvre of running as a pair. Some of the children decided this looked like great fun and copied their elders. Those without any means to tie their ankles tried to run in synchrony with their partner. Eventually the main participants lined up at the start. There were four couples which included Sian to make up the pairings. She was conjoined with the young man from Fochriw who had refereed the football; he had chosen his partner well.

At the whistle they streaked off into the lead as one couple struggled to get into a rhythm and clung desperately to each other before they tumbled over. Another pair hopped, skipped and jumped along but managed to keep on their feet while the fourth pair had adopted a strange high kicking style which kept them in contention at first. But nothing was going to stop Sian and her newfound partner who crossed the finish well ahead of the others and then took a dramatic and well-timed fall after crossing the line. The others straggled across the finish and the last pair who, eventually having re-found their feet, brought up the rear and were cheered just as loudly as the first.

It had been a great afternoon everyone agreed. All present gathered into a large circle to give thanks to God for their good fortune, fully bellies, the fine weather and finally to ask his blessing on their efforts in the forthcoming concert. It was going to be a long day for those taking part and they were very pleased to hear there was ginger beer and iced buns waiting for them at the chapel in Fochriw. It was time to move on the last few miles to the village and the waiting refreshments.

No one had noticed that John Baldwin had caught them up with his empty milk cart and horse and now he was patiently watching and waiting on the mountain track. His mare had her nose in a feed bag so they had been there some time. It was only those children taking part in the concert and the adults that were going on to the chapel in Fochriw. The other children were returning home across the mountain road in broad daylight. Most of them knew the common like the back of their hand although Walt did impress on them to stay near the track and try to stick together as a group. He doubted they would heed his advice once they were out of sight as some of the boys were already racing off back in the direction they had come.

Before Jack could run after them Walt beckoned him over.

"I thought if you were here then Dan would not be far away. I haven't seen him since the tea. It would be nice to get him to join in more with the other children," he said.

Jack had no idea how to address Dan's father, him being a deacon at chapel as well as the new miners' agent. Jack's father was eager to impress on his son what an important man Mr Lewis was these days and one deserving of respect.

"Oh, he wouldn't come to something like this would he?" the boy blurted out. "I mean most of the kids ignore him or else call him names. And he can't join in, can he? When he runs so funny I mean and falls over so much. They'd just laugh and think he doesn't understand. Not that they'd do it in front of you being his Dadda and that," Jack added lamely. Walt smiled weakly at the boy's honesty.

"Well off you go and make sure the others get back safely. Give my regards to your father... and don't stay out too late now," said Walt. He ruffled the boy's hair and turned back to take his seat alongside John Baldwin in the cart. Jack ran off running his fingers through his mop of thick dark hair wondering what it was with these old chaps and his hair. Miah chose to walk alongside leading the horse while the young concert party followed behind and chatted happily.

68

"Well that was a grand idea," said Miah as he strolled alongside the cart. "It has been a real change for me at least. I cannot remember the last time I was invited to take part in such an informal and enjoyable capacity. It's not often I get the chance to slough off the responsibilities of my position. I found the whole thing thoroughly refreshing and actually enjoyed watching the football match."

"Yes," said Walt, "I may have had my misgivings about this event but the young people have enjoyed themselves... And it is good for them to see that their elders joining in the fun. I only hope the return journey this evening does not prove to be an error of judgement on the part of our young folk... Some of these children will be very tired to troop across the mountain in the dark."

"But what an adventure," said John Baldwin. "They will remember today for the rest of their lives as will I. These are our first bible scholars in our new chapel, Gwallt, with my little Cecelia and your Trefor among them. There's a proud father I am and not ashamed to admit it."

"Yes, indeed John," said Walt "there is satisfaction to be had in the achievements of our children... I understand how you feel. This has been an occasion well worth celebrating."

As the cart reached the turn down into the village they had a good view of Fochriw dominated by the huge winding gear and pit head across the valley. Miah noticed a large standing stone silhouetted against the skyline on the high ground. It was several hundred yards further on beside the track as it reached its summit. "Is that what I think it is?" he asked his companions pointing to the monolith in the distance.

"Yes, quite an ancient landmark on the common. I was born and raised in Bedlinog down in the Taff-Bargod valley over the hill from here to the west," replied John

Baldwin pointing vaguely in the right direction. "I remember the standing stone was much taller when I was a lad. And this trackway is thought to be the remains of a Roman road leading to the fort at Gelligaer. Heol Adam it is called perhaps because it is as old as Adam. Who knows? The newspapers have reported that antiquarians from the museum in Cardiff have been digging at the site of the Roman fort again this year."

"Yes," added Walt "They have made some interesting finds including a stone inscription in Latin. I was given a tour of the site... they plan to unearth more of its secrets over the next few years. That standing stone pre-dates the Roman times... harks back to our most ancient Celtic ancestors... We also passed the site if Capel Gwladys a mile or so back. This common hides many more of Gwalia's ancient secrets in its lumps, bumps and platforms no doubt."

"Although there is no mistaking the imprint of mankind on the landscape of the present day," said Miah looking across to the industrial activity at Fochriw pits on the other side of the valley as they turned to descend into the village itself.

Chapter 8

The audience for the concert that evening was growing steadily and, when the contingent from Bargoed arrived by train, Noddfa chapel was full to capacity. The large united choir from Bedlinog had already taken up their places in the impressive choir stalls looking down from a height on the congregation below.

Walt, Miah and David Price were given seats at the front along with the minister from Fochriw, Mr Leyshon. He started the proceedings by welcoming the guests from Bargoed and the choir from Bedlinog. No gathering in chapel could be complete without some congregational singing and they all joined together in some favourite Welsh hymns to begin. The sound was majestic, thought Walt as everyone present knew their parts for the harmony, not just the choir. The large pipe organ added to the depth of sound which made the hairs on the back of his neck tingle.

Miah was introduced as their distinguished guest that evening and gave a brief address as was expected. He had been given an order of events by Mr Leyshon scribbled on an old envelope in pencil. Without his introductions, the performers and audience would not know what was coming next. He complimented the singing but chose to highlight the contribution of the young people to the evening's entertainment. This was a very special event for those starting out in life with an excellent knowledge of the Bible for which he thanked the hard work of their Sunday school teachers.

The choir started the programme with a hymn sung to the tune Cwm Rhondda written in 1905 during the revival for a Gymanfa Ganu in Pontypridd. It was already a firm favourite with Welsh congregations. They followed that in a

71

contrast of style with John Roberts Welsh translation of the hymn known as to all as Gwahoddiad. The beautiful tune and heavy Christian sentiment was beloved up and down the land. Music had played a significant part in the recent Welsh revival. This chorus repeated over and over at revival meetings put those gathered in a meditative mood. The audience joined in the final chorus:

Arglwydd dyma fi
Ar dy alwad di,
Canna f'enaid yn y gwaed
A gaed ar Galfari.

The next item was John Williams, our scholar, who was to play the pianoforte. It was a variation on *Dafydd y Garreg Wen* he had arranged himself. His youth coupled with his proficiency as a pianist quite stunned the audience as they listened to the beautiful and familiar Welsh air in an unfamiliar setting. Without a break in the performance and a nod from the pianist he was joined by little 12-year old Celia who sang the words of *Dafydd Y Garreg Wen* in her beautiful clear soprano to his piano accompaniment. The applause was deafening as both young people stood together to receive the plaudits, both embarrassed but overjoyed at the response.

"Well," said Miah aside to Walt "the boy may not be much of a footballer but he knows how to play the piano." He stood up as the applause continued.

"Was that your own composition?" he asked John scholar.

"Yes Sir," replied John scholar abashed. His mother in the audience was visibly moved by her son's performance as she dabbed away a tear with her lace handkerchief.

"What a talent we have witnessed tonight," said Miah to the audience, "a young composer in the making and beautiful singing; wonderful musicianship from both performers." The applause continued as they took their seats.

Trefor's contribution was the next item on the list and, as the applause died, away Miah introduced him. He was doubly nervous to follow on such a well-received item and stumbled taking the few steps up to the front. He chose his place and took a few deep breaths as his father had taught him; at least he did not have to sing he consoled himself. He had already performed this monologue once before at a much smaller gathering very successfully and, settling himself for a few seconds as the audience looked on in anticipation, he announced the title "The Highwayman by Alfred Noyes." It was an unusual choice since it was in English but he had his father's approval which was enough for him. Walt had said it was time the audience was treated to something new.

During the first lines of the narrative poem he gained in confidence as he heard his newfound baritone voice, so reminiscent of his father, ring out across the hall. When he got to the bit about the highwayman came riding-riding- riding he remembered all the dramatic inflections learned from reading plays at school and which he had practiced in the front room at home. He knew he had grabbed the audience interest for the story and encouraged by their rapt attention continued with the narrative not hesitating once, even at the word 'breast'. He remembered all the actions, the rhythm and pace of the words like the hoof beats of the highwayman's horse. He took his audience on the journey with him right up to the end when he staggered as the highwayman lay dying in his own blood and leaned against the pianoforte for dramatic effect.

He had given his best performance yet and, as the audience applause rang out, he could not resist taking a bow. Most of those present had never heard this particular narrative poem but it was highly effective and proved very popular. Trefor had managed to add a few highly individual actions to the version he had rehearsed before his father at home. But the audience seemed to appreciate his rendition and he beamed across at his father looking for his approval.

"It looks as if you have an able elocutionist in the family…" said Miah to his old friend as Walt continued to applaud and smile at his son, "… a talented actor even."

The next item was a family contribution from Fochriw who sang another traditional Welsh air *Clychau Aberdyfi* unaccompanied and in close harmony. Miah was amazed to see the young brute of a man who had felled Jack Williams singing like an angel in the group with his parents, brothers and sisters. Many of the evenings' contributors were trying out their performances for the many eisteddfodau held locally. The popularity of these events had done a great deal to improve and perfect the musical talent in the valley.

Next some older children and two adults of the Fochriw Sunday school performed in a concertina band with a very elderly white-haired man providing percussion on the spoons. It was a light-hearted item very much appreciated by the audience. The choir contributed last to the evening with some familiar passages from Handel's Messiah concluding with that great crowd pleaser the Hallelujah chorus, their winning entry in the recent Bargoed May Day eisteddfod.

The evening could not finish without giving the congregation another opportunity to exercise their vocal chords. They sang a few more favourite hymns ending with *Ar hyd y Nos*. The music and singing had been exceptional this evening, a reflection of the traditional Gymanfa Ganu or community singing organised regularly by all chapels in the area and across Wales and beyond, wherever the Welsh congregated.

The audience seemed reluctant to leave after the final thanks and blessing expectantly awaiting a cup of tea. Parents collected their children together and Walt saw John Williams scholar leave to catch the train down the valley with his parents. Wise boy, he thought to himself at the prospect of the trek home by horse and cart. Others stood around chatting, greeting friends and acquaintances while tea was served from the chapel's very own kitchen. Walter always attracted a lot of interest with several people eager to make themselves known to the miners' agent and his guest.

One man in particular descended purposefully on Walt, obviously a miner given the visible blue scars on his hands and face. The man was intent on using this opportunity to bring up the question of the 8 hour Act introduced the previous year by the Liberal government which limited the hours a miner could work underground per day. He wanted to know Walter's opinion on the matter and, like many disgruntled miners, did not look as if he would be easily put off.

"Please excuse me," Miah said softly to Walter having noticed the small deputation gathering around them, "I think I'm wanted." Walter looked across the hall and recognised one of the deacons of the chapel with Mr Leyshon the minister who was beckoning across to Miah obviously keen to speak to him. "It's probably about the arrangements for tomorrow." Walt nodded to his friend and returned his attention to the group now gathered about him.

This one piece of legislation had proved unpopular with both miners and pit managers alike. Even the miners' wives complained their husbands would be at home under their feet too much if they only worked 8 hour shift. It had become especially unpopular with those who worked in the older deep mines in the north of the valley like Fochriw and Bedlinog pits. Here the work force faced a reduction in wages because they were paid by ton of coal extracted. It took them so long to walk to and from the working coalface underground it soon eked into an eight-hour shift. The situation was made even worse if they worked under less favourable conditions. The managers likewise bemoaned the reduction in productivity were it to be implemented. The South Wales coalfield had the worst accident record underground in the whole of the country and it was hoped the accident rate would be reduced if miners worked less long shifts.

It was a difficult situation for Walter as the union official representing the workers but one which he had plenty of practice at dealing with. His profile and significance among the miners of the Rhymney Valley meant there were few who did not recognise him now or take every opportunity to seek his opinion on some issue or other. While the Act was a positive step towards improving the welfare of the miners, it was the other implications when it came to pay and the effect on living standards which were uppermost in the thoughts of these men. The situation highlighted the need for more fundamental reforms in the working conditions underground which could not be addressed by simply reducing the hours of the working day. But these were long term goals that did not placate the immediate concerns of members of the Fed.

The matter was not helped with the ongoing development of new mines further south in the valley which employed the very latest technology to increase productivity. Here the new Act was welcomed. Just a few months ago Bargoed colliery had achieved its record coal output in a single shift albeit 10 hours long. Penallta colliery had just gone into full production using the new scheme and plans were well underway to open the first all-electric mine at Britannia the following year based on an 8-hour shift pattern.

Walt thought carefully before answering the man's concerns knowing how change, even for the better, was met at first with deep suspicion by the workforce.

"We cannot ignore the law," he said to the men, "especially when it aims ultimately to improve working conditions underground... The aim of the Fed is to ensure it does not reduce the workers' pay along with their hours'. Few of the pits at the top of the valley are intending to comply with the Act... But this is a national issue... in my opinion it could escalate into industrial action if it comes to a ballot."

The men gathered around him nodded sagely and listened intently as Walt continued. "You must have been aware of the Fed's drive to increase membership in the valley? Paying your penny due gives our voice strength in unity. We... the miners' Federation... will work towards improving pay *and* working conditions. Are you a paid up member of the Fed?" Looking at the shamefaced miner Walt could see he had made his point. Another man in the group reached out to shake Walt's hand enthusiastically.

"It's a penny well spent in my opinion," he said beaming at Walt. "You're one of us after all and I for one am proud to be represented by a union who elects men such as you."

Walt knew this was a reference to the fact that he had spent more than 20 years underground himself, working in every capacity except as haulier. Walter smiled and nodded at the man's appreciative remarks.

"I started underground as a pit boy aged 9 years old... because the iron masters of Tredegar chose to ignore the legislation... passed many years before... preventing children under 12 working in any capacity... never mind underground. I do not want to see the law ignored again. We must make it work for us... that is my aim at least," said Walt. "Now talking of children... I am needed to escort our young party back over the mountain... if you will excuse me, gentlemen. I hope I will see you at the next meeting in the area... which will be tomorrow afternoon in the Victoria Hall, Rhymney... Join us," he said to the first miner "and add your voice to the debate."

Walt was relieved he had got out of that situation relatively lightly compared to others. Whether it was the fact that they were in chapel or the way in which he addressed the group he did not know, but he could never escape his responsibilities as the miners' representative. He took his empty teacup back to the ladies in the kitchen and thanked them for making the tea before making a quick exit out of the back of the building. He went in search of his companions and hoped to bid a final farewell to Miah and thank him for his contribution to the success of the day.

It was much cooler outside in the advancing twilight and, looking around, Walt saw the tall dark silhouette of his friend Miah at the corner of the building. But before he could hail his attention a young woman appeared from the shadows and stood before Miah. Walt clearly saw her pale, shining face looking up at the tall man before her and heard her say "Father it is me, Mary. Do you not know me?" Miah seemed to hesitate but opened his arms to embrace the young woman. "Can it really be you my child? Praise the Lord, my prayers are finally answered," Walt heard his old friend speak into the night over the young woman's head. "Our Saviour, Jesus Christ is good indeed."

"There you are," said a voice behind him. Walt turned startled to see it was John Baldwin. He quickly ushered him back into the kitchen and away from the scene behind him, "We've been waiting out front, cart loaded and all eager to be off on our adventure."

"I'm coming," said Walt, "held up with union matters again I'm afraid." As he walked away he was deeply puzzled by the scene he had just witnessed, especially by the exchange he had inadvertently overheard.

Chapter 9

Rae carried baby Henry in her woollen shawl, Edith held May's hand and Cath and Nell skipped along ahead on their weekly parade to the early morning service at St Cadoc's church in Bedlinog. All the girls looked neat and tidy having had their weekly bath in the old tub in front of the range the previous evening. Their long hair shone in the sunlight. Rae always felt proud of the way the girls turned out each week but she would have felt even better if the men in the household would join them at church. Sam seemed indifferent to religion but, not to offend his wife, would accompany them on the odd occasion. He preferred to use his day off for one of his many projects. The family had left him amid the pieces of an old bicycle he was repairing; something else he had salvaged and hoped to sell on.

Rae had long since given up on the souls of her brothers Seth and Lewis who, more often than not, disappeared for the whole day at this time of the year with a shotgun and dog. At least Henry had no choice in the matter of church attendance yet, or for some time to come, she thought to herself as she felt the weight of his baby warmth against her breast. Rae had never seen the young couple from No 6 at church either, but then again, they could be chapel of course.

Ahead of them Lydia Waters, dressed up to the nines and carrying her fox stole despite the warm weather, with her husband and boys was heading in the same direction. As they passed number 3, Billy Prosser sat on the doorstep in the sunshine and stuck out his tongue making raspberry noises at the Waters family.

"'Ark at 'im, Billy Bully Prosser," said May. Lydia ignored them and walked on straight and tall. But Albert Waters turned behind his mother's back to make a very rude gesture at his protagonist. He blushed scarlet when he saw that it had not gone unnoticed by Rae and her girls.

"Did you see that Mam?" whispered May in shocked tones. "Ignore them girls," Rae said holding her head up as dignified as she could as they passed the neighbour's house. The Prosser's were church too but Rae knew that Maggie and Bert could not cobble together a decent outfit for any of their children to attend the Sunday school even in summer.

"I think I may have found a position for you Edith," she said to her oldest girl. "Mr Beynon the baker's sister-in-law, a Mrs Roberts in Trelewis is looking for some help with her household. Her youngest boy is going down the pit at the end of the year when he leaves school. Her only daughter is married and expecting her first and living at home so she is going to need help in the house." Edith said nothing.

"You will be old enough to leave the schoolroom at Christmas. I have discussed it with your father and if this woman and her family keep a good home then we should settle the matter sooner rather than later." Rae waited for a response but still Edie said nothing, she only squeezed little May's hand a little tighter. "We are eager to find you a suitable position. You'll not be needed for a while yet mind you. At least not until the baby comes so you have some time to get used to the idea." There was still no reply from her daughter. "I shall keep you and Nell from school tomorrow," Rae added.

"What for?" asked Edie suddenly surprised since the girls never, ever missed a school day.

"Nell is coming with me to the opticians in Pontypridd to have her eyesight tested. Your father thinks it time she has reading glasses of her own. And you will help me choose some cloth for a new dress and blouse. Coarse calico for some new pinafores for the girls obviously, but you have grown a lot this last few months and nothing seems to fit you tidy anymore," said her mother looking at the girl's increasing bust.

Edith blushed awkwardly at this obvious reference to her developing figure. "We cannot keep you in a pinafore for ever now can we? There's nothing of mine suitable to cut down for you and I have some sweet money saved. I cannot think of anything I'd rather spend it on at the moment," she added.

Edith suspected her mother had included her in this rare term time expedition as a treat to soften the news she had just imparted. Fancy her leaving school at the end of the year and going into service? It was a big step, one for which she felt ill prepared. Her mother had done it before her, keeping house for her elderly grandmother and older brothers, and Edie bowed to the inevitable fact that she was indeed growing up fast. It was not the work she feared but leaving the familiarity of her childhood home; her father, the uncles, the animals and especially her sisters. As if reading her mind, Rae put her free arm around her daughter's shoulders as they strolled along.

"We will miss you too," she said quietly to which Edie responded with a weak smile and fought back a tear. "And at least you will be close to home," added her Mam. "It's not as if we're packing you off to London town now, is it?"

*

During the morning service at chapel, David Price gave an impressive sermon based on Corinthians 12:10, '*Therefore I take pleasure in infirmities, in reproaches, in necessities, in persecutions, in distresses for Christ's sake: for when I am weak, then am I strong.*'

Although it could be apply to many areas of life, Walt found it particularly apt for his work with the Fed and regretted Miah had not had the opportunity to hear the young man in action. He asked his wife's opinion on the sermon and the preacher as they walked home to Ty Gwent. Elizabeth confirmed his good opinion of David Price.

Unusually the house was empty when they arrived home. The children attended Sunday school immediately after the main service and had already left. Sunday was the day when the family used the front parlour. It was the best room in the house with its ornate fireplace and mantle, horsehair stuffed three-piece suite in burgundy, glass display cabinet for Elizabeth's best pieces of china, bookcase and the small wooden cabinet from which her Singer sewing machine miraculously unfolded.

Walt retired to the room alone to read while his wife prepared an early lunch for him, leftover cold meat and potatoes, with boiled beetroot and bread and butter. He opened his bible to find the text for the sermon that morning and ponder further on the words of sermon which had resonated strongly with him. Young David Price had quite a gift as a preacher; a talent that eluded Miah despite his reputation as a bible scholar and a limitation that he was always the first to admit.

Walt then closed his bible and opened it at random, something he often did to find solace when troubled even without realising it. His eyes lighted on the page and read the first verse that came to view:

Train up a child in the way he should go: and when he is old, he will not depart from it - Proverbs 22:6

This unsettled his peace of mind reminding him, yet again, of the strange scene he had witnessed between Miah and the young woman claiming to be his daughter the previous evening. Or that was what he assumed. A Baptist minister would never encourage any of his flock to address him as Father, at least not in his experience and he could not imagine ever Miah doing so.

The only conclusion he could come to was that the young woman must indeed be Miah's daughter. But Miah had never spoken of his family except to say he had been an only child and all his nearest kin were now deceased which did not encouraged Walter to enquire further. It was not impossible for Miah to have a daughter he thought. She looked very young and did not have Miah's height being quite petite although, he had to admit, it was difficult to tell her age from a brief glimpse in the twilight. It all seemed a mystery since Miah had never referred to her in all the years he had known him.

"Your dinner is on the table," Elizabeth's voice broke his reverie. "You have just enough time to eat it before the Fed meeting this afternoon."

There would to be no play or games for the young Lewis children despite the fine weather on the Lord's Day. Fortunately, attendance at Sunday school left them little time to get bored. No sooner had they finished their meal than they returned to chapel for the afternoon session. Great store was given to Bible study and even the little ones like Ceridwen and Gwladys knew their bible stories well. Gwladys loved it since she was not yet old enough to attend proper school like her sister Ceridwen. She was proving to be the most precocious of Walter and Elizabeth's children in that she could read fluently already; even bible text which she could not possibly understand she read almost faultlessly.

The girls loved to play at school with Ceridwen teaching Gwladys everything she had learned herself during the week. This meant Gwladys had an extensive vocabulary of Welsh and English words and often spoke in a mixture of both. Playing school was by far their favourite pastime which their parents had encouraged by providing a blackboard and easel for the girls' Christmas surprise. It was only during their classroom role play that Gwladys allowed her sister to tell her what to do which meant Ceridwen relished being teacher as much as Gwladys wanted to be pupil. After Sunday school both girls would be eager to relate to their parents the full content of their Bible instruction that day.

Walt would much rather spend the day with his family and accompany his wife to the Gamanfa Ganu at Ainon chapel in Gilfach later but today, and far too often, his Sundays would be taken up with union matters. Many public meetings were held in the area on Sunday, the only day that the majority of the workforce was available to attend in the significant numbers needed. This afternoon he was off to Victoria Hall, Rhymney for a meeting with the miners employed by Rhymney Iron Company.

Not all the pit managers in the valley were as willing to listen to the men's concerns as Powell Duffryn who were expanding their enterprise in the lower Rhymney Valley. At least they acknowledged that output, and hence profit, was directly proportional to the miners' welfare. Walt used this argument successfully to avert disputes as the management were more receptive to the wellbeing of the workforce.

The company fully supported the building of the miners' hospital in Aberbargoed, providing the land and covering the initial costs to implement the project. Running costs would be funded by a deduction from the wages of the men employed in Powell Duffryn collieries. Mr Hann had spared no expense in the development of Bargoed colliery travelling throughout Europe to source the latest equipment for haulage and ventilation. He had put in place even greater improvements for Britannia and Penallta which contrasted sharply with conditions in the older mines still reliant on naked lights, ponies and door boys.

Later again that same evening his attendance was required at a charity concert at the English Baptist Church in Hanbury Road. The concert had been organised by a group of singers from Abergwynfi where a local colliery had been shut because the managers claimed it no longer paid under present conditions. Nine hundred men and boys were without a job which resulted in 1500 women and children suffering for want of food. The singing party, under the direction of a local councillor, had been performing in the streets and organising concerts in the valley to collect money to help the families affected.

Somewhere on the South Wales coalfield there always seemed to be a long-term dispute causing real hardship for the miners and their families. Although far from the Rhymney Valley, Walt knew that the miners of Abergwynfi had been locked out because of a wage claim made under a clause in the South Wales Miners' Federation agreement and the dispute had nothing to do with the local geology as the management claimed. He could only hope there would be a good turnout for the singers to reward their efforts towards the Abergwynfi miners' hardship fund.

As he put on his suit jacket and straightened his tie in the hall mirror, he thought of the conflict between serving God and serving the members of the Fed on The Sabbath but, on this occasion, he hoped the one would result in the other; the plight of the striking miner's families, especially the innocent children, being uppermost in his concerns. So, this evening the miners of Abergwynfi and their families had priority over his own and, in making a speech in support of their predicament, he could encourage the congregation to show good Christian charity and give generously in their donations.

He quickly checked his pockets to make sure he had sufficient funds on hand to set a good example through his own generosity to the cause. Putting on his best Homberg hat after quickly combing his hair and moustache, he left the house and his family still comfortably closeted in the front parlour. His working week was not limited to the office but, over the years, service to the members Fed and concern for the welfare of their families had increasingly occupied most of his waking hours. He could not do it without the support of his dear wife and his faith in the Lord. Between them they kept his body and soul fuelled for the fight.

*

Esau was enjoying a cigarette as he strolled with a large group of other single men down the High Street. They were soaking up the sunshine and admiring the single girls who walked arm in arm showing off their Sunday best outfits. Ostensibly they were on their way to or from the church or chapel but the girls noticed the young men who, in turn, noticed the young women. The 'monkey walk' had become quite a Sunday tradition and the fine weather had bought them out in larger numbers than usual. Esau was enjoying the view. His height often attracted admiring glances from the young ladies who pointed out the 'tall one' to each other. His height gave him another advantage as he spotted Walt's black Homberg hat bobbing around in the crowd outside the Hanbury Road chapel.

He crossed to the other side of the roadway, stubbing out his cigarette under foot in the mud. It would be a pity to spoil a lovely evening by being collared into attending a dreary concert for some miners' hardship fund by his brother-in-law. There were several of hours of daylight remaining and Esau intended to linger a little longer with his companions doing nothing in particular. He had quite forgot that he had promised Elizabeth he would sit with the children this evening so that she could go to the Gamanfa Ganu.

Chapter 10

Elizabeth was feeling anxious after everyone had left on Monday morning since the Post Office were coming to put in the new telephone line. She had no idea how much disruption it would cause or if she'd have any mess to clear up afterwards. She'd had enough of all that during the recent building work although Walter had done his best to reassure her that, today, it would only be a wire through the door frame. The rest of the work would be confined outside and did not involve any major act of demolition he assured her.

The post that morning had bought a letter for Esau calling him for an interview later that week for one of the jobs he'd recently applied for; cashier and invoice clerk in the office at the new Peglars grocery opening in town. The job would suit him she thought as everyone in the family had a good head for figures. He would prefer a desk job to labouring in the colliery. This could be a good opening for him if he was successful and, with money in his pocket, he might feel less of a burden to his sister's family. Esau was not in her good books after letting her down last night. He still seemed to lack any sense of responsibility to others. And that wasn't his only fault. Elizabeth was thinking particularly of her brother's smoking habits.

Walter never asked where Esau got his tobacco but Elizabeth had been buying it on account from the Co-op with the housekeeping. Luckily her husband had long since given up scrutinising the household bills since she had more than proved capable of managing within the budget he allocated for the household. By making a few economies, which had gone unnoticed by her husband, she had succeeded in not asking for an extra penny since Esau had moved in. But if Walter found out he was paying for Esau's cigarettes, well, he would not be happy and she felt guilty about keeping a secret from her husband, even more so after Esau's oversight yesterday.

She was too soft with him just because she still treated him as the youngest and most vulnerable of her siblings. At least Esau had the good sense not to smoke in front of Walter or anywhere else in the house that she was aware of, other than the kitchen with the back door open. As Elizabeth fretted about her torn loyalties between husband and brother, she had no idea that outside the Post Office engineers were already on the job extending the line to install the telephone at Ty Gwent.

Walt had left home early that morning to attend an inquest into the death of a haulier in Deri. He decided to walk over the Graig to the village just a few miles distant rather than take the train. The early morning walk might do him good on such a fine day. An urgent message had come into the office on Saturday morning requesting representation by an official from the Fed at the inquest to be held that Monday morning. It was the practice of the union to send a representative to every inquest on a fatality involving one of its paid up members. Looking in the diary Walt realised he was the only senior official without a prior engagement so had taken on the responsibility himself after writing the details neatly in the engagement diary.

When he arrived at the inquest, which was being held in a local public house, he made a point of introducing himself to the widow who was relieved to hear that he was here to represent her interests on behalf of the Fed. He did not add that he had no details of the incident other than the name of the deceased which was not unusual. He had attended far too many inquests during the years he had been a Fed official.

Walt sat in the airless back room of the Darren Inn and listened intently to the proceedings and evidence of the witnesses, occasionally appearing to making notes. It seems the 48 year old haulier had incurred severe multiple injuries commensurate with being crushed by a de-railed tram, sadly an all too common hazard of the job. The only witnesses at the inquest had arrived after the incident and could attach no blame to the rail or equipment. This was examined by the safety officer as part of the routine at the site of an accident after the severely injured man had been removed to the pit head for medical attention. This exonerated any blame which could be directed at the pit management but the family were still entitled to financial support. The deceased had paid his weekly penny to the Fed and was not in arrears, something Walt had immediately checked on first hearing of the incident.

It seemed a straightforward case to Walter but there was an unusual twist to come. When the medical evidence was put forward, the duty doctor, who attended to the injured man at the pit head, differed in his opinion of the cause of death to his medical colleague, a local practitioner, who had attended the victim during the two days and nights immediately following the incident until his death last Friday night. The family had called their local physician to attend the badly injured man at home in the hope he could be treated despite the cost. This doctor's evidence stated death was due to kidney failure. In his opinion, the symptoms of kidney failure were obvious and could be due to a pre-existing condition unrelated to the accident.

His colleague the duty doctor, however, argued that kidney failure could also be a direct consequence of crushing injuries to the lower abdomen incurred at the time of the accident. Both men were insisting on putting forward their different medical opinions at the inquest. As the purpose was to determine the cause of death their evidence was crucial to the coroner's decision and, based on that, whether Walter would be able to authorise compensation for the widow.

"Has a post mortem examination been carried out to determine whether the loss of kidney function was owing to the man's injuries or to long term degeneration of the kidneys?" asked the coroner to both medical men. Both doctors admitted it had not. "Would such an examination settle this issue?" Both doctors agreed it would. "Well I fail to understand why you have not undertaken this procedure before now. Since the remains of the deceased are on the premises I suggest we adjourn while you carry out the post mortem."

Walter was repelled by the idea of the post mortem being carried out in a storeroom of a public house with the widow on the premises. But he reluctantly admitted to himself that it was the only sensible suggestion to resolve the case today. He folded his notes into a pocket and followed the coroner outside for some fresh air and relief from the airless back room of the inn.

"An unfortunate business this," said Walter who knew Mr Rees the local coroner from previous inquests. He steered the gentleman away from the group gathering outside which included a local newspaper reporter who he knew well and was not averse to eavesdropping on a private conversation. Walter accepted the man's congratulations on his election into office before continuing. "The completion of the miners' hospital cannot come too soon in my opinion. This is no place to conduct a post mortem. We all deserve some dignity in death whatever the circumstances."

"I could not agree with you more Mr Lewis," the coroner replied. "How advanced is the hospital project?"

"It is proceeding apace at last... At the last meeting of the committee which I was privileged to attend... we were shown the finalised architects' plans. There is to be a mortuary and post mortem room in the basement... The building work has been out to tender... Powell Duffryn have released the land and given the go ahead now the contractor has been appointed. All being well... it is hoped it will be staffed, open and running in the New Year."

"Excellent," said the coroner, "that should put an end to the less than satisfactory situation we find ourselves in this morning."

"How long do you expect them to take over this post mortem examination?" asked Walter.

"In my experience, not very long if the evidence is clear cut," said the coroner.

"I hope that proves the case... Without evidence one way or the other... I cannot see either of our distinguished medical men willing to back down over their opinions on this issue. It's not a matter of professional pride... You realise a verdict of death by natural causes will leave the widow without the financial support I can authorise on behalf of the Federation."

"I hope you are not trying to influence the outcome of these proceedings," said the coroner with a wry smile.

"Simply stating a fact Mr Rees," said Walter with a firm gaze at the coroner, "although you might like to bear that in mind... should the medical evidence prove inconclusive." They did not have long to wait which looked as if the coroner would be able to make his decision before midday.

*

That afternoon Walter was back in the Fed offices in the Bank Chambers in Bargoed. He completed the paperwork relating to the inquest and dictated a letter to the coroner's office requesting a copy of the death certificate in order to authorise payments to the widow. Both doctors had agreed that the kidneys showed evidence of physical damage and, with the absence of any signs of atrophy typical of long term kidney disease, concluded the cause of death was kidney failure caused by crushing injuries to the lower abdomen. Thus the duty doctor, with his experience of attending mining accidents, had been vindicated. The coroner returned a verdict of accidental death. Relieved at the outcome on behalf of the widow and her family, Walter turned his attention to other more routine matters in the week ahead which included his presence at the executive meeting in Cardiff.

When Walt arrived home, he was greeted unexpectedly by Elizabeth at the door.

"It's here," she said excitedly and ushered him in. The children all stood on the threshold of the study staring in wonder at the black candlestick apparatus on their father's desk.

"How does it work?" asked Trefor. Walt was amused by the family's curiosity since the telephone was no longer a novelty to him in the office.

"Now, that depends on what sort of answer you want... I have no idea how it works," said Walt smiling, "but I can show you how to use it. It would be useful for you Elizabeth... if there is a call when I'm out." Walt lifted the earpiece from the side cradle and then tapped it several times. Putting the earpiece in place and holding the mouthpiece up to his face he spoke to the operator.

"Good day operator… This is Mr Walter Lewis speaking... miners' agent… I am at home at Ty Gwent. The new apparatus has been installed today... I was simply checking it was in working order. Could you put a call through, please? My wife will answer… Yes I will, thank you," and returned the earpiece to its cradle.

"Is it that simple?" asked Elizabeth.

"Yes, my dear. When making a call you speak to the operator... then ask to be connected to the number you want. Our number is written here... Bargoed 27." Suddenly there was a loud ringing behind them which made them all jump at the volume of the unfamiliar bell high on the wall in the passage.

"Come on Elizabeth," said Walt handing the telephone to her. "Just put this to your ear... And speak into the mouthpiece."

"Is that you Miss Davies, in the Post Office? Well I never. I can hear you clearly… Yes very well… and the family? How is your mother's rheumatics these days?"

Walt turned to the children "Your mother's a natural," he said. "Put the earpiece in the cradle when you've finished your conversation," he said to Elizabeth and shooed the children from the doorway out to the kitchen before he removed his jacket to hang on the stand in the hallway.

*

Rae and her two girls had returned home from Pontypridd before the rest of the family and in time to put the tea on.

"Put those packages away before your father sees what I've been buying," said Rae. "In the front parlour, he never goes in there," she added. "Let's get some tea on I could do with a cup, I am parched."

"Sit down Mam, we'll do it," said Edie as she stoked the fire to get it going again and added more coal. Rae looked tired after carrying Henry around all day in a shawl. Her back really was getting worse. At least she hoped it was just her back or could she possibly be expecting again?

"It'll be awhile. Shall I peel some potatoes while we're waiting?" asked Edie.

"You are a good girl," said her mother unpacking the groceries from her basket. "Let's scrape some of those new potatoes we bought today, it will be a nice change. Put some eggs in to boil too. We'll finish that cold ham tonight. Nell take Henry's wet nappies off, there's a good girl. Put them in with the others in the bucket in the yard. I must do some washing tomorrow after spending the day away from my chores," she added. "Let some air get to him or he'll be getting sore again and grizzling." Rae watched her girls set about their tasks, relieved to take the weight off her feet before enjoying a nice cup of tea when the kettle eventually boiled.

They heard May and Cath coming before they burst through the open door into the kitchen after school.

"Did it hurt?" asked Cath excitedly. "Do they use needles?" Nell looked baffled. "Testing your eyes - was it painful like when we had those jabs in school?"

"Oh, nothing like that," replied Nell. "I just had to read letters while the man held up different rounds of glass 'til we found the ones that worked best. Nothing painful at all," she added. Both Cath and May looked disappointed.

"Where are they then? The spectacles? Can we try them?"

"I shall collect them on Saturday morning after work," their mother replied. "Now have a drink and a piece of bread and butter and go out and enjoy the sunshine all of you. Let me have a whiff b' here before the men come home."

*

There had been no sign of Dan at Ty Gwent all afternoon and he had not yet come home for tea. The fine weather had kept him out wandering further afield than usual. He was sitting among the bracken on a rise near the ancient site of St Gwladys' chapel on the common watching a group of children playing noisily on the track below. He didn't want them to see him because he did not recognise them. He decided he might as well go home.

He was tired, hot and thirsty and he had a long trudge back. It was no fun being on his own and Jack Williams had not mitched off school today which is why he'd just wandered aimlessly further afield than usual in his disappointment. He liked being with Jack. It reminded him of the times he had his brother Will for company.

Dan crawled away from the spot on all fours hidden by the tall fresh green bracken growing down the slope until he felt it was safe to stand up out of view of the road. He looked behind him just to check no one had seen him before heading back down the hillside and was horrified to see a man stumbling through the reeds towards the rise. Dan and the stranger stopped and stared at each other both equally alarmed.

The man was tall and athletic looking with dark hair and clean shaven. He was dressed in typical working clothes and hatless. The noise of the children playing in the distance made him suddenly look around. With one last look at Dan the dark stranger turned and headed back in the direction he had come, away from the noise of children playing. The children had scared the man too, thought Dan as he rose

97

awkwardly to his feet. Dan wondered who the man might be but quickly forgot the brief incident as he started his journey home with a little more urgency than before.

*

His mother was getting uneasy about Dan missing his tea although it was not the first time.

"He'll appear soon," said Walt "you wait and see... His stomach will tell him when it's time to come home." He picked up the copy of the Journal he had not seen since Friday as Elizabeth cleared the table around him. Criddy asked her parents politely if she could go out to play.

"Not tonight," said Elizabeth. "Have you forgotten you are going to the magic lantern show at chapel this evening? 'The life of Admiral Lord Nelson' now there's interesting. Miss Thomas will have put in a lot of hard work preparing for it. We cannot disappoint her."

"Must I go too?" asked Trefor. "I have some Latin verbs to learn for tomorrow."

"You'll have to go with your sisters. I cannot leave the house with Dan not back yet. It will only be an hour and you can stay up late to learn your verbs if you must." There was no arguing with his mother when she used that tone of voice, thought Tref resigned to his baby-sitting duties.

"Come on you two," he said to his sisters. "We'd better go if we're going."

"And come straight home mind you after it's finished. No hanging about the streets like vagabonds," said their mother. Or like Dan, Trefor thought to himself but would not have dared to say out loud.

"Have you anything planned for this evening?" Elizabeth asked her husband in a more pleasant tone.

98

"The outdoor meetings of the Independent Labour Party have been on all summer... I have only attended one so far. They usually clash with the fortnightly council meetings... but there is no council scheduled this week. The ILP have a speaker... from the regional office in Cardiff... I'd better stroll across and show my face" said Walt. "Do you fancy it Esau?"

"Rather not, if you don't mind. Not quite my cup of tea," replied the brother-in-law. "Elizabeth tells me you are resigning from the Gelligaer council come the next round of elections. It seems you have your sights on higher office. It'll be the County Council next no doubt."

"Well yes... my predecessor Evan Thomas was a County Councillor... I am to stand for his vacant seat at the next election. The Fed policy is for miners to have more representation in both local and national government... I will also be standing for election as the official ILP candidate... for the House of Commons in the general election... to be held next year."

Esau looked at Elizabeth quite taken aback. "Did you know about this?" he asked her.

"Of course," she replied calmly. "We have discussed it in private and I'd be very grateful if you would keep it that way at present. Nothing is settled yet."

"Elizabeth is right," said Walt, "the general election is still some time off... there is nothing officially declared yet. The difficult part will be getting elected as the local candidate for this constituency... the Fed intends to ballot the members. There will be stiff competition from other local agents... It is a big constituency... but I may as well throw my hat in the ring."

"And then there's the election itself. Can you see the electorate voting for the ILP candidate around here if there is a credible Liberal put up against him?" asked Esau.

"You may have a point there... but the Independent Labour Party stands for the rights of the working people... the very men I represent..."

"But Lloyd George as a Liberal is doing more for the working class with his People's budget last year than any previous government and he's Welsh to boot. He is practically worshipped in this valley. Anyone who stands against a Liberal will have to fight a very good campaign to convince them otherwise."

"You must keep up with the times, Esau... It is clear to me that the ILP is the future... Remember we may inherit the past... but the future we build... as Mabon is so fond of saying. You fail to realise that when all working men get the vote... and not just householders... there will be no stopping the rise of the Labour Party who represent them and fight for their rights... not just the interests of the wealthy few. They are the political future... and when that day comes, and it will... you mark my words... it would my greatest honour to represent them in Westminster... if, with God's grace, I am the men's choice."

"But even your precious Mabon was elected as a Liberal at the last parliamentary election in the Rhondda. Will he be standing as an ILP candidate in the next election? That's if he stands at all," said Esau. "He is losing support within the Fed itself as you well know however much you admire him personally."

Esau was getting over enthusiastic in his political discussion and Elizabeth felt very uncomfortable. Walt was renowned for his patience but even he had his limits. Esau might offend her husband if he kept on like this. In her eyes, Walt put up with enough argument and opposition outside the home not to have to endure it within it.

100

"I forgot to tell you Esau's news," said Elizabeth abruptly to change the subject. She went on quickly to tell Walt of the upcoming interview. Walt was pleased to hear it and Esau fortunately took the hint. The two men had a more amicable conversation about Esau's prospects for success at the forthcoming interview and Elizabeth felt more at ease.

"Well I must get going if I'm to walk over the Graig again today," Walt said getting to his feet. "If the telephone rings take a message," he said to his wife smiling.

"So, I'm to be your secretary now as well as maid of all work," she replied matching his teasing tone.

After Walt had left the front way Esau disappeared out the back for his cigarette. The children had left for their magic lantern show and the house was quiet. Elizabeth sat down to enjoy a rare quiet interlude in her busy day. When she opened her eyes in what seemed barely a moment later Dan had appeared in the kitchen just as his father predicted.

"Where have you been?" she asked sharply in sheer relief. He smiled at his mother.

"Up the mountain," he said pointing vaguely behind him. "Sunshine… tired, thirsty."

"You're lucky your father's out. What time is this to come home for tea?" Elizabeth could not scold the lad now he was safely returned and set about getting him a drink of water and the leftovers for what was now going to be his supper.

Chapter 11

With all the family accounted for and safe in bed Elizabeth was alarmed to hear the bell ring for the telephone. It was dark outside and must be well after 10 o'clock.

"Who on earth can that be this time of night? Go answer it quick," she said to her husband. "That bell will wake the whole house and the neighbours an' all." When Walt returned to the bedroom just a few minutes later she asked who had called at this hour.

"Don't be alarmed," he replied. "It was Dr Dan Thomas... There's been an accident."

"God forbid! Not the pit?" she asked at once.

"No, no... not the pit. I cannot understand it... he says Miah Thomas was brought to him with a head injury... I must go and find out what's been going on... perhaps he is mistaken," he added putting on yesterday's shirt and reaching for his tie. "Miah should be safely at home before now... that is if he caught the train to Brecon this morning. I'll be back as soon as I can... don't wait up." He discarded the collar and tie in his haste to leave.

Elizabeth heard the front door close quietly behind her husband before she wrapped herself in her dressing gown and went down stairs to the kitchen in the dark. She struck a match from the box always kept on the mantelpiece and lit the old oil lamp. Dan was fast asleep on the chair and did not stir, no doubt exhausted after his afternoon roaming the common. She poured a cup of water in the back kitchen and carried it and the lamp into the front parlour. She decided to wait at the window for her husband's return and turned the flame down before placing the lamp carefully on the high mantelpiece over the fireplace. This had become far from a typical Monday, she thought, and sat on the arm of the chair to keep her vigil at the bay window.

*

"Sam, Sam, wake up Sam," shouted Alf Waters banging loudly on the front door of 4 Club Row. It was very late, already dark and Alf was holding an oil lamp to light his way since there was no moon that close, muggy night.

"Heisht man, you'll wake the dead with all that racket," Sam shouted down when his head and shoulders appeared through the open bedroom window. "What in God's name is going on down there?"

"We need some help here. The young woman at number 6, she's in a dreadful state. Lydia's with her but we cannot understand a word she's saying. Can you come? Bring your wife. I'll wait here for you with the lamp."

"Give us a moment and we'll be down," Sam replied. Rae was already out of bed and putting her coat over her nightdress.

"What's happened? Is it Mary? We must go and see what we can do," she said to her husband who was pulling on his trousers and braces while tucking in his night shirt. The noise had wakened the girls and Rae could hear whispered comments from their bedroom. "Go back to sleep, you have school in the morning. Make sure they stay put, Edie, we won't be long," Rae said in urgent tones as she followed Sam out of the house.

"There was a terrible commotion next door. The noise and the screaming woke us up. Lydia said to leave it but it sounded as if he was wrecking the place. And that poor girl's screams, I'm surprised they didn't wake you up," said Alf as they walked the short distance to the end cottage. "Well, you can see for yourself. I left Lydia with her through here in the kitchen at the back."

103

Rae and Sam followed him through the tiny parlour in the cottage to find the two women crouched on the floor behind the upturned table amid a wreckage of broken crockery. They had few possessions and it seemed all of them lay strewn across the floor and the furniture upturned. Lydia was holding young Mary Brown in her arms, rocking back and fore in an effort to comfort her. Rae knelt quietly beside them.

"She seems calmer," said Lydia "but she is in a dreadful state. She was babbling hysterically when we found her. I thought it must be Welsh. I could barely hear what she was saying and couldn't understand a word so sent Alf to fetch you."

"I think we need the doctor here," said Rae looking up at Sam who was shocked at the scene of devastation around him.

"We'll go," said a voice from the doorway. It was Lewis and Seth with a storm lamp. "And rouse Evans police from his bed and bring him back with you too," said Lydia. "That husband of hers deserves to be punished for this. Look at the state of her clothes. And the mark on her neck, it looks like he tried to kill her." Rae lifted back Mary's hair and saw the reddened marks around her throat. Her blouse was torn, one sleeve hanging away at the seam.

"The brothers will be a while by the time they've got them out of their beds. Let's see if we can get her upstairs and into her bed and then straighten the mess here. Has anyone checked on the little boy Robbie, where is he?" asked Rae.

Sam stepped closer and bent to lift Mary but she recoiled clutching at Lydia. Sam was visibly shocked by her reaction. "Leave her to us," said Rae, "we'll cope won't we, Lydia? Alf, take Sam to your house and see if you can make a pot of tea between you. It's going to be a long night," she added.

"Come on," said Alf clapping a hand on Sam's shoulder. "I might be able to find something a little stronger than tea." Gently the two women helped to lift the young woman to her feet. She groaned and leaned heavily on Rae who noticed the vacant look in her eyes as they lead her to the stairway.

An hour or so later the doctor was getting ready to leave having given Mary something to make her sleep. "Rest is a great healer," he said to Rae. "Can you stay with her?"

"They won't be left alone," she replied. Miraculously she had found little Robbie awake but unharmed in his own makeshift cot where he now slept soundly. She looked at his sleeping form and could just about see the slight rise and fall of his chest with each breath. Although he was only a year or so older than her Henry, he was still a baby and seemed thankfully unaware of this night's events.

"She will sleep at least eight hours, possibly more, after that injection," the doctor said. "I'll come back after my morning surgery. If Constable Evans requests an examination of our patient I'd much rather assess the full extent of her injuries in the light of day and with her consent. I'll call next door to tell him not to attempt to question her until I've seen her again tomorrow. She should not be agitated and upset any more than proves necessary for his enquiry."

Lydia knocked lightly on the bedroom door and came in with a cup of tea in her hand. "Thought you might need this," she said handing the cup to Rae. "Will she be alright doctor?"

"She has had quite a shaking up but I do not think there will be any long term physical damage," he said. "The bruising will develop fully over the next few days. But in cases like this Mrs Waters it's her state of mind that I am most concerned about."

"The Police constable is next door. He asked if he could speak to you before you leave. My husband has a drop of brandy too if you'd like one. For medicinal purposes only, of course. There's a slug in your tea," she said to Rae.

"I cannot do more tonight," the doctor replied "but send for me if you think it necessary. I trust I'm leaving her in good hands," he smiled at Rae who was looking with some distaste into her cup of adulterated tea.

Later the house was quiet and Rae was finding it difficult to stay awake by the dim light of a single candle. She heard heavy footsteps ascending the stairs and, for a moment, froze in fear. "It's me, love," Sam whispered, "can I come in? The girls are sound asleep in bed and Henry has not stirred. How is the poor girl?"

"Oh Sam, how could he do this to her?" she said and leant into his strong arms for comfort.

"So, you think it was Hugh as well," he said. "I cannot believe it of him."

"Who else could it be," she asked "and where is he?"

"He should be at work if he is innocent of this. Evans has gone with the brothers to check and bring him to the police station if he's there. Alf insists he saw a man rush out of the house after the rumpus woke him up. He only saw it from the bedroom window but is prepared to swear an oath it was Hugh, dark though it was. Evans has it all written down."

"Go home love and get some sleep if you can. There's work in the morning," said Rae.

"I'm not leaving you here alone for the rest of the night," said Sam. "What if this mad man comes back? Go lie on the bed in the other room and try and get some rest," he said noticing how bone weary his wife looked, the dim light accentuating the deep shadows under her eyes. "I'll watch her for a while and will fetch you straight away if she stirs. I'll get Nan Evans to sit with her come first thing. Nan will have had an unbroken night's sleep and will want to do her bit to help. You know what she's like, kindness itself. All the neighbours will want to pitch in once they hear what has happened," he added.

Rae opened the door across the landing to the only other small bedroom. It was obvious Hugh slept here. The single bed was neatly made but men's clothing hung on the nails behind the door and there was shaving soap and brush in an enamel bowl and a razor and strop on the shelf with a piece of broken mirror. She lay on top of the blanket but did not think for one minute she could sleep.

Rae could not help thinking there was far more to this than a marital row. Bert and Maggie Prosser had had some real scraps over the years she had known them but Bert had never tried to strangle his wife no matter what the provocation. These separate rooms, avoiding the neighbours and then she remembered Mary Brown's reference to 'my boy'. Yes, she thought, there's definitely more to this than meets the eye.

*

Back at Ty Gwent that same night, Elizabeth did not have long to wait for her husband who returned less than half an hour after he had left. Dr Thomas' house and surgery was just minutes away on Cardiff Road. She saw Walt coming wearily up Wood Street from her vantage point at the window and, picking up the lamp, met him at the door. She could tell by the stern look on his face it was not good news. Putting his fingers to his lips he ushered her by the elbow into the front parlour and quietly closed the door.

"It is indeed our dear friend... and in a poor way he is too. Dr Thomas has informed the police... Sergeant Harris arrived just after I got there... But Miah was knocked senseless... a blow to the back of the head," said Walt.

"But how?" asked a very shocked Elizabeth. "Who could have done such a thing? When did it happen and where?"

"That's exactly what the police will need to find out my dear... Miah is in no fit state to tell them... The doctor cannot be sure how bad his injuries are... but Miah is in good hands there... Dr Thomas and his sister will keep a close eye on him. His wound is cleaned and dressed and they have him in their little spare bed... although he is not stirring yet."

"What can we do?" asked Elizabeth.

"There is nothing we can do tonight but pray for our dear friend's complete recovery... In the morning I will meet with the police sergeant... see if I can help with their investigation into this strange occurrence... I really am at a loss to understand what might have happened." Elizabeth held her hands before her in an attitude of prayer and looked heavenward as Walt began. "Almighty Father, our help and support in times of need, we beseech you to give us strength..."

Chapter 12

That next morning, Walt and Elizabeth left the house together with Esau nominally in charge of little Gwladys while the older children got ready to leave for school. Elizabeth could not be dissuaded from going with her husband to see the patient for herself and, if needed, help nurse poor Miah.

When they arrived at Dr Thomas' surgery they were greeted with the news that Miah had earlier regained his senses and was reported to have a strong and steady pulse. The doctor was optimistic about his patient's condition if given some time and peace to recover from the shock of the blow to his head. He had given his patient a very mild sedative and now Miah was sound asleep leaving little Elizabeth could do to help.

"I will call into the police station briefly to check on any information they might have on this incident… and offer what assistance I can," said Walt.

The meeting he had inadvertently witnessed between Miah and the young woman after the concert that last Saturday was weighing on his mind. If it did have any significance in relation to his old friend's current predicament, he really should tell the police. But it was little enough for them to proceed with. He had no idea who the woman was who claimed kinship to his friend or where she might be found. Miah had spoken very little of his family and Walt had always assumed Miah to be a bachelor. Now his conscience troubled him greatly should the existence of this mystery woman, possibly Miah's daughter, turn out to be of any relevance to a police investigation. He desperately wanted his dear friend Miah to recover sufficiently to guide them on the matter.

"Try not to worry too much about Miah my dear," Walt said to his wife before they parted. "With God's help... and the ministrations of the doctor..."

"But I do worry," said Elizabeth. "I slept not a wink last night. To think something like this should happen to the dear man, and on our doorstep. I feel responsible."

"Now you are being silly," said Walt, "but I understand your concern... We can be responsible for making sure this matter is resolved... and that Miah recovers from this injury."

"I will make some chicken broth for when he wakes up," said Elizabeth. "And he can always stay a few days with us if he is unable to travel home. I will suggest it to the doctor and dear Cissy..."

"Yes, you do that my dear," said her husband "and I will hopefully have some news when I come home at midday." Elizabeth left for the Co-op to buy the ingredients she needed for her broth feeling somewhat dejected as Walt continued his walk to work via the police station.

When Walt came through the front door at midday for his dinner, Elizabeth had been waiting for him at the window of the front parlour. "Come into the front room," she told her husband. "We won't be overheard." Walt sat back with a sigh in the armchair and related all the details the police had told him that morning, mainly provided by the farmer who had brought Miah to the doctor's surgery the previous evening.

Farmer Jenkins from Heolddu was returning from the Dowlais horse fair late yesterday afternoon when he was stopped on the road above Fochriw by two farm labourers struggling to carry a body between them. They had been looking for stray livestock and had chanced across Miah's inert form lying on the ground near the old monolith.

Realising he was alive but in need of medical care, they carried him as far as the trackway and intended to seek help at the White Horse public house.

Luckily for them Farmer Jenkins was passing with his pony and trap. He recognised the two farm labourers and agreed to give what help he could immediately. Between them they manhandled the unconscious man into the trap. Farmer Jenkins decided it would be better for him to continue into Bargoed to seek medical attention for the stranger rather than risk being out after dusk on the mountain track without light.

On passing his farm on the way to Bargoed the farmer stopped and, alerting his son, they had done their best to make the unconscious man more comfortable before proceeding the short distance into the town. There the unidentified patient was left in the capable hands of Dr Thomas before Jenkins the farm went on to Bargoed police station to report the incident.

Miss Thomas, the doctor's sister, had been out all evening at the magic lantern show and was late home having stayed to practise the organ before locking up the chapel. When the good doctor eventually called on his sister to help nurse the patient and make him more comfortable, it was she who had recognised Miah despite his dishevelled state. She was one of the Sunday school teachers who had taken part in the events on Saturday and assured her brother that his mystery patient was indeed the preacher who had officiated that day and a good friend of Mr Lewis, miners' agent.

"Well thank goodness for the farmer's caution," said Elizabeth "or Miah could be lying in some public house still unidentified and us in total ignorance."

"Yes," agreed Walt "but we still need Miah to recover before any further light can be shed on the matter." He had decided on the spur of the moment not to tell the police sergeant about the young woman he had seen briefly talking to Miah or, indeed, what he overheard. If it was of no obvious relevance then such speculation could be damaging to Miah's reputation. Everyone enjoyed a salacious story, especially about a minister, regardless of any element of truth in the telling and he did not want to be the source of unfounded gossip.

Using the same reasoning he had decided not to tell his wife either. Not that he feared Elizabeth was a gossip, but the fewer people that knew about it at this stage the better. He was not comfortable keeping information from Elizabeth or the police but felt his silence justified under the circumstances. He sent a private prayer for Miah's speedy recovery which the doctor assured him should be soon.

"I shall, of course, thank Farmer Jenkins for his troubles... on Miah's behalf. His actions have been that of the Good Samaritan... and he still has no idea who he has helped..." said Walt.

"...and the two labourers both. Did the police give you their names?" asked Elizabeth.

"I will inquire after them," replied Walt reaching across to give a reassuring touch on his wife's hand. "The police have probably only told me this much because of who I am..." he said with a rueful smile. "I also suggested they telephone through to the Brecon police station and inform them of Miah's... predicament.   Someone in the chapel or his home should be told... his absence will be noticed eventually and could cause alarm. The police there will know who to contact..."

"Yes, that should put their minds at rest. Someone may be very concerned if Miah was expected home yesterday," said Elizabeth.

"I have never asked Miah about his living arrangements… and he has never talked about family come to that… But if he does not return home for several days… it is bound not to go unnoticed by someone as you say… of that I am sure."

Elizabeth nodded her agreement. "Now you have mentioned it, it is surprising how little we know of Miah's life," she said.

"Probably because like many laymen... we don't expect a minister of God to have a private life," he replied looking rather concerned by the thought, "never mind a history."

"Come and eat your dinner now. You don't have much time but say nothing in front of Gwladys. You know what she's like for repeating stories," she added ruefully.

*

Mary Brown slept right through to the following afternoon as the doctor had predicted. "Like a corpse she has lain there," said Nan Evans who had sat snoozing beside her all morning. Rae had taken Robbie into her home telling him her Mam was not feeling very well that day and needed her rest. He was an unusually quiet and well-behaved toddler, thought Rae. All morning he had played on the floor under the table engrossed with the contents of her button box, sorting them into colours and shapes and even trying to count them. She was able, at least, to get on with some washing.

She had just pegged out the last of the washing and was thinking of make some tea when her domestic peace was shattered. Evans police knocked sharply on the open door with Lydia Waters sticking her nose behind him too. Rae dried her reddened chapped hands on her apron as they entered her kitchen and removed another boiling kettle from the range.

"Well I really cannot tell you anything you may not know already," said Rae to Evans. She found his pencil and notebook very disturbing when she realised he intended to write down anything she might say. "I would have thought the person you should be questioning is poor Mary Brown," she added in a cautious whisper aware of little Robbie under the table who might overhear and understand the adults talking in the kitchen.

"I am on my way to do that," he said "and hoped that you would come with me. The doctor suggested it because you have a calming influence on the young woman. He has been to examine her first thing this morning and insists she is not to be distressed further than need be. And I'm sure I can trust your discretion not to repeat anything you will hear to all and sundry," he added with a look towards Lydia.

Rae was flattered by this trust in her and agreed to accompany him if Lydia would wait and mind the two little boys until she came back. Lydia could hardly refuse under the circumstances although being excluded piqued her neighbourly curiosity somewhat.

"Well it must be that husband of hers. He didn't turn up for his shift yesterday, did he? Why else would he have run off?" asked Lydia. "Nearly killed her he did. If it hadn't been for me and my Alf she could still be lying there stone cold dead right now with no one the wiser."

"But fortunately, she is not," said the police constable. "Now, I need to see what the young lady has to say on the matter before I can bring charges. Otherwise it will be dismissed as just another domestic argument."

"Just another domestic argument!" Lydia shouted. "He tried to kill her, believe me I heard the commotion. Let me tell you there is more crime going on behind closed doors than you or I can ever imagine. You should be out there hunting down that husband of hers for what he did to her last night." Rae thought Lydia had made a good point given her knowledge of domestic life on the row. But Constable Evans looked nonplussed.

"I have my duty to do Mrs Waters and procedures to follow. Now, if you'll permit me. After you, Mrs Jones," he said with as much dignity he could muster after that dressing down. Lydia watched Rae leave followed by the policeman. Only when they disappeared into the house along the row did her head withdraw into the room and her attention back to the two little boys inside.

After the policeman had left it was very quiet in the cottage and, to all intent and purpose, Mary was asleep. The last time Nan checked, she had turned to lie facing the wall.

While her body lay still Mary's mind was racing. Hugh no longer deserved her compassion, not after this she thought. She would never have believed him capable of using such violence towards her. No longer would she blame herself for his actions. She shuddered as she recalled that anger in his face. She was lucky to be alive and, for the sake of her son, she must get away; now while she still had the chance. Let him run and keep on running, she thought, as long as it is far, far away from me. And she dared hope that, after recent events, she might find forgiveness and comfort back with her own family. But she would need to be brave and tell the whole truth; no more lies and half-baked stories. Hugh's murderous intent had finally severed

115

any bonds of loyalty or gratitude she may had felt towards him in the past. Her hand ran along the edge of the ticking fabric on the pillow until she felt the little hard bundle of coins she had wrapped in a cloth and pushed inside. Good, he had not found the money at least.

*

When Sam came off his shift later that afternoon, Rae had a lot to tell him when they could find a moment alone. Telling her husband was not breaking the constable's confidence as Sam could keep a secret if he had to. She waited for a quiet moment once the family had all finished the stew she had made with the ham bone. The girls were packed off on an errand to the village shop to buy cheese and told not to hurry home.

"Well, she didn't deny it. It was Hugh," said Rae having explained to Sam her presence when Evans police had spoken to Mary earlier that afternoon. "She said very little if truth be told, must be the shock still or the bruising to her throat. I do not know if she'll bring charges against her own husband. She must be afraid or what he'll do if the police cannot find him and he finds her first. Evans was very patient with her but she did agree to make a full statement when she feels stronger. That gives her a while to wrestle with her conscience. But I don't know how she'll do without him. And her with that little boy to care for an' all," said Rae. "Do you think he'll come back? Hugh, I mean."

"He would be a fool to show his face around here again," said Sam. "Now I have had time to think on it his behaviour is that of a guilty man. And I wouldn't be the only one willing to give him a taste of his own medicine after what he did last night. What did the doctor say when he saw her again today?" he asked.

116

"No bones broken, rest; not a lot he can do for her that time won't heal," said Rae. "Nan Evans is sitting with her and Robbie again this evening and I'll call in now just. Evans police asked for a description of Hugh, his height, colouring any distinguishing marks or features," she added.

"I expect he will put out a wanted notice on him if she presses charges. Then, if he gets picked up for vagrancy or anything else, they'll know he's wanted for questioning in connection with an assault," said Sam. "But with so many young men on the tramp looking for work this time of year, it's not likely he'll attract much police attention. That is unless he walks into a station to confess."

His wife looked deep in thought. "What's on your mind love? You have that look on your brow that something's not been said." Rae gave a little rueful smile. She could not get away with much between her and her Sam.

"Well you have asked so I will tell you. Between us me and Lydia gave Evans police a fair description of Hugh, good height, near six foot and dark, clean shaven, lean and strong but we could have been describing one of any number of young men in the village. I was wondering love. Could you do a likeness for them? Your sketches of the girls and me are so good. Would you try? You knew him best on the row if anyone did. Then if you are pleased with it, I could give it to Evans police if needs be."

"Well I could have a go but whether it'll be any good from memory," he said.

"There's your pencil and some nice paper on the dresser. Try now, before the girls get back and you have the light still. I'll go and check on Nan, see if she needs anything and make them some tea." Rae put the sleepy Henry down in his crib. With a sigh and a smile of resignation Sam watched her leave. It was difficult to refuse

117

his Rae anything, even this unusual request. It might not be much good but he'd try his best. He closed his eyes, visualising Hugh's face in his mind's eye, as the pencil moved over the paper.

Chapter 13

The telephone bell rang out loudly in the passage making Elizabeth jump in alarm. "It's the tephalone bell Mam," said Gwladys, stating the obvious. "You must answer it for Dadda."

In a mild panic Elizabeth nearly knocked over her chair in her rush to get to the study before the bell stopped ringing, just remembering in time to shut the door behind her.

"Gosh that was quick," said Gwladys barely a minute later. She was sitting on the first step of the stairs outside the study when her mother came out of the room closing the door behind her. "Is it more bad news about Uncle Miah?"

"Now then, what do you know about Uncle Miah?" she asked grabbing the little girl by the arm. "Have you been listening at closed doors again?" she asked giving the child a shake. Gwladys burst into tears and Elizabeth let her go in exasperation. "If you have been, you are a very naughty girl and Dadda will have to hear about it," she said wagging an accusing finger as Gwladys wailed louder. "I have no time for this now. I need to go out. And you, madam, I'll deal with you later."

With her covered bowl of broth in her basket and dragging a reluctant Gwladys by the hand, Elizabeth left the house. "You will sit quiet with Mrs Jones the shop while I am gone. If she says you have been a good girl, well, I shall not be too harsh with you when I get back."

"Where are you going?" asked Gwladys through her sobs.

"Where ever, not for you to know," came the reply.

119

The telephone call had been from Dr Thomas at his surgery. Miah was awake, although not fully aware of what had happened to him. Elizabeth could not wait to see the patient herself before reporting the news to Walt in the office. Praise the Lord, our prayers have been answered she thought. He was back with them at least.

"He still needs his rest Mrs Lewis," said Miss Thomas taking the chicken broth. She had taken the visitor through to the kitchen of the house which acted as surgery, infirmary and home to Dr Thomas, his wife and sister and their widowed mother. "He is still not quite himself so my brother has forbidden any visitors just yet. He hasn't even told the police our patient is awake until he finishes his full examination. He thought you and Mr Lewis should be the first to know as he is your friend."

"I suppose the doctor knows best. But tell Miah, Mr Thomas that is, that I have called in with some restorative broth. Now I must let my husband know straight away. He will be glad to hear his dear friend is on the mend," said Elizabeth.

"Well not quite recovered yet," said Miss Thomas, "a head injury can have lasting effects, you know."

"Dew, dew," said Elizabeth "I had not imagined anything like that. Join our prayers for him dear Cissy, that he should make a complete recovery, God willing."

"I will indeed and I'll tell you as soon as Mr Thomas is up to receiving visitors. Now you have a telephone in the house my brother can give you regular bulletins on his progress," said Miss Thomas.

"You are most considerate, my dear. Yes, use the telephone if you must." Elizabeth wondered if Walt might expect her to telephone the office with the news but decided, as she was already in town, she would get to the office just as quick as walking back up the hill to use the apparatus. She set off pleased to be able to tell her husband the glad tidings knowing how relieved he would be that Miah was conscious if somewhat the worse for his ordeal.

No one was happier with the patient's condition than Dr Thomas as he examined Miah and noted his reflexes were all in order.

"You've had a lucky escape my man," said the doctor cheerily. "That was a bad blow to the back of the skull which put you quite out of it for a while but it looks like no lasting damage has been done. You're not completely out of the woods yet though. I'd like you to rest here for the time being where I can keep an eye on you."

Miah raised his hand to his head, touching the dressing and asked "How long have I been here doctor?"

"You were brought in last evening by the kindness of a local farmer. Some labourers luckily stumbled across you prone on hillside and sought help, fortunately for you. You have taken some time to come around during which you displayed bouts of extreme agitation and seemed unaware of your surroundings. You had me worried for a while there. My sister has sat with you almost constantly overnight." The doctor took his pulse and felt his brow. "But you have no fever or other symptoms we cannot account for given the blow to your head. You must have been hit very hard by a rock or similar hard object. The wound is quite clean. Do you not remember anything that happened man?"

"Yes, I can remember Sunday... but I have no recollection since," said Miah hesitantly.

"That might be expected after a head injury, but I'm afraid the police will want to speak to you. Given the circumstances under which you arrived here at my surgery, they have already been informed. I cannot put them off indefinitely now that you are clearly recovering. Do you have any idea who did this to you or was it an accident? Did you fall and strike your head on a rock?" asked the doctor.

Miah sighed. "Perhaps, I do not know and the police will have to be content with that. Unless I might remember in time, doctor, do you think?"

"Yes, in time," he answered reassuringly. "You've had a visitor already today. Elizabeth Lewis has brought you some chicken broth. My sister is heating it for you now. It will do you good to try and eat something. By then you might feel up to answering a few questions from the police sergeant." Miah nodded. "He has already been through your possessions and found nothing of value in your pockets but an old watch with no fob and a train ticket. No purse or any money. Perhaps it was robbery or the men who found you helped themselves to any cash as a reward. That is unless you are in the habit of travelling with no ready cash about you?"

Miah looked embarrassed as he admitted to the doctor that he had not had any money on him.

"Well, I can prescribe you something stronger for the pain if you need it but it could make you drowsy. It would be better to see if you can cope without it given your propensity for sleep. But if you get a severe headache, then don't suffer in silence. Some headache powders should not make you any drowsier that you are already."

"You are too kind doctor, thank you for your care. It seems I am also indebted to your sister's nursing," said Miah looking around the neat but Spartan room that served as an infirmary. Dr Thomas noticed Miah taking in his surroundings for the first time and saw it as a positive sign that his patient was recovering.

"Don't worry, I shall be sending you the bill when you are finally discharged," said the doctor with a smile. "That is if you can find some cash to pay it."

"Can I ask you one special favour? I need to talk to Walter Lewis if that's possible. Will you tell him? Both he and his wife are my good friends in the town…"

"Don't worry, Walter Lewis was here soon after you were brought in last night. He confirmed your identity to the police. We had no idea who you were at first until my sister thought she recognised you. Miss Thomas, one of the Sunday school teachers at Noddfa, perhaps you remember her? Walter Lewis will indeed be overjoyed to see you on the mend."

"Dear Gwallt… and kind Elizabeth. It seems I owe a debt of gratitude to many people for my rescue. I have been the cause of a great deal of inconvenience and concern," said Miah

"Here is Cissy with your broth and I will leave you in her capable hands for now," said Dr Thomas holding the door open for his sister carrying a tray. Miah watched the young woman who entered room.

"Ah yes, indeed, I do remember you now; at the prize giving and the outing. Was that only Saturday? It seems an age ago," he said sinking back on the pillows. Another good sign, thought the doctor with a smile.

Dr Thomas left the room to telephone the police station in the town before asking for the operator to put him through to the Fed Offices to pass on Miah's request to speak with the miners' agent at his earliest convenience.

Chapter 14

"Soft boiled eggs for tea today," said Trefor, "my favourite, mmmm, runny yolks."

"Ych-a-fi," said Gwladys pulling a face. "Ch-a-fi, a-fi, fi, I," she added for emphasis making Esau laugh.

"Well you don't have to have one," said her mother. "Put some jam on her bread and butter for her Trefor, there's a good boy... and lucky she is to be having that after her performance today."

Gwladys puffed out her cheeks in a full pout for the benefit of the others sitting down at the table.

"I cannot believe our Gwlad has been a naughty girl," said Esau giving the little girl a chuck under her chin. "Come on cariad, give us one of your best smiles."

"Leave her be," said Elizabeth, "I am still deciding on a suitable punishment for listening at closed doors. Caught her red handed when I answered the telephone in the study today. So, before she can pass on what she overheard, with added embellishments no doubt, I can spoil her fun by telling you all once we've had our tea." At that moment she was interrupted as Ceridwen sidled in through the open back door.

"And where have you been my girl?" asked Elizabeth.

"Ty bach," was her blushing reply.

"Go swill your hands and face then before joining us at tea," said Elizabeth. "And there's room for you at the table too," she said to Dan. It seemed their mother was not in her usual even-tempered mood. The Lewis children knew it was time for best manners and speak only when you're spoken to this tea time or they might be in for a good tongue lashing from their Mam.

Tea progressed in silence while Elizabeth picked up the large teapot to pour and handed out the cups and saucers. "Now did you all enjoy seeing Uncle Miah this weekend?" she asked when their plates were cleared.

"Yes mother," said Trefor who, as the eldest, acted as spokesman for his siblings in these situations when his Mam was cross.

"Well, before he could return home Uncle Miah met with an accident somewhere up on the mountain," Elizabeth continued. "He has been in Dr Thomas's infirmary since yesterday evening so that the doctor and Miss Thomas could look after him. He is getting better but your father and I have been beside ourselves with the worry of it. I have barely slept a wink the last night. Your father is to visit him from work and, if he is well enough to move, he will come back to us here for a day or two. Hopefully then he can manage the journey home. It is the least we can do for our friend. So Trefor, you'll be back in with the girls for a night or two and I'm afraid you, Esau…."

"I am in the way," said her brother. "Have you asked Mrs B next door? I have my interview at Peglars Stores tomorrow as well remember. And I want to make a good impression."

"I had not forgotten," said Elizabeth "and will sponge and press your best suit before Walter gets home for his supper. Leave your boots and Dan will clean them tonight. Now I want you lot out of the way for an hour or so. Go and enjoy the fine weather, it might be the only bit of summer we get this year."

"There might be football down the farm field," said Trefor,"the girls can watch".

"Not Gwladys today. That will be her punishment. She can stay and help me and learn how to do something useful rather than listening at doors," said Elizabeth. "Now

off you go and Dan, go with them, there's a good boy."
Trefor was about to protest at having Dan tagging along too.
Criddy was bad enough, but given his mother's mood he
thought there was little point in arguing as they left the
table. Little Gwladys was still pouting.

*

Some local lads were knocking about an old deflated
football when the children arrived at field at the bottom of
the street. Not enough numbers to have a game, they were
practicing their goal shooting. Jack was there with some of
his butties from West Street and they were more than happy
for Tref to join in. Criddy sat down in the grass to make
daisy chains and chatter with some girls from their street.
Dan stood on watching self-consciously as the boys took
turns to shoot at goal. Tref added his school blazer to one of
the two piles of jumpers and jackets substituting for the goal
posts.

"Why don't we let Dan have a go?" suggested Jack.
"Come here Danny boy, let's see if you can kick the ball at
goal."

"I don't know why you waste your time with him,"
said Tref, "he's useless at this sort of thing."

"Doesn't mean he can't have a go," said Jack. He
didn't mention that it was their father who had suggested it
might be good for Dan to join in more with the other
children.

"You'll be letting the girls play next," replied Tref
laughing.

Jack patiently retrieved the ball for Dan placing it at his feet
each time he tried and missed the goal. The others shouted
encouragement at his efforts to kick the ball but he really
did not have the co-ordination and control to strike it

cleanly never mind in the right direction. For once the laughter was good natured and Dan did not seem to mind.

"Right, practice over Dan. It's best of three," said Trefor throwing the ball back to Jack. At that moment 'Nobby' Harris and two of his gang appeared through the hedgerow on their way home to Gilfach.

"Playing with cripples now are you boys?" shouted Nobby as they headed towards them across the field.

"Watch who you're calling a cripple," replied Jack standing protectively in front of Dan.

"Come over here and say that you little runt," said Nobby. Jack strode across the field and shouted straight into the bigger boy's face. "You heard me, less of the name calling," said Jack threateningly.

Nobby pushed him back and looking over his head he sneered at Trefor, "Why don't stand up for the cripple? He's your brother, isn't he?"

"Why don't you just shut your big fat gob," said Jack and threw a punch at Nobby's jaw. He was quickly set upon by the other two of Nobby's gang. Tref did not stop to think in his anger and waded into the fray legs pumping and fists flying. Before he knew what had happened he was on the floor and a boot connected with his face. He curled up into a ball in the grass as boots stamped over him but Jack was still on his feet swinging out at their attackers as he moved to stand over Tref protectively.

"What's the trouble over b'there?" shouted the Farmer Edwards across the fence at the milking parlour.

"Come on lads, let's get out of here," shouted Nobby. They needed no further encouragement and all three antagonists legged across the field in the direction of the Black Path. Jack bent over to get his breath.

127

"You alright?" he asked Tref. "Never thought I'd see the day when you'd stand up for Dan," he said offering his hand to help him up from the ground. Tref got onto all fours and let the blood drip from his nose onto the earth in front of him. Some of the warm thick fluid trickled down into his mouth and he spat it on the ground before taking the hand proffered to help him up onto his feet. Jack slapped him on the back. It hurt as he straightened up and rotated his head slowly just to check.

"Well I couldn't just watch those three beat you into a pulp," said Tref grinning. Criddy ran over with her pure white hankie in her hand. "Mam will kill us all," she said dramatically which made Tref laugh. Odd he should feel so good, he thought to himself as he took her hankie to wipe some of the blood from his face.

"Be off with the whole lot of you now," shouted the farmer waving his arms. "I'm not running a boxing booth on this field. And you'll answer to your father young man," he said to Trefor, "he'll have something to say about this I know. I won't want to be in your shoes when you get back home with blood all over your shirt and mud on your trousers."

Trefor took Criddy's hand and looked around for Dan. "Come on you two, let's go home and face the music. Although quite what Mam will say when she sees this I have no idea the mood she was in today. Tamping she was."

"I'll come with you and explain if you want," offered Jack.

"Kind of you but perhaps best you go straight home and clean up. Your lip is split, must have taken a direct hit from Nobby or one of his gang. He's a bad lot that boy, always looking for trouble. His father's no better according to the old man. Walk up with us," said Tref. "What will your Mam say when you get in?" he asked Jack.

"Surprised if she'll notice the state I get in most days," Jack answered grinning and showing his rotten stumps.

*

The Jones girls were playing hopscotch down the garden path when their mother called them in for supper and bedtime. Edith had watched her three younger sisters and cradled baby Henry on her knee. That evening it dawned on her that this would be her last summer at home all together with the family. She savoured the evening sun over the row and her mother's flower garden at its best with bees, heavy laden with pollen, labouring in the lavender. When Mam called she rose reluctantly, shifting the baby's weight onto her hip as she followed the girls inside. It seemed very dark in the kitchen compared to the bright sunlight outside.

"Check Henry before you put him down for the night, Edie," said her mother.

Chapter 15

It was gone 6 o'clock when Walt left the Fed offices. The fine summer evening was still warm and bright, drying out the road surface which had been levelled earlier in the week by the council steam roller. The roadway looked quite tidy for once. He made his way past the shops and businesses on Hanbury Road but instead of taking the hill up to the house strode on to Dr Thomas' surgery.

"Good evening Mr Lewis," said Miss Thomas as she greeted Walt at the door of the house. "Our patient is eager to see you. He seems to be recovering well despite his sore head and has been resting most of the afternoon. Come on in and I will bring a cup of tea when the kettle has boiled."

"You are too kind," said Walt. "I came as soon as I could get away... Is Miah, Mr Thomas, up to a visit so soon?"

"My brother is very pleased with his recovery although Mr Thomas is still a little weak and may feel light headed. The wound on his head will take a while to fully heal. He is in full possession of his senses although he cannot remember the incident. Come into our infirmary and I will leave the two of you alone while I get the tea. Just let me know if he seems to be getting tired, use your judgement."

Walt was pleased to see his old friend propped up on a bank of pillows in the neatly made bed which just about accommodated his height or length when prone. His face looked a little grey and drawn against the whiteness of the pillows and accentuated by the large white dressing on his head. Miah pulled himself up in the bed as Walt drew up the only chair in the room.

"Dear Gwallt," said Miah "there's pleased I am to see you."

"Not as pleased as I am to see you... alive and well... thank the Lord," said Walt. "You gave us a fright but God, in his infinite wisdom, has answered our prayers and brought you back to us."

"Amen to that," said Miah. "Excuse my recumbent position, the doctor has forbidden me to attempt to get up until tomorrow and has taken my clothes to be on the safe side." Miah gave a little laugh which encouraged Walt in the belief his old friend really was over the worse effects of his injury. "But I am far from death's door as you can see. I am grateful to the care and consideration of those who have put me on the road to recovery. Even the police it seems have been interested in my plight."

"The circumstances were very unusual... it is not surprising they were informed. Do you have any recollection of what happened? What were you doing alone up on the mountain?" asked Walt.

"In answer to the first question, no, I cannot remember how I received this blow to the head," said Miah. "I told the police as much this afternoon, unhelpful as it is. However, I do know why I went to that isolated spot but... it is a strange story."

"Does it involve a young woman with red hair?" asked Walt to Miah's surprise. He proceeded to relate what he had observed after the concert the previous Saturday. "Do not worry... I have not mentioned it to anyone... not even Elizabeth. I was not meant to witness the scene... and had no idea who the young woman was. What use could the information have been to the police? But it has laid heavily on my conscience... given everything that has happened since," said Walt.

"Thank you for your discretion. I owe you a debt of gratitude and will repay you in part by telling you her story. I have been thinking about her all day while I have been confined to this bed. Perhaps it is the blow to my head but my concern for her has been growing by the hour and I find myself in no position to do anything while I am lying here helpless," said Miah. "I must have lain out on that hillside most of the day until I was found and brought here yesterday. And now another day is nearly over. Gwallt, I need to find my daughter, for that is indeed who she is."

At that point, there was a gentle knock at the door before Miss Thomas entered with two cups of tea and a plate of shop bought biscuits on a tray. "I hope I am not disturbing you gentleman," she said putting the tray on the bedside table. "Now don't overtire yourself. Just ten more minutes, doctor's orders. My brother would also like to see you before you leave Mr Lewis if you have the time." Walt smiled and nodded as he picked up his teacup and helped himself to a biscuit.

"Thank you, Miss Thomas," said Miah, "you have been kind to let me see my old friend here. I promise we shall not be long if you don't mind..." Cissy smiled indulgently at the two men before quietly closing the door as she left.

"She reminds me of Mary. She must be about the same age as my daughter who you glimpsed that night outside the chapel in Fochriw. My long-lost daughter, I might add," said Miah "born in wedlock when I was but twenty-two. You have always accepted me for who I am, or rather, the minister I have become, but my early life before I chose this path was not uneventful. I married young to a beautiful young woman with red-blonde hair, just like our

132

daughter's. But God chose to take my dear young wife from us after the birth of our baby girl…

"It was a sad time and I know you, of all people, will understand my situation. Even now I cannot help but regret some of the decisions I made for my daughter's care at that time. But what is a young man to do with a new born child? When my mother-in-law took on the responsibility for her I was more than relieved for the sake of the infant's wellbeing. A woman's touch was just what was needed at the time as I adjusted to a life without the responsibilities of a wife or, indeed, a child."

Walt nodded in agreement as he sipped his tea and Miah continued.

"To cut a long story short given the brief time we have this evening, my daughter grew up with her grandmother on her family farm not far from the town of Brecon where I have a house. My mother-in-law kept a good Christian home and had a large extended family. It was where my wife had lived until our marriage and as good place to raise a child as any. Mary seemed to thrive, she was always such a happy child. I took advantage of my change in circumstances to pursue my theological studies and train for the ministry. During that time, I rarely saw her growing up but once a year I made it my duty to visit them in May, around the time of Mary's birth.

"When she was barely sixteen, however, her grandmother came to me in much distress. The girl had disappeared and could not be found. We assumed she had met with a terrible accident. There was no evidence of foul play and all our enquiries lead to nought. The police were not encouraging. You can imagine the remorse her grandmother felt having failed in her duty of care but I could not blame the woman for this sad turn of events."

Miah cleared his throat and accepted the handkerchief his friend offered him before continuing.

"My only ray of hope in this tragic affair came when we learned that some local estate workers known to Mary had left their employment around the same time to seek their fortune elsewhere. I held on to the belief she might have run away in their company. All I could do was pray that my daughter was safe somewhere and making her own way in the world. It is terrible to be devoid of hope; to think that her body lay somewhere undiscovered as the police suggested.

"In the years since her disappearance, I always hoped that in my travels I might hear some news, a face in a crowd. Well my prayers were answered last weekend. It was Mary who sought me out. She heard of the concert and events at Noddfa and that I was a guest of the chapel in Fochriw that weekend. The happy outcome I had long prayed for materialised. It was like a miracle, as if she had risen from the dead" Miah cleared his throat again, something he did frequently when nervous. "Does this shock you, Walter?"

Walt said nothing at first as both men reflected on what had already been said.

"Tell me, dear friend... what has finding your daughter after all these years got to do with your present predicament?" he asked.

"It explains what I was doing on the mountainside on Monday morning instead of taking the train home. Mary would not receive me at her lodgings. She made it clear my presence would not be welcomed by her husband. The more I think of it now, she seemed to be afraid of him. If not that, at least wary I might cause any confrontation." Walt looked surprised knowing Miah was not the sort to cause trouble.

"Given the circumstances, I suggested we meet near that monolith, the one high over the village. It was the only landmark I could think of and would find easily. After fulfilling my obligation at Fochriw on Sunday I met her there as arranged on the Monday morning instead of catching my train." Miah looked earnestly at his old friend. "She has a son, Gwallt, my grandson. She brought the boy with her to meet me. He is nearly three now, a beautiful, innocent child." Miah cleared his throat and sipped his tea before continuing. Walt was a good listener.

"Mary asked my forgiveness for running away and seemed most concerned that, should anything untoward happen, I would recognise the child as my grandson and give him a home. I did not hesitate. I assured her that both she and the boy will always find a home with me if the need ever arose. All that had passed could be forgiven if she prayed to the Good Lord. She seemed both relieved and grateful to hear it. Now I have no idea where she is. I let her go and she is lost to me again. I must find her or news of her and the boy and I cannot do that lying here in this feeble state. That's where I need your help, old friend, if you will give it?"

"Do you think the assault on you might be related to Mary's troubles?" asked Walt.

"That is my worse fear. She might have been followed, our conversation overheard by her husband. But I remember nothing except watching her leave our trysting place carrying the boy on her back over the rough ground. Perhaps I did slip and hit my head on a rock as the doctor suggested. On the other hand…"

"Rest easy now… do not tire yourself," said Walt as he sat back in thought. "I have a suggestion… I am confident I can convince Dr Thomas to release you into my care... for your convalescence. Elizabeth has already suggested it... We can use the excuse of his mounting charges if nothing else. Tomorrow I must be away most of the day.... it cannot be avoided... duty calls," he added apologetically.

"You must take that time to recover and get back on your feet... Elizabeth will be only too happy to have the chance to make amends for this calamity in her eyes. But the following day... we will see if we can pick up the trail of your errant daughter. Leave all the arrangements to me." He rose from his seat. "I will leave you now... I shall have a word with the doctor on my way out... and you must try and rest if we are to follow this plan through. And I only ask one favour..."

"If it is in my power to do it, you have only to ask," said Miah.

"Can you find time tomorrow to tell Elizabeth what you have told me about Mary and your grandson? I will leave it to you to choose the moment... but we cannot keep her in the dark... And it would sound more credible to her if it came from your own lips... She holds you and our longstanding friendship in great esteem. Let us pray for a satisfactory outcome to our quest."

After arranging with the doctor for Miah to be discharged into Elizabeth's care the following day Walt eventually made his way home hoping Elizabeth had kept something tasty for supper. As he reached the crossroad outside the house who should he meet coming up the street but Trefor, Dan and Ceridwen on their way home accompanied by Jack Williams heading for West Street.

"Look out," said Tref to his siblings "there's father. Leave the talking to me." At that point Criddy burst into tears and ran to her Dadda.

136

"What have we here?" he asked lifting her up with some difficulty, "why the tears?"

"It's my fault father," said Tref putting away the blood-soaked hankie in his blazer pocket, "a bit of trouble with Nobby Harris and two of his louts."

Walter was amazed to see his eldest son had clearly been fighting and had the wounds to prove it. "What sort of condition is this to come home in? Inside all of you," said Walt. "Wait until your mother sees the state on you, my boy."

Chapter 16

The following morning Alf Waters caught up with Sam as they walked the path to work for the day shift. The morning sun was already warm on their faces as the headed for the pithead.

"Hey, Sam," he called, "my Lydia was convinced she heard someone clattering around that house next door in the night. Do you think Hugh might of come back to finish her off?" asked Alf a little out of breath.

"To be honest Alf, Hugh Brown had me fooled. I thought I was a good judge of people and I would never have thought he was the type to attack a woman as viciously as that. The fact he ran off just confirms his guilt in my eyes. He was a good ostler and gentle with the horses, mind. It seems strange he could turn on a woman like that."

"She must have done something bad to provoke him," said Alf.

"No excuse, if you ask me," replied Sam. "Our Rae reckons she never went anywhere other than the local shops and then he always went with her. No visitors as far as she could tell. Most un-natural how they kept themselves to themselves these last few months."

"Who knows what goes on behind closed doors," said Alf "that's what my Lydia says. Well, I just hope we've seen the last of him. The police won't do anything…"

"What can you expect Evans to do? Goodness knows where Hugh has got to by now, he could be in Swansea for all we know."

"Well Lydia's convinced he's lurking around here. She was up and down twitching the curtains all night but I was in no hurry to go and see. So, when are they going to replace Hugh in the stables? A nice job that, always fancied it myself - bit of an easy life," said Alf.

"Easy life? It' a bloody dangerous one if you don't have some knowledge of horses," said Sam. "You need a calm and steady manner with them underground if you don't want to get crushed. Horse can kill a man with its weight alone in a confined space. But there's no point bending my ear, man. I don't hire and fire. It's my job to make sure the shifts are covered, not necessarily who covers them. Although I could do with a few more men with Hugh Brown's skill." They walked on in silence, Alf not sure if he had offended Sam with his remark.

"That Hugh, he had been a stable lad before he came down the mines, you know. One of the few things he did tell me," said Sam. "His experience showed, worked on some big estate since he was a young boy. Like I said, he was good with the horses and I am responsible for their welfare or not much coal would get hauled out of that mine."

"Aye, those ponies are treated better than the men. And that's a hard job, haulier, and not that well paid either," said Alf. "Perhaps I'm better off as a hewer, at least I know what I am doing after all these years. Worked on the Staffordshire coalfields before a long term lock out in the local pit made a load of us head out looking for work; never thought me and the family would end up so far from home."

"…you and a thousand others. Yes, stick with what you know and can do best. That's the surest way to stay safe down the pit," Sam said as they headed down the grassy track to the pithead buildings.

*

Rae had seen the men off out to work as usual that Wednesday morning and now the girls were up, dressed and seated at the table with Edie in charge.

"Eat up your bread and jam and off to school when you're done," said their mam. "I'm just going to step along the row and see Mary and little Robbie, Edie."

"How is she Mam? Is it true Hugh tried to kill her?" asked Edie in an innocent voice. "Now where did you hear such tall tales?" asked Rae.

"All the children in school were talking about it yesterday," Edie replied.

"Bully Bertie down the row said he heard it all and saw the murdering Hugh run into the night covered in her blood," said May.

"Now stop that at once. It is a wicked story and it is not true I am telling you. So you do not repeat it. Do you hear me?" said Rae.

"But Evans has all the police out hunting for him Bertie said…" said May tearfully. "Enough of what Bertie said. I will not have tales told in this house. Don't you learn anything from Sunday school? Hugh has done something very bad but, as for murder, it is all too much."

"You go and see to them Mam. I can make sure that we get off to school," said Edie.

Rae wrapped Henry in her shawl and left the house quickly before her temper got the better of her. She found Nan Evans sitting on the chair at the unlit range of the Brown's end cottage. The old woman was leaning forward with her head in her hands. Snoozing again probably, thought Rae until Nan lifted a sorrowful face towards her.

"You won't find them - gone they are," she said.

"What do you mean gone?" asked Rae.

"She sent me away last night," said Nan, "after you went. Said she could cope with Robbie and I needed my bed. Very calm she was - insisted. I should have told you. You've done so much for them. I did not want to disturb you with it again last night. I came back here first thing. Now I've looked everywhere, out the back an' all. They are not here."

"Dew, dew, what can she be thinking? Doing a moonlit flit with the little one an' all and her in that state," said Rae "I suppose we should let the police know."

"Will they blame me, the police?" asked Nan. "Never trusted that Evans. Known him all his life – my husband's nephew's son. A sly little boy he was and a thief. Never trust a thief."

"No Nan, none of this is your fault, you have shown nothing but kindness itself," said Rae ignoring her remarks about Evans police. "But strange it is she should up and off without helping the police put that man behind bars after what he did."

"Something to hide that pair have. Wash my hands of them I do. And I'm telling you - do the same," said Nan before wiping her face with the skirt of her apron.

"You may be right there, Nan," said Rae. "Let's get back to my kitchen. You look as if you could do with a good strong cup of tea. The girls can take a message to the police house on their way, that's if they have not left for the schoolroom already."

Chapter 17

Walt leaned back to relax as best he could in his seat. He had already had a busy morning but had managed to catch the 8 o'clock train to Cardiff as planned. It was quite clear to him that Elizabeth did not like to have her weekday domestic routine disturbed; rather too much had happened already this week for her to maintain her usual even temper. Trefor returning home covered in blood had just about been the last straw and the children, all of them, had been dispatched to their beds without any supper. She sponged and pressed Trefor's school uniform for the morning having just done the same with Esau's suit in readiness for his interview today. She had shown more concern for the state of her son's clothes than the state of his face as she scrubbed away at his bloodied nose with a cold flannel.

Walt had sought refuge in his study where he busied himself preparing for today's executive meeting and for his planned excursion with Miah in search of his daughter and grandson the following day. Thanks to the telephone he was able to do most of that from the comfort of the chair in his study.

By bedtime, order reigned once again in Elizabeth's kitchen as she and her husband discussed the children. Walt agreed that stern words were needed to dissuade young Trefor from descending in to bad ways and fighting his way through life. He would need to get to the bottom of that incident since Trefor had been economical with the truth as to how he became involved in scrapping with the likes of Nobby Harris.

Economical with the truth, indeed, Walt thought. We are all guilty of that from time to time. He had decided not to tell the police or his wife about Miah's daughter to preserve the reputation of his friend. What was Trefor's reason for glossing over the cause of his uncharacteristic actions, Walt wondered.

He opened the newspaper and held it high in front of him for some privacy with his thoughts. The other occupants of the carriage were mainly school boys, Trefor's fellow pupils, traveling from up the valley down to the Lewis School in Pengam. Trefor would surprise them all turning up to lessons today with a cut across the bridge of his nose and two shiners of black eyes. He would probably earn a lot of schoolboy admiration into the bargain especially when they found out who had inflicted his injuries. The Harris' men had a reputation as a hard fighting family and often turned up at public meetings with the sole intent of starting a good scrap. Why should the boys be any different given the example they were set? *Train up a child in the way he should go: and when he is old, he will not depart from it.* The scriptures held many truisms thought Walt as a parent.

As well as predicting a future as a pugilist for her eldest, Elizabeth also seemed to exaggerate little Gwladys' habit of eavesdropping as the early signs of a life of delinquency. He had promised her that he would speak to Trefor in his study this evening. As for Gwladys, he suggested it was high time the girl went to school. That would satiate her natural inquisitiveness for the world around her. He would have a word with Miss Owen, the headmistress, to get her admitted early in September. Elizabeth had been mollified for the time being.

His wife was pleased to hear his update on Miah's progress and warmed to the news that he would be discharged into her care. It had, after all, been her suggestion which she saw as some atonement for the fact that Miah had been

143

injured, as she viewed it, practically on her doorstep. Walt had decided to withhold the revelation of Miah's runaway daughter and the existence of a grandson to a man she regarded as the epitome of bachelorhood. If he had been economical with the truth himself it was because he thought it better if she heard it directly from Miah, especially given everything that had conspired to put his dear wife out of temper yesterday. He knew his old friend would not let him down and would find an appropriate moment to speak to Elizabeth.

On a more optimistic note they had discussed Esau's prospects at his interview, agreeing that a desk job would suit her brother's temperament and talents far better than casual labour down the pit when he could get the work. Having set their world to rights, husband and wife retired upstairs to bed in a slightly improved humour.

Walt was used to a hectic workload but the unexpected events of the last few days, he conceded, had been a drain on them both. Now he must concentrate on the matter in hand. He had been to many executive meeting of the Fed as acting agent during his predecessor's long illness, but it was his first as the newly elected miner's agent for the Rhymney Valley. There were important matters to discuss, not least the prospect of a national ballot on the eight hour Act and the ratification of the affiliation of the Fed to the Independent Labour party. Walt would need his wits about him to follow the debate and all the legal arguments. But there was one consolation, he knew there would be a good lunch to sustain the delegates.

*

Elizabeth made Miah walk at a snail's pace the short distance from Cardiff Road and up the hill to Ty Gwent. He was ushered into the front parlour to sit on the uncomfortably overstuffed armchair with a blanket on his knees despite the warmth to the weather.

"What can I get you while I put the kettle on?" she asked, "something to read perhaps?"

"May I borrow your Bible there?" he asked. It still lay opened on the small table at the book of Proverbs.

"Better still I have your own. The police sent your bag over first thing. Walt must have arranged it although goodness knows where they found it," she said.

"I really have caused a great deal of trouble to a great many people. Can you forgive me Elizabeth?"

"There is nothing to forgive," she replied lifting his battered Gladstone bag onto the table at his elbow. "You take your time and I'll be back with some elevenses."

He checked his bag and it was just as he had packed it early Monday morning. He leaned back wearily in the chair and had his eyes closed when Elizabeth returned with tea and buttered Welsh cakes. The rich smell made Miah realise he was quite hungry after all.

"Now you sit down and join me," he said. "We have had little time to talk together during my visit. I'd like to know how you are coping with all these changes and responsibilities that have come with Walter's position. How are you, Elizabeth?"

"You are kind to ask," she replied. "But there are so many advantages to our present situation I would feel ungrateful to complain. My concerns are, as always, for my husband and children. That would have been the case if we were still living in the old cottage in Cwmsyfiog and Walter working as checkweigher at Coedymoeth pit. My family are constantly in my prayers."

145

"Family," said Miah "so important to a wife and mother. Sometimes I think we men dismiss the vital role our women undertake on our behalf, raising our children, managing the household."

"I am blessed in my husband's support on behalf of our family," she said. "Indeed. Have I ever told you anything of my family?" he asked. It was only fair that he should not be the cause of secrets between husband and wife after all.

He knew that his tale of Mary and his late wife would not surprise Elizabeth unduly. Death in childbirth was still all too common and his situation as a young widower was not unusual. But as he expected, she was shocked to hear of the girl's disappearance. Elizabeth had been unnaturally quiet during the telling, even when he mentioned his intention to find Mary and his grandson with Walter's help. What he could not know was that she was struck by the parallel between the account of his early marriage and widowhood and that of her husband.

Walter had been married before he met Elizabeth although she rarely dwelled on it these days. His first wife had died within a year of their marriage after giving birth to a surviving daughter, Margaret. Miah must know this she realised, yet he had said nothing. Miah had first known them both when they were courting and Walter's circumstances were well known in the village of Hollybush at that time. After his first wife died, he and his daughter continued to live with his mother-in-law and her family as lodgers. Elizabeth recalled for the first time in many years how that woman resented Walter's blossoming relationship with her.

When Walter and Elizabeth eventually married, his daughter Maggie was nine years old; it wasn't as if they had rushed into it with the impatience of youth. Maggie stayed with her grandmother when the newly married couple set up home and started their own family. At 12, when Maggie left school, she went to work as a servant for Elizabeth's parents in Argoed. Elizabeth had thought it an ideal solution for Maggie's future at the time. She herself had been sent to work for a family in Pengam at the same age. After all, it was a common enough fate for girls from working families. Maggie was now a grown woman, married herself with two young children and still living in Argoed.

Since moving across the river to Bargoed, that episode in their life had been largely put behind them. The younger Lewis children did not even know of Maggie's existence as far as Elizabeth was aware and, if Trefor remembered her, he never mentioned his half-sister. Elizabeth returned from her reflections on the past to the practicalities of the present.

"I need to relieve Mrs B next door before Gwladys drives her up the wall with her endless chatter. She'll be wondering where I've got to this morning," said Elizabeth back to her daily routine which revolved around the family's welfare. "I have kept some chicken broth. Let us have it for dinner. Then I suggest you have a nap this afternoon; you will need to gather your strength if you and Walter are to fulfil your plan to return the prodigal daughter." So, she had been listening Miah thought to himself.

Chapter 18

After a refreshing afternoon nap Miah enjoyed the bustle of the Lewis family about him in the kitchen later that afternoon. Esau had returned home first and was pleased to announce to his sister that, as of next Monday, he would be the new cashier and invoice clerk at Peglars grocery store. The previous occupant of the post had been promoted to assistant store manager in Aberdare and Esau spoke enthusiastically of the opportunity for promotion within the company. He could not wait to rush back out to broadcast his good news to the neighbours after wishing Miah a full recovery from his injuries.

Ceridwen came home from school next and proceeded to tell them what she had learned that day while they waited for the boys to return for tea. She promised to teach Gwladys fractions later much to Miah's amusement.

Dan had earlier been sent on an errand to take an extra bundle of shirts and tablecloths to the Hop Woo laundry and had not yet returned. He had spent some of the time waiting out of sight of the house in the back lane behind Cardiff Road offering a light to any miner walking down the hill for the afternoon shift in the pit. His mother did not like him having matches but the men did. Matches, of course, were banned underground. Only when Dan saw Trefor go through the back gate into the house did he join the family for tea. Safety in numbers if Mam was out of temper, he reasoned.

Elizabeth had baked a rich fruit cake for a tea time treat and the homely smell of fresh baked cake enveloped them all in the heat of kitchen when the family sat down to tea with their guest.

"Grace, Miah please," said Elizabeth. The children bowed their heads on their clasped hands at the edge of the table. Miah cleared his throat and bowed his head. "For what we are about to receive may the Lord make us truly thankful…"

"AMEN," said Dan loudly. The other children peeked at their mother to see her response.

"Amen indeed," said Miah smiling at Dan. Elizabeth picked up the knife to cut the loaf of bread with a stern look on her face. The children ate in polite silence but, throughout the meal, Gwladys stared as if mesmerised at Miah's head much to her mother's consternation. Eventually she said "Don't stare Gwladys, it's rude."

"I must look strange to the child with these bandages," said Miah. "It looks as if I'm wearing a turban."

"What's that?" asked Ceridwen.

"Men from the east wear turbans on their heads. Like this, only yards of rich bright cloth not Miss Thomas' white bandages," replied Miah "and secured with a shiny jewel in the front."

"From the east - is that like the wise men who came from the east?" she asked.

"Yes, young lady, although not every man in a turban is necessarily a wise man," he replied looking meaningfully at Elizabeth.

"Now enough questions. Once she starts she cannot stop," said Elizabeth excusing her inquisitive daughter. "Don't encourage her, Miah."

"Oh, it does the heart good to see the curiosity of youth, Elizabeth don't you think? And I am enjoying the diversion," he admitted. "But I am not the only one who looks as if he's been through the wars. Those are two fine black eyes you have, Trefor. If I did not know better it looks as if you've been in a good scrap since the weekend."

"Yes, well the less said about that the better," said Elizabeth. "I am afraid his father will have to deal with him later and see if he can get to the bottom of that sorry affair."

"Well, thank you for the excellent tea, Elizabeth," Miah said realising that Elizabeth was not best pleased with the behaviour of her children at this precise moment. He had been insensitive to mention the boy's appearance but those black eyes were quite impressive. "What time do you think Walter will be home this evening? I am eager to get back to my business despite your generous hospitality. I do not want to outstay my welcome here."

"You must stay as long as needed. I will not be sending you home still unwell. As for Walter, it depends how long the executive committee sits. They stay as long as they must to complete their business. Sometimes it means an overnight stay in an hotel. But Walt did not think there was call for that today or he would have warned me," said Elizabeth. "Dan will go and meet the half past six train up from Cardiff. That's the one he usually gets and if he's not on it he can let us know. Meanwhile I have his supper to think of so help me clear away the tea girls. Homework, Trefor?"

After yesterday, there seemed little point in asking permission to go out to play. "Lots," he replied, resigned to an evening indoors despite the good weather. "I'll fetch my book bag."

The family settled to their early evening activities. Elizabeth with her work box was knitting. Miah was mesmerised by the speed and dexterity with which she wielded the knitting needles; barely needing to glance down as she worked. Trefor had his head in his school books at the kitchen table. The girls had put up their blackboard and were practising their handwriting. Ceridwen wrote letters which Gwladys then copied in her large, childish script. Dan had already gone to meet the trains up the valley from Cardiff to wait on his father's expected return.

"C is for Ceridwen. It is the first letter of my name."

"Add that and it's a G, the first letter for Gwladys," said her little sister.

Miah sat in deep contemplation of the domestic scene around him trying to ignore the dull ache in his head. Watching the Lewis family made him realise how the early death of his young wife had deprived him of the contentment of family life. Walt had a second chance at domestic happiness and he could not help but feel a tinge of envy for a man who had that blessing and enrichment in his busy life. It made him all the more determined to find Mary and her boy. While his daughter had seemed more than content in her childhood home, something had made her run away with the first man who had showed her attention.

It pained him further to think that his neglect of fatherly concern had forced her to stay estranged from her family when she was in need. How desperate her circumstances must have become, he thought, for her to overcome her guilt and shame to beg his forgiveness after all this time. If he could not give her the opportunities she had deserved in childhood he now had a second chance with his grandson; if only he could find them. If Mary's situation was now intolerable to her, he thought holding his head in his hands, well, no woman should have to live in constant fear of her husband whatever the law might say on the matter. It was a conundrum he had not really thought through until now, going as it did against many of the teachings in the scriptures he held so dear. The wedding vows he had heard so often resonated in his head. "Let no man pull asunder," he muttered audibly.

"Are you well Miah?" asked Elizabeth.

"But for this ache in my head," he replied. But it was the ache in his heart that troubled him.

"Perhaps you should put your feet up for a while," said Elizabeth, "at least until Walt returns. I will make up one of Dr Thomas' headache powders for you. It would be quieter for you in the front room."

"That might be a good idea. But don't let me drop off to sleep again. Let me know when Gwallt returns."

Ceridwen had cleaned the blackboard and was showing Gwladys how to write fractions.

"One over two is a half. Like a ha'penny is half a penny so you need two ha'pennies to make a penny," she said helpfully. "One over four is a quarter. A farthing is a quarter of a penny, so how many farthings make a penny, Gwladys?"

"Four?" she asked.

"Good girl," said Ceridwen and showed Gwladys how to work out four times a quarter on the blackboard. "We worked out how many farthings in sixpence and a shilling and a half crown."

"What's a half a crown? Do two half-crowns make one whole crown like the king wears?" asked Gwladys.

Ceridwen looked perplexed at her mother who was watching them over her knitting. "No dear, a crown and a half crown are coins of the realm," said Elizabeth. "You don't see crowns anymore but the half-crown is a big silver coin worth two shillings and sixpence."

"So that must mean a whole crown is worth five shillings if we had that much," said Ceridwen. "Five shillings is a lot of money," she explained to Gwladys.

"So then, clever clogs, how many farthings in a sovereign?" asked Trefor listening to his sisters.

"A sovereign – what's that?" Ceridwen asked.

"A coin made of solid gold that old misers keep in a secret chest under their beds and count at dead of night," answered Trefor.

"Does Dadda have sovereigns under his bed?" asked Gwladys.

"Of course not, twp, that would make Dadda a miser which he is not. A miser is someone who cannot bear to spend their money and hoard it instead," explained Tref.

"Now don't call your sister stupid when she is anything but. Although he is quite right, Ceridwen, your father is not a miser but quite the opposite. He is a very generous man who pays for the shoes on your feet and the food in your belly."

With all this to distract and amuse her, Elizabeth was unaware of the passing time until Dan returned ahead of his father and nodded vigorously in reply to his mother's question. Walt was on his way. Miah had also been listening out for Walt's return and she heard the sound of their voices in the passage.

It was almost another hour before Miah and Walt could retire to the study and finalise their plans for the following day. The girls were sent up to bed at precisely seven o'clock, even though it was still light, bidding goodnight to their father and Uncle Miah. Then the family caught up on the day's events most important of which was Esau's good fortune to find a job with prospects while Walt ate his food.

Despite Walt's enthusiasm for the following day ahead, Miah had several misgivings about the lengths his dear friend was willing to go on his behalf in his quest to find Mary and her son after they retreated to the study to discuss their plans.

"Now do you have any idea where Mary may have been lodging?" asked Walt. "It must be within walking distance of Fochriw... for her to have met you outside the chapel late on Saturday night."

"I watched her walk away down the other side of valley away from the monolith after our meeting," said Miah.

"The Taff-Bargod towards Bedlinog and Treharris... there are several pits in the area where her man could have found work. They are close-knit communities... If she is living there we have a good chance of finding her... so that's where we'll start. Bedlinog first... it is the closest village to the spot. We can ask at the local shops... even the inns if need be. She is bound to be known by someone. Do you think you're up to this?" asked Walt.

"I only wish we could have started sooner. Can you spare the time in your busy schedule?" asked Miah.

"Let me worry about that... one of the advantages of being in charge... I have an excellent deputy and devoted office staff. They cover my frequent absences on official business... they will do the same even it happens to be... shall we call it unofficial business? The diary is not full tomorrow... and I can catch up from home... now I have this telephone here... it is going to make life a lot easier for me. And as you said yourself there has been too much delay already."

"This idea of hiring a carriage, is that wise or even necessary?" asked Miah.

"Essential... how else are we going to cover all this ground … and all in one day? It is far too soon for you to be walking miles with a head wound... The carriage can take us direct to where ever we need to go… then onto the nearest railway station for a train to Brecon. We must think of getting you home soon," said Walt persuasively. "And it is not an idea… it is all arranged... Davis himself will drive us. The dry roads will speed our progress… God willing... and you will ride in comfort on this journey."

Miah could only smile at Walt's command of the situation and decided to raise no more objections.

"Now... is there anyone you need to contact by telephone tonight?" asked Walt.

"No, not at this time of the evening. I have a housekeeper who lives in, my mother-in-law in fact. Her son now runs the farm and she retired to keep house for me. But I have not had the telephone installed at the house. After the events of this week I can see that it has its uses in the home and shall be following your example and get one installed."

"Well, if you'll excuse me… I have some calls to make before supper. And, if you don't mind... will you tell Trefor I want to see him ... in here in a few minutes? Then I suggest we get an early night."

Miah left his friend in the study to finalise his arrangements and joined Elizabeth and the boys in the kitchen. He passed on the message to Trefor who nodded, resigned to the long-awaited interview with his father. He had hoped it had been forgotten but should have realised his father always made time to honour his family obligations… eventually.

"I cannot thank you enough for everything you have done for me Elizabeth but I have one last request before I retire for the night," said Miah. "Gwladys' reaction to my headdress over tea, well, I really must look quite a curious sight. Do you think you could help me remove Miss Thomas' turban?"

"If you are sure, I always think it better to let the air get to a wound myself once the scab has formed. Let me see," she said and set about the task of unwinding the bandages and inspecting the injury. "Now supper…"

"No more food for me tonight, thank you. I will take Walt's advice for an early night given the plans he has afoot for tomorrow. Good night and God's blessing on us all especially you, dear Elizabeth and your household."

*

Sam was late returning from work. He had to rearrange the shifts to cover for the missing Hugh. News travels fast so he already knew that Mary had disappeared sometime the previous night taking little Robbie with her. Perhaps that was the noise Lydia Waters heard from the end cottage. He was not surprised to hear the story repeated by his excited daughters.

"Let a man get his boots off first. So how are my best girls," asked Sam "been good today?"

"They took my message into the police house this morning on their way to school didn't you," said Rae. "I'm surprised Evans police hasn't been here asking questions again, not that I've got anything to tell him. Poor Nan was put out by it all. That young woman, what can she be thinking running off like that - there's the thanks you get."

"It's been a bad business, this whole thing from beginning to end," said Sam. "I expect Evans has better things to do with his time."

"Well let's hope this is the end of it," said Rae "at least as far as we are concerned. I feel silly now asking you

156

to do his likeness," she said as she turned over the piece of paper Sam had used last night and looked on the unmistakeable face of Hugh Brown. "Waste of time that was too."

"But it's very good, Dadda," said Cath "although he looks very evil the way you've drawn that look on his face."

"Perhaps I was thinking evil things about him after what he did to his wife," said Sam with a wry laugh. "Your mother thought it might help the police find him. There are no photographs in the house but I doubt they'll be interested now. There'll be no case against him without her evidence." Rae picked up the pencil sketch and placed it firmly between the pages of last week's newspaper in the box in the grate for lighting the fire.

The kitchen was quiet after the children had gone to bed. Sam sat reading some technical manual with his spectacles perched on the end of his nose while Rae was doing some mending. "Alf and Lydia reckon someone was prowling around the end cottage last night," said Sam. "Perhaps it was Mary or do you think he might have come back, Hugh I mean? No sign of anything unusual today?"

"Nothing that I've noticed. But we could take a look inside, there's no lock. Anyone could walk in there. Although the place is probably crawling with black pats with no one to scare them back into their hidey holes," said Rae.

"Leave it," said her husband. "It's none of our concern. Like I said to Alf, let's hope that's the last we hear of the Browns." He returned to his paper then added "I hope her and the boy are safe, though he can go to the devil in a hand cart for all I care."

Chapter 19

The presence of a horse drawn carriage in the street outside Ty Gwent the following morning caused quite a stir amongst the neighbours. Normally only hired for funerals or weddings it set tongues wagging and front curtains twitching. A group of the over curious gathered opposite outside the corner shop for a closer look.

Esau came out from the Braithwaite's house next door to admire the horse drawn vehicle and share a cigarette with the owner Dai Davis. Old John looked on from the corner of Ty Gwent and Jones the shop opposite came and joined him.

"Good morning gentlemen," said Walt smiling broadly and lifting his cap coming out of his front door. "It's a lovely day for a carriage drive, don't you agree?" They looked on in astonished silence for once.

Miah descended the steps behind his friend, bag in hand. Davis, wearing an over large coat and cap, hurriedly put out his cigarette and opened the door for Miah to ascend into the well upholstered interior. Noticing Esau among the group of men standing on the corner, Miah went to raise his hat in acknowledgment. Realising he no longer had his hat, it had never been found even though his bag had been miraculously returned, he waved instead. Elizabeth and the children stood on the threshold of the house to witness the unusual scene and wave off their guest. Walt got into the carriage alongside Miah and Dai Davis shut the door securely behind him.

"God's speed," cried Elizabeth and the children waved frantically as the carriage moved away from the house. A few young boys ran alongside, then lagged behind the carriage until the horse broke into a trot and left them standing in the roadway as the horse and carriage rattled and jingled on its journey. Once out of the town, they passed Heolddu Farm and bowled along the mountain track across the open common. Miah understood his friend's wisdom in hiring the vehicle. "At this pace, we shall be in Bedlinog in no time," said Walt.

Back at Ty Gwent the children had left for school and Elizabeth felt a little deflated after the excitement of her husband's departure with Miah. Then the dreaded telephone bell rang out from the passage. "Stay here and don't you dare move while I see who that can be," she said to Gwladys.

"Police Sergeant Harris you say? Well, I will have to speak to him, put him through… No, Mr Miah Thomas is not here. I'm afraid he left this morning with my husband to return to Brecon. They left by horse and carriage nearly an hour ago… The police in Brecon are trying to locate him? A message from his housekeeper you say… well, if you tell the lady to be patient he should be with them well before the day is out… I know they are stopping on their journey to do some family business which is why they are travelling by carriage... thank you. Good day." Elizabeth returned the earpiece to the cradle ending the call. "Now I wonder what that was about?" she said aloud shutting the study door behind her. "Carriages, telephones, what is the world coming to? Come on Gwladys, come and help me strip the beds" she called out; more business for the Hop Woo.

*

Davies used the brakes to ease the carriage down the steep hill before drawing to a halt in Bedlinog village square. Walt and Miah headed straight into the largest grocery store. Anyone who lived in the village would need to buy

159

their groceries somewhere had been Walt's logic in selecting this as their first destination. The local shopkeepers would be as good a place to ask for information as anyone. Inside the well-stocked shop, it was dark and relatively quiet. One elderly shopkeeper was behind the counter and busy serving an even older woman. They both looked round as the shop bell rang out to announce the arrival of the two strangers.

"Good morning," said the shopkeeper, "I shall be with you now just if you don't mind waiting."

"See to these gentlemen first," said his customer, "I am in no hurry. I can wait."

"Thank you dear lady," said Walt touching his cap. "Good morning sir... we are not here to buy anything... but we are looking for news of someone... a young woman and her child.... we believe they may be lodging nearby... and may use your shop."

"Her name is Mary and she has a little boy about three years old called Robbie," said Miah and described Mary's distinctive red-blonde hair so like her mother's. The shopkeeper looked meaningfully at his customer who happened to be Nan Evans getting in her weekly grocery order when the shop was quiet. "In what connection are you strangers looking for this woman and her child?" he asked suspiciously. Miah did not hesitate. He inclined his head and said "I am her father..."

"Dew, dew, dew, dew. Well I never," said Nan. "Would you believe it? I have a neighbour who fits that description, or rather I did..." and she sat down heavily on the wooden chair set aside for the customers.

"You are too late," said the shopkeeper dramatically. "Nan Evans here was just telling me. Mary Brown has left without telling a soul. Crept away in the dead of night, like a criminal if you ask me, and took the

160

boy with her. Looks like she was avoiding the police after all that trouble her husband caused. And him gone missing too with the police out for his arrest."

Miah and Walt exchanged an astonished look. They had not expected to hear news of her so quickly never mind news of this nature.

"'Ark at you, Sam Siop talking as if you know it all. Confusing these gentleman with your tittle-tattle," said Nan. "I knew these people you speak of, your daughter and her son. Or about as well as anyone hereabouts. Not that that is saying much. Kept to themselves, they did. As I said, I am a neighbour. But Sam Siop here is right about one thing. No one has seen her and the boy since Tuesday evening. And you are her father?" She looked quizzically at Miah, taking in his height and slightly dishevelled attire. "You will want to know the full story. I know who you can tell you everything, sensible like and no gossip. If you have the time?"

To locate a neighbour at their first attempt was good fortune indeed. "We have as much time as is needed… We did not expect to find news or her so readily... Is it far?" asked Walt. "We have a carriage outside."

"No, not too far to Club Row," replied Nan.

"I will have the boy deliver your order after school. Are you paying for it now or shall I put it on your account?" asked Sam Siop.

It was a squash inside the carriage, but having helped Nan up into the seat, Walt perched on the fold down seat opposite her and Miah in the cab. A few minutes later they descended in the lane outside the end cottage in small a row of six. "Lived here for nearly twenty years now," she said, "and seen a lot of coming and going in my time. But you don't want to hear about me. Let me take you to see Rachel

Jones. She will talk sense to you. She knows most of what's been happening here this week past; been witness to most of it. Her and her Sam tried to help your daughter. We all did."

Rae was quite taken aback to find Nan escort two unknown gentlemen to her door especially when Nan told her they were looking for Mary Brown. She was even more surprised to learn that one of the gentlemen was Walter Lewis, miners' agent and the other very tall gentleman none other than Mary's father and him a Baptist minister too. The kitchen was in a chaos of confectionary so she showed them into her neat but fussy front parlour where they sat side by side awkwardly on the chaise long. She gathered her thoughts while removing her apron and patting down her hair to check her hairpins were secure. Starting at the beginning she told them of the events that began last Monday night and had so scandalised the neighbourhood and now shocked the two gentlemen.

Rae answered their questions as frankly as she could and freely admitted when she could not give them all the information they needed. "You will need to ask Constable Evans if he intends to pursue the matter. The police house is back in the village square," she added helpfully.

"How badly injured was Mary in the attack?" asked Miah.

"The doctor who treated her injuries also lives in the village, in the big house. You cannot miss it and I am sure he will find time to talk to you. To me she seemed very withdrawn after the attack but physically the doctor said that there was severe bruising to her neck and some scratches. She was fortunate, he's a strong man and he did try to throttle the life out of her," answered Rae.

"The husband, Hugh Brown I believe, has anyone seen him?" asked Miah.

"No. He did not turn up for his night shift at the pit on Monday. Evans the police went straight there after the incident was reported. There are rumours among the neighbours that he may have been lurking in the area and even came back to the house on the night after Mary and Robbie left. But that's all they are, rumours," said Rae.

"Strange as it may sound to you Mrs Jones, I have never met my daughter's husband. Could you describe him to me? What does he look like, any distinguishing features?" asked Miah.

"I can do better than that if you'll excuse me a moment," said Rae.

"Well you were right to be concerned," said Walt when Rae left the room and they were alone for a moment, "the girl's circumstances are desperate indeed. Do you think this husband of hers knew or found out about your clandestine meeting on the hillside?"

"It is possible he might have seen or heard Mary leave the house. If he works nights he could well have been in the house when she left to meet me on the Monday morning. If he followed her, it is even possible he overheard our conversation and knew I tried to encourage her to return to Brecon with me and bring the boy with her," said Miah.

"Dear Lord forbid... you mean it was he who attacked you and was responsible for your head wound... then later took out his anger on Mary?" asked Walt.

"I cannot be sure since I cannot say with certainty that I saw him and did not know what hit me. But it all falls into place. The two attacks, both on the same day. It is too much of a coincidence to overlook," said Miah.

163

Rae returned and gave Miah the piece of paper she had retrieved from the newspaper box by the fire. "It's a very good likeness. My husband drew it at my request. I thought it might help the police to find him as there was not one photograph in the house. Sam, my husband, worked with Hugh so was familiar with his appearance. Hugh is a big athletic man, taller than my husband but not as tall as you sir," she said. "Six foot at a guess and probably doesn't know his own strength. But you cannot mistake him if you find him as he has a severe stammer and talks reluctantly. Sam also says he whistles like a lark if that's any use. And he is very good with horses. He worked with the pit ponies underground. My Sam is the head ostler but, excuse me, I'm prattling now."

"May I keep this?" asked Miah and Rae nodded.

"You are welcome. Can I offer you tea, gentlemen? Nan has the kettle on," she said.

"Mrs Jones you have been more than kind," said Walt "but I think my friend and I... we must be on our way. We cannot thank you enough for the information you have given us... It has been of great use to us... Thank you for your time," and he held out his hand to press a large silver florin into her palm. "There is no need..." she started to say. Walt smiled shaking his head and pressing her fingers over the coin. "Please accept it... a small token of our thanks... You have given us a clear account of the events leading up to Mary's sudden disappearance," he said. "Your neighbour did well to bring us to you... I expect there is much rumour and speculation about the village."

"Indeed there is sir, far too much. I only hope you find Mary and her boy safe and well," she said. "I am only sorry I cannot give you any clue as to where she might be. We knew little enough about where they came from. But if

I was in her shoes, the Lord forefend, I would be looking to my family." She looked pityingly at Miah.

"God bless you for your kindness to my daughter and grandson and thank your husband for this. I hope you are right. I will try to find news of them when I return home," said Miah looking at Sam's drawing before folding it and placing it carefully in his pocket book.

"There is nothing for her to come back to here," said Rae. "I hope you find them safe."

Once the gentleman had left in their carriage Rae added the coin to the rest of her sweet money in the wooden biscuit barrel on the dresser. Wouldn't Sam be surprised, she thought when she told him of her visitors today? Although why Mr Walter Lewis the miners' agent was looking for the missing Mary and not the police she had no idea. She had not chosen to tell the two gentlemen of her suspicion that Hugh was not the boy's father. It was based solely on a passing remark of Mary's and hardly warranted a mention under the circumstances. They had a lot more to worry about after learning of the attack, finding Mary and Robbie gone and Hugh's whereabouts unaccounted for. Quite a shock for Mary's father particularly. It was a bit early but she would have a break and enjoy a nice cup of tea with Nan for company.

*

Jack and Dan were wandering the mountain together. After three consecutive days in school already this week Jack had decided to take an unofficial day out to play and sought out his butty Dan for company. They headed for one of the many streams that gurgled through a wooded valley down towards Deri. Jack fancied looking for sticklebacks and having a paddle in the brook. He knew a good spot to while away a couple of hours on a summer's day.

"You should go to school," he said to Dan "not me. There's lucky you are being allowed out all day and no teachers. Come on, let's take our boots off and get in." Dan laughed in reply. That's why Jack liked him, he was always so cheerful. Perhaps he didn't always understand everything Jack told him but he was good company if you were not looking for conversation. Jack stepped onto the wet boulders up to his ankles in surprisingly cold water but nothing he could do or say would persuade Dan to join him in the water. Dan preferred the relatively safety of the bank and followed Jack carrying his worn boots as he made his precarious journey downstream stepping from one boulder to another.

"I can smell smoke," said Jack. "Can you smell smoke? Where's it coming from?"

Dan tried his best to give him a hand up onto the bank and Jack put his boots on hurriedly. "Over b' there, come on," he said to Dan and heading for a partly collapsed dry stone wall. "Keep down," he added ducking below the wall and heading down hill with Dan crawling behind him on the grass. Several yards further on the smell of damp wood smoke grew stronger and Jack could see the thin grey wisps rising from the field on the other side of the wall. Jack peeked over the top of the wall and could see a man kneeling by a small fire. He had an open razor, an enamel bowl and his shaving soap and was stooping in front of piece of broken mirror propped up a pile of stones out of the wall. Just then, the man began whistling a sad little tune. Beautiful it was, like the larks over the Graig.

Jack pulled Dan up by his sleeve to take a look too and managed to dislodge a loose stone in the wall. It fell onto another fallen stone with a sharp crack. The stranger rose immediately looking in the direction of the noise and saw the two faces staring at him over the wall.

"Gerroff with you," he shouted shaking the razor angrily at them. Jack did not hang about and, pulling Dan by the sleeve, headed back in the direction they had come. He prayed the man would not chase them as Dan did not move fast on his feet as they stumbled away to safety.

When Jack thought they'd put sufficient distance between them and the stranger to be sure he was not following, he stopped pulling Dan and they sprawled on the grass to get their breath back. "Just some bloke on the tramp looking for work I 'spose. He gave me a scare though," he said.

Dan was shaking his head. "Seen him before," Dan said, "up there," he added pointing to the hill above them. "When?" asked Jack. Dan shrugged "Days ago," he answered. "Well I guess he's not doing any harm, just living rough. We must have startled him that's all. Come on, let's find something else to do away from here. I know, let's go see the roman fort. The teachers took us there last week over Gelligaer. The whole school walked over the mountain from Bargoed. It's not far if we don't rush boyo," he said to Dan encouragingly "and we've got all day."

Chapter 20

On his return to Bargoed with Dai Davies in the carriage, Walt asked to be dropped off outside the house. He was back earlier than he expected and had time to call at home, have something to eat and tell Elizabeth of the morning's revelations before returning to the office. He had his monthly report to prepare for the lodge meeting on Monday and could make a start on that this afternoon. Then there was a miners meeting in Bargoed at the end of the day shift on the waste ground near the Hanbury Hotel which he would be able to attend. The men referred to the area where they gathered as Trafalgar Square because of the number of open air meetings that took place there; although few others in the town knew it by that name.

Walt and the other Fed officials were organising a 'show cards' campaign against non-unionism in the valley. It was hoped the men would turn out to support them for next week's show cards at Bargoed colliery. It was an opportunity for Walt to remind them to make sure they were clear on the books. Then he remembered he was due to appear before the magistrate on Friday morning; tomorrow in fact. Now, how could he possibly have let that slip his mind he thought with a smile to himself. There were probably messages awaiting him at the office in relation to that fiasco.

"You are back early," said Elizabeth after she heard the front door open and close. Walt was the only one who routinely came in and out through the front door. He carried a key while everyone else came the back way. The back door was rarely locked except at night.

"Is everything well? Did you find the girl?"

"No but we have news of her. And Miah took the train from Fochriw onto Brecon at five and twenty to twelve. He should be well on his was way home... quite a few days later than expected of course. Perhaps some food before I go back to the office? A bit of bread and cheese will do."

As Elizabeth got cut the loaf he told her what he could in front of little Gwladys, leaving the more sensational details of the story for later.

"We had a word with the constable in Bedlinog and the local doctor... But the neighbours at her lodgings have not seen her since Tuesday. Miah is optimistic that the girl will turn up back at her childhood home... eventually. Let us pray that he is right," said Walt in conclusion.

"I almost forgot. There was a telephone call for Miah, just after you left this morning. Police Sergeant Harris at Bargoed had a message from his housekeeper," said Elizabeth.

"Did he give you the message?" asked Walt.

"No. Perhaps she simply wanted to know how Miah was and when to expect his return. I told him Miah had already left and intended to be back in Brecon sometime later today, although he might be delayed by this business."

"Well I will see if I can find time to ask Sergeant Harris at the police station... I shall see you for supper. There is a meeting of the miners at the end of the day shift... It's on the doorstep so I should not be too late this evening."

"There are some letters came in the first post. I put them on your desk," said Elizabeth.

"I'll take them with me," said Walt as he picked up the neatly written envelopes on his way out.

*

169

"I had two gentleman visitors today," said Rae smiling at her husband. "They arrived in a carriage. You'll never guess who?"

"You will have to tell me then as I cannot imagine who arrives in a carriage around here other than the doctor and he rarely carries passengers," replied Sam.

"Well, one was very tall gentleman, a Baptist minister named Mr Thomas…"

"Was he trying to convert you?" asked Sam smiling. Any reference to religion never ceased to amuse her husband much to Rae's consternation.

"Get on with you. Now listen, I am being serious mun," she said laughing. "This Mr Thomas was looking for Mary and little Robbie. Believe it or not he said he was her father." Now that did surprise Sam. "Didn't seem to know much about her at all he didn't. The attack on her this week came as a surprise to him I could tell. A strange coincidence he should be looking for her within days of her running off. Even admitted he had no idea who Hugh was so I gave him that likeness you drew. Lucky it was I did not use it to the light the fire this morning. He was very pleased and said to pass on his gratitude for it."

"Well I doubt it is coincidence, bad news travels fast," said Sam.

"No, I'm telling you, he was shocked by what I had to tell him. He was hearing it for the first time. Whatever brought him looking it was not news of the attack or Mary running off like she did."

"Who was the second gentleman then? You said there were two."

"Well that was strange an' all. It was Mr Walter Lewis the new miners' agent from Bargoed. Now why he is looking for Mary and not the police I have no idea," said Rae. "Have you ever met him?"

170

"No," replied Sam "but you have had some distinguished visitors today, quite the toff I expect this Walter Lewis."

"Not really, he looked an ordinary sort. Even wore working boots and a cap except they were clean. But he had a collar and tie and his jacket and waistcoat fitted him well. He spoke lovely, he did, slow and very clear like he chooses his words carefully and beautiful Welsh. He seemed a very polite and generous man to me.

"Now that Mr Thomas the minister, Mary's father. He was very tall and so thin. His clothes were well worn almost scruffy and hanging off him, looked like he'd slept in them the past few days. And he looked tired and drawn, anxious that's the word unless he's sickening with something. I doubt anything I told him was welcome news either. I did feel sorry for the man, just a few days too late to find Mary here."

"I'd be more than anxious if one of our girls ended up in such a pickle as young Mary Brown," said Sam as he tamped down the tobacco in the bowl of his pipe.

"Well, our girls should be back from the Band of Hope in the village now just. Don't speak about the visitors to them although they'll probably hear of it off someone tomorrow if they haven't already. I seem to be wasting my time trying to discourage the gossip. It will rumble on for weeks this story…and grow in the telling I am sure."

Sam lit his pipe with a wooden spill from the bundle he kept in a pot on the mantlepiece and Rae resumed her mending. When the girls came in all was quiet.

"So, have you signed the pledge Edie?" he asked his eldest daughter laughing. Why thought Rae, she had no idea. Never drank a drop her Sam.

*

171

At Ty Gwent that evening everyone was engrossed in some task or other. Walt was in his study reading. He had several internal circulars from the Fed's solicitor to study to keep up with the current legislation on trades disputes. Included in them was one on the legal implications of the union collecting a levy for political purposes, specifically to fund the ILP. It had become essential in the last few years that any strike action was properly organised according to the law and Walt was ultimately responsible for keeping the Fed out of the law courts. That's when he was not being arrested for obstructing the highway. That incident had caused some wry amusement at the executive meeting yesterday.

Trefor was in the front room studying the bible. More specifically he was trying to memorise Psalm 37 about the fate of the wicked. It was a long and repetitive psalm. The task had been set by his father in the study the previous evening and Tref did not want to find out what would happen if he was not word perfect by Sunday afternoon. Trefor took it as his punishment for the scrap earlier in the week although Walt regarded it as part of his religious and moral education. It was not the first time he had to learn a psalm by heart but he fervently hoped this might be the last. Elizabeth wanted to use her sewing machine that evening but left Trefor in peace knowing the rhythmic whirr of the machine and clatter of the treadle was not conducive to his task. She had heard him repeating the lines aloud to commit them to memory when she fetched her work box.

At seven o'clock the girls were dispatched to their bed after putting away the blackboard and chalks. Elizabeth did not like the girls playing out in the street especially without their older brother to watch over them. She still hoped that Walter would manage to push through the development of the park and play area at the top of Wood Street before he stepped down from his position on the parish council.

It had been a lovely evening and she would have appreciated a walk with her girls around a park with neat flower beds and seats under the shade of a tree. Walter persevered with the idea of such an amenity for the town although his fellow councillors had been barely luke warm about the proposal given the more pressing issues facing them. It did not help that Walter thought Bargoed was as much entitled to a facility on the scale of Bedwellty Park in Tredegar. Perhaps if he reigned in his enthusiasm it would stand more chance she thought. But she knew the main stumbling block was the expense of getting the land on the hillside levelled to establish the site. Inevitably it always came down to money in the end.

"Say goodnight to your father on the way upstairs," Elizabeth reminded them the girls. "Knock on the door and wait mind Gwladys until he bids you enter." She returned to her embroidery at the table and heard the clatter of the girls' feet up the stairs a few minutes later.

Gwladys had been a very good girl today and had not repeated anything she had heard earlier about Miah's 'girl' as Walt had referred to Mary throughout their earlier conversation. The only thing she was overheard saying was that she hoped Uncle Miah would find his 'little girl' soon as she would not like to be lost and her dada so upset he had to wear a turban to keep his head warm and stop the ache. Perhaps details of the events that week had gone over the child's head for once.

Elizabeth was keen to hear more of Walt and Miah's expedition but it would have to wait. It was an unwritten rule that Walter was not to be disturbed in his study even if he was in there all night as had happened on more than one occasion when he had fallen asleep in his armchair. But he did make an exception if there was a cup of tea on offer; he took it in the study with his books and papers.

"Dan, go and tell you father I am putting the kettle on. Ask would he like some tea."

Dan waited until his father called out in answer to his knock before opening the door to the study. It was a small dark room even in summer with a new built in cupboard in an alcove, one wall lined with books and papers on oak shelves salvaged from the Farm, Gilfach Fargoed at the bottom of the street and Walt's desk against the wall by the door. The candlestick telephone stood on the desk at which Walt sat on a wooden office chair with castors. There was an upright armchair by the cast iron fireplace where Walt sat to read and a small Turkey rug on the floor boards. The effect combined business-like efficiency with the homely. Walt was at his desk writing as Dan stuck his head round the door.

"Tea?" he asked in a whisper. "Yes, some tea," replied Walt "tell your mother I'll take it in here."

As Walt turned his chair back to face the desk he knocked some of the papers piled at his elbow which tumbled onto the floor. Dan stooped to try and pick them up and noticed the drawing among them. The face he saw on the paper shocked him and he let out an involuntary shriek.

"What's the matter, boy? Do you know that face?" Walt asked his son holding up the paper for him to see it clearly. "Come here... tell me."

Dan was alarmed by his father's questions and his insistent tone. All he could do was nod his head in assent. "Now this is important. I want you to tell me… as best you can… when and where you saw the man... the face in the

174

drawing. Can you do that?" Dan stared mutely at his father. Walt rose from his chair and placed his hand gently on Dan's shoulder. He steered him back along the passage to Elizabeth in the kitchen.

Walt showed the drawing to Elizabeth and explained its significance and how he came to have it in his possession.

"There is little doubt this man cruelly assaulted Miah's girl before running off... He might still be a danger to her. No one knows the current whereabouts of either Mary or her assailant but... if his daughter does not turn up safe and well in the next few days... it is Miah's intention to turn the matter over to the police... He will start by enquiring after Mary and the boy in the villages around her home in Brecon... but I insisted he leave me the responsibility of informing the local police. They can start looking for the man here... in the area where this Hugh Brown was last seen... That is why he gave the likeness to me... If I have not heard by Monday that Mary and the boy have been found... I am to take it to the police. They can use the drawing along with a description to distribute a notice... countrywide if needed. Hopefully the police might get information to apprehend him... Miah is even willing to offer a considerable reward for information."

"But why delay?" asked Elizabeth. "This is a serious matter which the police should be dealing with."

"It was me who persuaded him not to act rashly and in haste. If this man is on the run... there is little the police can do. Miah will simply attract a great deal of unwanted attention and publicity. The neighbour in Club Row... in my opinion... was sensible in her assessment of Mary's predicament. I think between us... we have convinced Miah that his daughter could well turn up in Brecon... seeking his protection. Hopefully that is where she has headed. Miah has no fear of the consequences of any scandal... recent events have not yet roused the interest of the local newspaper reporters. But if Mary disappearance remains unresolved... and I act on Miah's wishes on Monday... well... we could have the reporters knocking at our door."

"Yes, I can see your dilemma. The safety of Mary and her child could well be at risk while this man is still at large. But why should you worry for Miah's reputation when he has so little concern for it himself?" asked Elizabeth.

"Miah has done nothing sinful in all of this. He is not thinking of himself... only the safety of his daughter and grandson. He has no other family... to find them and lose them again in the space of a few days. He is impatient... I understand that... but I do not want him to rush headlong into a situation which... for the sake of a little delay... might prove unnecessary. Now if Dan here has seen this Hugh Brown... and recently... in the last few days," said Walt prodding the drawing on the kitchen table "it is possible we might avert the publicity a manhunt would invite."

"I understand. Now Dan," she said drawing the boy to her where she sat and putting an arm protectively around his shoulders "tell your mam, have you seen this man before?" He nodded vigorously. "Recently in the last few days?" she asked. He nodded again. "Now tell me where," she encouraged him. "Mountain... Jack," he mumbled.

"Jack? I wonder if he means Jack Williams... from the shop in West Street? You know Richard Williams' son from chapel. They have been spending a lot of time together recently those two... Even I am aware of their friendship," said Walt.

176

"Now did you see the man with Jack up the mountain?" asked Elizabeth. Dan nodded more hesitantly this time. "Jack… my butty." He did not want to get Jack in trouble for mitching school. "Good boy," said Walt smiling and ruffling his son's hair. "You have not done anything wrong, quite the opposite. Elizabeth, keep him here. I need to talk to Jack Williams before it gets dark and the shop closes." He left hurriedly taking Sam's drawing with him.

The Lewis family rarely used the corner shop in West Street with Jones the grocer opposite the house only a few paces across the road and an account at the Co-op. Richard Williams owned and ran a small grocer shop and had a popular side line in firewood which had earned him his nickname with the locals, Dick the stick. Most of the streets in the town had a house converted into a shop, usually on the end of the terrace, with the family living in the back room and over the shop. It was some surprise therefore for Nellie Williams to see Walter Lewis standing before her at the counter. She had not heard him enter as the shop door was propped open in the dry weather.

"Is your husband at home?" asked Walt.

"Richard is in the back. I shall fetch him now, straight away Mr Lewis," said Nellie a little flustered. "Well it's your eldest I am eager to speak to, Jack."

"The children are all in bed by now, school in the morning. Except for Jane who helps me with the young ones. But I don't know if Jack is in yet. No idea of the time in the summer, that boy. I shall have to go and check. He's not in trouble again is he? Dick," she shouted. "Dick, Mr Walter Lewis is here. Come and see to him a minute."

Richard Williams emerged from behind a curtain separating the shop in the front room from the family's living space as his wife disappeared up the stairs to the

177

bedroom. The shopkeeper was stripped down to his grubby vest, trousers and bracers and was not expecting visitors. "Now what's the boy been up to this time?" asked Jack's father. "Not causing you trouble I hope Gwallt."

"No indeed not but he may have some information, a matter of some urgency if I can speak to him tonight," answered Walt. "I doubt the lad is even aware that he may be able to help me... It is a somewhat unusual matter."

Jack had sneaked in the back late, tip-toeing past his slumbering father straight up the stairs to bed. Even his mother had not noticed him creep upstairs. He now appeared to be asleep like an angel in bed with his younger brother Tom. "Jack," she said rousing him roughly. "Get your clothes on now this minute and get down those stairs. If you have been up to no good boyo it's the strap for you. We have Mr Walter Lewis in the shop wanting you now... Hurry!"

Jack had no idea why Dan's father wanted to see him at this late hour but he did as he was told and joined his parents in the shop where Mr Lewis was waiting. Nellie had not invited Walt through to the kitchen as the place was a mess, not fit for the likes of Mr Lewis.

When Walt returned home he went straight into the study. Elizabeth could hear him talking on the telephone and did not disturb him. All the family were tucked up in bed except for Esau who had not long returned home. She did not ask Esau where he had been these last few evenings, afraid of the reply. If he was frequenting the mid-week entertainments at the New Hall Theatre it was something else Walt would disapprove of. She only hoped he did not have any friends who would lend him the entrance fee as she drew the line at giving her brother the cash out of her purse. The moving pictures were a great attraction but some of the acts on stage were very crude, of a music hall variety and not the sort of thing that she could condone never mind her husband. The stage was very much frowned upon by most in their circle.

"I'll be off up now then," said Esau. "My last few days of leisure before I start work on Monday, must make the most of them. I'm looking forward to having steady work and some money in my pocket. I can pay you keep then and start planning for the future at last."

"Good night," said Elizabeth, glad she had not brought up the topic of the New Hall theatre. It would be good if Esau could settle down, find himself a good wife and start a family. And it would be not before time she thought.

"I knew you'd be waiting up for me," said Walter emerging from his study into the kitchen. "It seems that Dan and Jack were out roaming the common most of today. Jack was truanting school I'm afraid. They came across someone who could be our missing man… Hugh Brown … He is living rough on the hillside near one of the old quarries above Penybanc… Jack Williams confirmed the drawing was a good likeness of the man they saw. He says Dan has seen the same man before on the mountain and seemed afraid of him… but then Dan does not like strangers. I have arranged over the telephone with Sergeant Harris to take some men up there… in the morning… first light. Jack has agreed to show the police exactly where he is camping out. I am going with them to make sure the boy stays safe. The police are doing me a great favour getting involved at all... I finally persuaded them that Miah may consider donating his proposed reward to their benevolent fund... That is if we successfully apprehend and question the man."

"Is any of this wise?" asked Elizabeth tentatively. "This man, Hugh Brown or whoever he is, he could be dangerous especially if you bring the police. He might do something desperate."

"Don't worry, my dear. If he is still sleeping out near the quarry in the morning... I will leave his apprehension to the police constables. But I feel responsible for involving the boy... The police wagon will be here to pick us up on the way. And Jack thinks it is an adventure... an excuse to have another day off school. I need you to keep Dan close tomorrow. I do not want him getting involved... he could be a liability in the circumstances. Now... to bed. It will be an early start tomorrow... sunrise is very early this time of year... five of the clock." Elizabeth started putting her needlework away.

"And I forgot to tell you with all this distraction. The hotel in Builth Wells has written to confirm our booking. It was one of the letters in today's post," added Walter.

Chapter 21

Jack was enjoying the ride high up front in the police wagon. He was sat between the driver and Sergeant Harris to show them exactly where he and Dan had last seen the man he had recognised from the drawing Mr Lewis had shown him. He only wished they had set off later so more of the neighbours could have seen him up there with the police officer. Perhaps there would be more people up and about when they got back to see him Jack thought hopefully. Otherwise he doubted very much his friends would believe him when he told them what he'd been up to first light. The two constables and Mr Lewis were in the back of the wagon. Walt hoped this was the last time he would find himself in the back of a police wagon as it most definitely was not the first.

Sergeant Harris had his doubts about this whole expedition fearing it might be a waste of police time. If it had been anyone other than Walter Lewis who had come to him with such a plan he would not have gone along with it. Mr Lewis could be very persuasive, furthermore his friend Mr Miah Thomas, he promised, would reward them well for bringing the man in for questioning.

When they came to the track adjacent to the site Jack identified, the wagon pulled off to the side. "We'll have to continue on foot. We cannot take this wagon over rough ground and the noise would quickly announce our presence," said Harris. "Stay with the horses and wagon" he said to the driver. "If there is a problem I will blow my whistle. But we should have enough men between me and the two constables if our suspect offers any resistance. That's if there is still anyone to find. Now boy, exactly where was his camp?"

"You won't see it from here," replied Jack. "It's beyond the trees down b'there and across the stream. He was in the field camped in the shelter of the wall. Part of the wall is down just before so I think I will know the right spot when I see it again."

"He'd best come further with us then," said Harris to Walt "Any objections?"

"No," said Walt "provided you do not mind me coming along with you as well."

"This is all very much against my better judgement, but I will not argue. I know you will insist and convince me otherwise. But I want both of you to stay back and leave it to the police to approach him once the boy has identified the exact place. No argument."

"Just as I would have suggested... I will make sure Jack stays close to me," said Walt in agreement.

"Our main advantage is surprise," said Harris addressing them all. "If he's still there we do not want to announce our presence too soon. No talking, look where you are going on the rough ground and hold your equipment to you to stop it rattling, especially the handcuffs. Only draw truncheons on my command. On this turf we should be able to creep right up to the wall without giving ourselves away and mind your step crossing that stream."

It did not take long to cross the ground down to the woods alongside the brook where Jack and Dan had been yesterday. Jack led them several yards downstream and pointed across at a section of tumbled stone wall. He indicated with his thumb that the camp was just to the right of that spot. Harris held up his palms to indicate to Walt not to go any further. Walt gripped Jack by the shoulders to keep him close, out of harm's way. Harris turned to his men to wave them forward over the stream and indicated they stay low. When they got to the wall Harris looked over tentatively, just as Jack had done the day before, then stood up. "Someone has been here but he must be an early riser. Looks as if our quarry has flown," he said.

Jack looked crestfallen and squirmed free of Walt's grip to cross the stream to get a closer look. He could see the remains of the fire and the stones which the piece of mirror had been propped up against but there was no sign of anyone nearby.

"Hey Sarge, look at this," said one of the constables lifting a bundle partly concealed in the wall. "Must be his stuff which means he might intend to come back for it."

Harris took the loosely packed bundle and shook it out on the ground. It did not reveal much, a small enamel bowl, shaving brush and cake of soap wrapped in muslin, a few candle stubs, the piece of broken mirror, a flannel shirt and a cap wrapped up in a worn blanket. "Well he's left nothing of value worth coming back for. No food either," said Harris. "We might as well have a look around in case there is anything…"

"Sir, sir I think you'd better come and take a look at this." It was one of the constables shouting from the other side of the wall. He was pointing downstream and started to run towards a large dark shape in the water that looked very out of place. Before Harris could get back over the wall, Jack had sprinted off after the constable. "Catch the boy… hold him back," shouted Walt who had a dreadful feeling as soon as he spied the object in the water over which the constable was now bending.

It was a very subdued ride in the wagon back towards the town. It had taken a while to retrieve the body and carry it back to the wagon but they could not have left it where it was. Walter insisted Jack go back to Ty Gwent with him

183

and have a strong cup of sweet tea. They both needed it as Elizabeth, ever calm in a crisis, poured out the tea.

"Suicide," said Walt "undoubtedly. I would have come to the same conclusion as the police... He still grasped the razor in his hands... It was a dreadful sight... There will have to be an inquest... but I cannot foresee any difficulties with the verdict."

"He was shaving with it when we saw him yesterday and waved it at us to scare us off," said Jack quietly.

"Odd he should be shaving yesterday... if that's what he had in mind. But perhaps shaving was his daily habit... Try not to dwell on it Jack," said Walt. "I must explain to your parents why I involved you in this... If I had any idea what we were going to find..."

"It is not your fault," said Jack "how were you supposed to know he would go and do something like that?"

"You are a sensible boy," said Walt. "If I were you... I am not sure I could be so forgiving. I have been very foolish... I was trying to help a friend..."

"Nothing to worry about, honest Mr Lewis. I try to help my friends if I can," said Jack and looked over to Dan who was huddled in his customary place by the range, looking as if he would rather be anywhere else than in the family kitchen right this minute.

"I hope your parents take the same view as you, young man. Let's get you home," said Walt, "or perhaps you would rather be in school today... It might take your mind off things... to be busy at your studies."

Jack looked surprised at the suggestion but then thought it might not be such a bad idea. He could tell his classmates about the events of the morning while Mr Lewis told his mam and da about their gruesome dawn adventure.

Jack already had a few embellishments in mind to add to the story as if the reality was not hair-raising enough.

"Must you rush off so soon?" Elizabeth asked her husband. It was still not long after nine o'clock. Ceridwen had left for school only minutes before they had returned and Gwladys was passed over the front wall to next door. Mrs B always enjoyed the child's company with her husband out at work all the shop all day.

"Have you forgotten…? I am expected in court this morning...Now, let us get it over with," he said smiling weakly at Jack.

Walt left the house with Jack on the short walk to the Williams' shop on the corner of West Street.

"One last thing young man," said Walt. "Can you tell me exactly what happened the other evening... down on the farm field? That time Trefor was fighting with Nobby Harris. I understand you were there."

"He won't get into trouble, will he? I am not one for clecking on my friends," replied Jack.

"No, I am sure you are not a clecker… and Trefor will not get into any more trouble than he already is. I would just like to understand… it is quite out of character for him to get into a fight."

"Oh sir, you would have been so proud of him. Never thought he had it in him but he gave them what for. There were three of them, calling names on Dan…"

"Ah...was that so?"

*

Rae was loading her confectionary cart carefully when there was an unexpected knock on the open back door. "Excuse me coming in the back way," said Evans police stepping into the kitchen "but thought I'd find you here in the kitchen. Now those look interesting."

"Hands off!" said Rae throwing a tea cloth over the tray of sugar mice. "They are for Beynon's shop, not for you. Now, what can I do for you? You have become a regular visitor this past week. No news of Mary and her boy I suppose."

"No, but there has been a related, if unexpected, occurrence. Police Sergeant Harris from Bargoed station telephoned through to the police house. He had a tip off from a member of the public about someone sleeping rough and scaring children. Well, they recovered a body of a man on the mountain this morning. A suicide he said and they think it more than likely it is Hugh Brown."

"Good Lord," she said putting her hands to her head in shock as she sat down heavily on the kitchen chair behind her. "Well, I never... are they sure it is him?"

"Identified him using a drawing your Sam made by all accounts. Asked me to see if people round here knew any more about Hugh Brown. They want to trace his family, other than Mary of course who is still missing as far as I am aware. Parents, brothers or sisters" said Evans. "There will have to be an inquest into the death and it is our duty to try and find the next of kin. It will be reported in the paper no doubt but if they are not from 'round these parts any family will be none the wiser."

"You do know Mary's father turned up here yesterday? Looking for her he was but had no idea what had happened here this week. I thought his coming was just a coincidence but now I am not so sure," said Rae. "He might know more about Hugh though I doubt it. That's why I gave him Sam's sketch. He admitted he had never met his own son-in-law; had no idea what he looked like. And that was strange in itself, don't you think?"

"Yes, I met Mr Thomas when he called into the police house after he saw you yesterday. Very worried he was about Mary and the little boy. But he took your suggestion to heart and hopes she will turn up back in Brecon where she came from. That sketch of Sam's is a good likeness, I am told; clever of you to think of it."

"Sam said Hugh came from around Brecon way if I remember. Look, I'll ask Sam when he gets in if Hugh ever mentioned family. I doubt if anybody else round here knows anything. They had not been here long, only since the new year and they didn't say much about themselves. No visitors I know of until her father turned up – too late as it turned out."

"Well thank you for all your help with this. It's been a strange affair all told. I can see you are busy so I won't keep you from your work. I best be going. You can tell Lydia Waters that she need not fear that Hugh Brown will be back creeping around the row after dark again ready to murder her in her bed."

"I'm surprised she troubled you with that bit of tittle tattle." Baby Henry stirred in his cot waking from his afternoon nap. "Do me a favour before you go back," said Rae. "Go tell Lydia yourself. I have my hands full here. She's only next door and I am sure will be relieved to hear it from you. Not afraid of her, are you? Her bark is worse than her bite, I assure you."

*

Elizabeth spent a very anxious day what with worrying about how her husband would get on in court and mulling over the unexpected events of the week. The latest revelation had come as a shock, not that she knew the man but it was a travesty nonetheless. There had still been no news of the missing Mary and her boy. At least Miah need not worry about this Hugh Brown ever threatening her again. He was well out of the picture now.

Esau should not get into temptation's way today she thought. He was busy helping a neighbour move home, giving a hand lifting the furniture on and off the cart and no doubt would earn a bob or two for his trouble; enough for a night out at the New Hall. The Williams family at 55 were moving back to Gelligaer village to take up work in the new pit at Penallta.

Both children sensed her preoccupied mood and were well behaved all day. She wrote out a grocery order for the Co-op which Dan delivered with strict instructions to come straight home after and no wandering off. Walter did not return for his usual mid-day meal but he had warned her not to expect him. Dan even spent some time out the back garden with Gwladys turning the end of the skipping rope attached to the pole for the washing line. She could hear the child telling her brother off as she stopped and started her skipping rhyme over and over never getting very far before she tripped over the rope. It seemed it was always Dan's fault.

The groceries were delivered mid-afternoon and Elizabeth set about preparing some fishcakes for a nice tasty meal later. And some jam tarts she thought, that will be a nice treat. It would be good if they could all sit down together later this afternoon. It had been a week ago that Miah had shared their Friday supper with them. And what a week it had proved to be.

*

The news of the discovery of Hugh Brown's body spread like wildfire through Bedlinog village. Rae was not surprised when Sam and the girls already knew about it before they came home. But Sam was not pleased to discover that Evans police was still bothering his wife for information about the man.

"Hugh was hardly one for conversation given his speech difficulties and we rarely worked the same shift. All I know was he had worked in the stables of some place near Brecon. He did not say where but they should be looking for information about him in that neck of the woods. They barely lived here six months, hardly time to find out their life story even if the pair of them had been more forthcoming," he said to his wife.

"That's what I told Evans. But why kill himself, Sam?" she asked. "It seems a drastic act unless there is more to this than the attack on young Mary. Did he know he had not killed her when he ran from the house?"

"Perhaps not. He may have thought she was done for and him a murderer. Guilt, desperation; who knows the mind of a man that would take his own life? Although half the village have him murdered and some dangerous lunatic on the loose in the area. I was told to make sure to lock the doors at night or we might all be dead in our beds by morning. Would you believe it? Who comes up with this rubbish?"

"Well Lydia Waters was relieved to hear the news. Seems to think it was God's vengeance on the poor man. Convinced she was that he had come back here the other night. I had to listen to her for half an hour after Evans left this afternoon and with me trying to get ready for work tomorrow," said Rae.

"Well, the only way he'll come back now is as a ghost," said Sam.

"Now surely you do not believe that? And mind who you say things like that to. Next you know the row will be haunted," said Rae in shocked tones.

*

Walt and Elizabeth were discussing Hugh Brown's tragic suicide after the children had gone to bed in Ty Gwent that night. No doubt the news was the topic of conversation and speculation up and down the valley that evening and would be in the papers next week after the inquest.

"Do you think he thought he had murdered Miah?" asked Elizabeth.

"There is no real evidence that he was responsible for Miah's head wound. Miah never saw his assailant... although he is as convinced as anyone can be that he did not hit the back of his head in a fall. He was not robbed as the police might think. He had given all the cash he had on him to Mary that morning... to buy something for the boy. That Hugh Brown carried out the attack on Miah is only speculation on our part... but there is little doubt that he assaulted Mary. Why else would he abscond and be living rough? He obviously never went far from the scene... The neighbours may have indeed heard him return to the lodgings."

"But what drives a man to kill himself?" asked Elizabeth.

"Perhaps if he discovered Mary and their son were no longer there... he feared the worse... Remorse may have been the cause of his final act... and a desperate one it was. Self-murder is a sin... but the depths of someone else's suffering and torment can be impossible to fathom. I shall never forget seeing his lifeless body... the stream having washed away his life blood and leaving him white as the driven snow. Perhaps he thought he has atoned for his sins by this act.... I only know that he was a poor ignorant and misguided soul."

"Should we pray for him?" asked Elizabeth.

190

"Our sins cannot keep us from salvation… if we but accept the grace of our Lord," replied her husband. "If we cannot pray for the troubled soul of Hugh Brown... we can at least pray that he sought to made peace with his Maker."

Chapter 22

The Lewis family had not managed to eat together the previous evening contrary to Elizabeth's expectations. Walt returned home just in time to bid the girls goodnight before their bedtime. Friday had been a very long day even by his standards. This morning, to placate his wife, he sat down to take breakfast with the children. Elizabeth was determined to get back into her domestic routine starting today after the unusual week they had experienced. The various demands on her husband's time, however, made any routine difficult enough without him traipsing over the mountain side at dawn with the police in search of goodness knows who… and finding goodness knows what.

Unsurprisingly, given his dawn antics, Walt had arrived late at the magistrate court the previous morning. The magistrate was even later and fortunately his was not the first case to be heard. He was all present and correct by the time his case, along with the other two miners arrested at the scene, came before the bench. The solicitor appointed by the Fed had advised Walt not to contest the charge on the grounds of the prohibitive legal expenses. He was to plead guilty and get it over quickly. Annoyed on principle, Walt found himself fined and bound over to keep the peace. He did manage to say his piece in the court to the annoyance of both the magistrate and his solicitor who thought it an inappropriate moment to be reminded of the responsibilities of the elected representative to the miners during a legitimate industrial dispute.

The Friday afternoon saw Walt and his deputy Albert Thomas, sub-agent and lodge secretary, in the office processing the build-up of claims during the week and balancing the books. It was routine work but no less important for that and had kept them busy until late. The only outstanding business of the week was the completion of his report for the lodge meeting on Monday now the claims and accounts were finalised. A few hours in the Fed office this morning should see that done. He also needed to review his diary engagements and to plan the next few weeks ahead if he was to take his furlough as planned.

"Your father has some exciting news for you children," said Elizabeth looking at her husband over the breakfast table. Walter stared back blankly wondering what Elizabeth could possibly mean. "The holiday," she prompted. "Yes, we are going on holiday this year... to Builth Wells. We will all stay in a posh hotel," said Walter.

It was the first time the family would stay in a hotel even though it was only for four nights. In previous years they spent their holidays visiting family but rarely stayed from home for more than one or two nights at the most. Accommodation was more cramped than usual when the whole family descended on their relatives but no less enjoyable for that. This was the first year that both Elizabeth's parents were no longer with them and, with Walter's aged widowed mother living with his married sister and her family, such gatherings in future would be limited to day trips. More often than not they now hosted their scattered family, welcoming them to their home in Bargoed. Walter's sister and her family from Yorkshire were regular visitors every summer and Elizabeth put them up for a week. All the children doubled up in bed to accommodate their cousins and leave space for the adults' comfort.

It was the first time the Lewis family could afford such an extravagant holiday together. Builth Wells had been highly recommended to Walter as the place to be seen.

Many of his colleagues on the executive committee visited the town during the summer with their families to take the waters and be seen at the concerts, talks and other entertainments put on for the visitors. Being a cautious man, and not quite knowing what to expect when they got there, Walter decided to limit their stay to reduce the expense and the risk of disappointment. He was entitled to a week's leave during the long school holiday and Walter was hoping to spend a few days later in August at the National Eisteddfod at the Albert Hall in London. Prime Minister Asquith was to be the guest speaker. London was not a suitable destination for all the family in his opinion but Walter was thinking of taking Trefor along with him. It might broaden the boy's horizons before he knuckled down to his scholarship year at school.

"Builth has a lot of history," he told the children. "There is a castle we can visit. It is where Llewelyn... the last Prince of Wales... was turned away when fleeing the English. There is a story... the local blacksmith put the horse's shoes on backwards so that the English thought he was going the other way. That helped the prince escape capture... Now there's a clever Welshman."

"Where is the prince of Wales now?" asked Criddy. "Is he still hiding from the English?"

"It was all a very long time ago... That's what history is... the things that happened in the past... hundreds of years ago in this case. The story is so old no one can be sure if it really happened... but it has become a local legend," he explained. "Now, children, you must all be good and help your mother prepare for our holiday. Only one week left of school before term ends... then we're off to the Metropole Hotel in Builth Wells."

"And we can visit the springs that have made the town such a famous holiday destination," added Elizabeth.

194

"I may even take the waters myself although I understand they taste quite foul."

"Will I have to wear my school uniform on holiday?" asked Trefor.

"We are all going shopping down the town today for summer outfits and accessories. The Emporium has some lovely white shoes and stockings for the girls to complement their new summer frocks which I am making. Perhaps some straw bonnets too if the weather stays so lovely. And Trefor, how about a summer blazer, white flannels and a boater from the men's outfitters for you?" said Elizabeth looking hopefully at her husband. Trefor beamed in delight, anything but the old wool and worsted, Eton collar and tie he thought. A striped blazer, flannels and a boater would be the height of sartorial elegance for any young man.

"Get the bills sent directly to me. I know I can trust you to buy what may be needed... but I am sure I do not need white flannels," said Walt. "Can you imagine you what Old John down the street might say if I stepped out in a pair? I would not hear the end of it." Elizabeth and Trefor joined in his laughter at the idea and Criddy added a giggle politely, not quite sure what the joke was.

"Is Uncle Esau coming too?" asked Gwladys with a concerned frown.

"Uncle Esau has barely started his new job. He cannot expect a holiday this side of Christmas," replied her mother. "He is looking forward to having the house to himself. He will act as caretaker in our absence, a most responsible role that he is more than happy to do."

"Oh good," said Gwladys "I am glad you are not banishing him to England again. But what about Dan, is he coming with us?"

"Of course Dan is coming with us. Why did you think otherwise?" asked her mother shocked.

"I am glad but he might not want to come away from home," said Gwladys. How perceptive of the child thought her mother who was not sure herself how Dan might react to the journey and the public rooms of a hotel.

"Yes, you are Glad," said Tref, "get it in english-glad? Gwlad short for Gwladys."

"I like being glad or Glad or Gwlad. Being Gwlad is good," said the child unperturbed by her brother's silly play on names.

"Now time I was going into the Fed office," said Walt. "Don't worry about dinner today... not if you are out shopping. Take your time... I will have something to eat at the meeting of the Rechabites this afternoon... in the Hanbury tea rooms. So only a light tea for me this afternoon, please dear."

"We must get ready to leave too children," said Elizabeth. "A good wash with soap and flannel everyone and in hot water if we are going down the road. I shall check, mind you; and you too Dan. Brush your sister's hair out with the soft brush Trefor and then I'll tie it back off her face. Criddy you can do your own hair." Walt left the hustle and bustle of his family's preparations for their outing for the sanctuary of the Fed office and his monthly report.

*

Rae had bought half a dozen lardies home from Beynon's bakery for the girls' tea. The children of Club Row had spent the day playing on the hillside, in and out of the stream, chasing each other through the ferns and playing hide-and-seek. The sunshine banished thoughts of Hugh

Brown and the missing Mary and Robbie far from their minds. Even Edie joined in the fun still mindful of her sisters and baby Henry on her hip. When the boys decided to wander further afield, however, Edie put her foot down.

"No May, we must not go wandering off too far from the house. Mam will not like it if we are not home when she comes in from town. Tonight is bath night or have you forgotten? And you look right now as if you need one." Her sister's bare feet were filthy dirty from running around after paddling in the stream. "I must put this lump of a lad down too. Look you, there is a rip in your pinny, b'there," said Edie pointing at the pocket of May's very grubby pinafore. May looked down perplexed lifting her pinafore to inspect the damaged pocket. "Do not worry. If we go home now I may have time to sew it up before Mam gets in. At least we can stop the tear getting any bigger. Come on Nell, Cath. Let's get back to the house and play in the garden. You can feed the hens if you want, then we can put the kettle on for tea when Mam and Da get home."

Nell and Cath unpacked the cart putting Rae's groceries in their place in the larder while Edie saw to baby Henry. Rae cut the lardies in two for her and the girls ready for when the tea had brewed. She did this ritual nearly every Saturday keeping two whole lardy cakes for the brothers. When Seth and Lewis came in later for supper they would always say they did not want them. The girls would then get another half each after their shared bath in the galvanized tub in front of the fire.

Edie had always found her mother's little charade with the lardy cakes a bit pointless, until recently that is. She realised it was Rae's way of including Seth and Lewis as part of the family even though their home had been taken over by her husband and children. It was one of those silly little things Edie would miss about the family when she was sent out to service. Even sharing the bath with her sisters and brushing out each other's hair afterwards. All these seemingly inconsequential routines took on more meaning for her now her time at home was finite.

"Do you think we will ever find out what happened to Mary and little Robbie?" Edie asked her mother before they went up to bed.

"We will if it's bad news," said Sam coming in from pottering with his latest project out the back yard. "Bad things will be sure to get reported in the newspapers. But if she has found safe refuge we will probably never hear any more about her. She has no reason to come back here."

"Does that mean that what Hugh did will be in the paper next week? I mean him being found dead up the mountain," asked Nell.

"There will have to be an inquest into his death. That will be reported in the paper. Perhaps then everyone will stop speculating about murder when the facts are printed in black and white," Sam replied.

"Lydia was in town today and came by the shop. She said some men came by and cleared out the end cottage early this morning. Not that there was much else but a few shabby bits of furniture, no good to anyone. New tenants on Monday I expect… so life goes on," said Rae.

"I wish I had been about when the place was emptied. Could have been something to salvage," Sam said. "If nothing else the wood from the furniture might have been useful to light the fire."

*

"I am looking forward to a quiet night reading at home… and not legal documents from the Fed solicitors,"

198

said Walt later that evening at Ty Gwent. "Next week looks very busy with show cards up and down the valley. We organised it today… Albert Thomas and I hope to cover everywhere from Rhymney down to Caerphilly between us. Members' contributions were up again this month… but so were the claims. Inevitable with the increase in numbers… but it is a very encouraging sign Elizabeth. One day we will get all the miners behind us… Unity will give us strength."

"You have an hour or two to yourself, my dear," she said clearing away the table. She had bought sausages from the Hereford Butchers for tea and they were quite delicious hot with last summer's rhubarb chutney and fresh bread and butter.

"How did the shopping trip go? Did you find what you needed?" asked Walt.

"Indeed, the Emporium compares well to any shop in Cardiff. It is stocking some nice quality clothing even if it is ready made. You should see Trefor in his white flannels and boater, so grown up and quite the dandy," she added. "We will look the part holidaying in Builth Wells if nothing else."

"I am proud of my family, never doubt it," said Walt sternly. "And I do not want you worrying about this trip. I hoped staying in a hotel would be a welcome break for you... a pleasant change. No food to prepare and no cleaning... now there's a thought."

"You know me I worry about anything and everything, it's a mother's place," she smiled. "Now off you go to the study, the children will be in soon wanting their supper I expect."

Elizabeth heard the telephone ring out but left it to her husband to answer. He'll get no peace, she thought now we've got that thing in the house.

Several minutes later Walt emerged from his study and came out to the kitchen where the family were seated together around the table enjoying their sausage supper.

"That was Uncle Miah speaking on the telephone. He has good news for us… as we hoped and prayed… the missing girl and her boy have turned up at a farm… nearby in Brecon. His search proved fruitful… and has ended more happily than mine. He has seen her today… and hopes to welcome her to his house in town next week… when she is fit to travel. He has invited us to visit him… when we are on our way home from Builth in a few weeks' time, Elizabeth. He wants to thank us all for our help... and is most insistent. I have accepted his invitation. It looks as if our holiday together will be extended a day or two... with Miah's hospitality," said Walt.

"Oh, thank the Lord, that is very good news. And we get to visit Brecon town too and see where Uncle Miah lives. Now there's exciting children," said Elizabeth. She had a thousand questions for her husband wanting to find out what had not been said in front of the children. She would have to wait until the children were safely tucked up in bed before they could discuss the matter in detail.

"Now Trefor… a word with you please… in private. Finish your supper and come into the study... when you are ready," said his father.

Trefor had no idea what this might be about. Surely he had not done anything wrong since his scrap with Nobby Harris? His behaviour the last few days had been exemplary and he already had Psalm 35 memorised almost word perfect. He knocked on the door and waited feeling a little anxious as he always did when summoned to a private interview with his father.

"How have you got on with the task I set you this week?" asked his father. Trefor stood with his arms behind his back and started reciting the words of the psalm. When he faltered near the end his father joined in *"put your hope in the Lord and obey his commandments, he will honour you by giving you the land and the wicked will be driven out*. I have heard enough Trefor... you have done well. It is an uplifting psalm... reminding us that to do good means the Lord will never abandon us and we will prosper."

"Yes father, the message is very clear" said Trefor.

"Now... you never made any excuses for your behaviour last Tuesday... but I have been talking to someone who was there and witnessed everything. Will you enlighten me as to what lead up to the incident? I want the truth mind you... and I want to hear it from you," said Walt.

Trefor hung his head in shame knowing he could no longer avoid telling his father the full version of events. "Have I understood you correctly? You waded into the fray to help Jack... who was standing up for you brother against these bullies. Is that the full story?" asked Walt.

"Yes father, it was Jack who tried to defend Dan, not me. I could not stand by and watch him get beat up by three bigger boys. It was not Jack's fault. Nobby Harris started it."

"I can well believe that," said Walt "but you should never resort to fist fighting as a solution. You alarmed your mother... fighting like a street urchin. Let's make sure it does not happen again... even in the defence of others. Dan gets a lot of bullying from the other children... I am aware of that. And we must not stand by and let it happen... but fighting is never the solution. If you are strong and speak up for him in these situations... there will be no need for fighting in future. Not all children are wicked... it is ignorance as much as anything... if you speak up for Dan they will learn from your example."

"Forgive me father. I have been a coward in the past and I am ashamed to say it. I have stood by and let others make fun of Dan. That must make it seem to them that it is an acceptable thing to do. I was ashamed of Dan. Now I know that I should have been ashamed of myself."

"Well... you have learned a valuable lesson my boy. The strong must always look out for the weak... those that cannot help themselves. You know that Dan looks up to you as his elder brother. He misses Will... while I do not expect you to be saddled with him wherever you go... we must all include him in all our lives. He is as God made him... and we cannot change that. Remember Uncle Miah last week? He was not ashamed to be seen with Dan around the town. You would be well rewarded with his loyalty if you acknowledged Dan more outside the home... Do we understand each other?"

"Yes, indeed Sir," replied his son.

"I am thinking... after Gwladys' remarks this morning. Dan may not settle too well in unfamiliar surroundings... especially the formality of a hotel. He cannot stay home with Uncle Esau... he will be out of the house for hours at work... the boy left to run wild. Your mother cannot bear the sole burden of looking out for Dan and the girls all week. We must both step up to the mark... take some of the responsibility... or your mother will have no holiday at all. Do you understand what I am asking of you, Trefor?" asked Walt.

"Yes, I think so," said Tref hesitantly.

"Now off to bed with you too. I want to get Dan back sleeping upstairs... before the winter. It cannot be good for him… sleeping in that kitchen chair. Since you both share the room …you may be able to help," said Walt.

"But he always slept sitting up in bed with Will, father. That's why they always pushed the bed against the wall even though Mam always moved it back. I think he finds it more comfortable in the chair than lying down flat. Perhaps we could get some more pillows or something to prop him up in bed," said Tref.

"Thank you for that suggestion… I shall speak with your mother about it," said Walt. "Good night now… and do not forget Dan in your prayers. We must all pull together… united as one family… and with the help of our Lord… make sure we look after one another."

Chapter 23

The train was on time as the Lewis' alighted onto the platform at Brecon station. A porter quickly came to take their luggage and there was Miah waiting for them, his shiny new tall hat raised in greeting.

"I have transport outside waiting," he said. "Welcome one and all. It is good to see you again looking so well and under much happier circumstances." He spread his arms wide as if he could embrace husband, wife and all four children at once. "We will be at my house in minutes and Mrs Kelly my housekeeper has put on a luncheon in honour of our guests. I entertain rarely and then only fellow ministers like myself. Mrs Kelly is eager to meet the family and especially the children. And you, no doubt, are eager to meet my daughter and grandson; but all in good time."

Miah lead the family out of the station to the waiting horse and wagon where their luggage was already being stowed in the back. Miah introduced his driver, Llewellyn, who helped lift the girls up to sit on top some hay bales, telling them to hold on tight while their parents took the seats up front behind the driver, not without some difficulty given the height of the vehicle. Dan stood looking up at the horse, a beautifully turned out cart horse in full harness and bigger than any he'd seen before.

"His name's Goliath," said Llew "he will not hurt you, a real gentle giant this old boy." Dan stood in front of the horse which lowered his head to sniff him. They stood nose to nose quietly. "He likes you. Now let's get you all aboard," and with that he swung Dan up besides his brother and sisters before the boy knew what was happening.

It was not a long journey through the town but there was a lot of traffic and progress was slow and steady. This was a great treat for the children to travel atop a farm wagon and Gwladys could not resist standing to wave enthusiastically at pedestrians passing by on the high street. Trefor held onto her pinafore, just in case she fell out, and Criddy held onto him complaining loudly that he should stop Gwladys showing off like that.

"Sit quietly children," said Elizabeth turning around "or we'll have you all tumbling out onto the road." Gwladys sat down demurely and poked her tongue out to Ceridwen, a bad habit she'd picked up from the spoilt child of a family staying in the hotel in Builth Wells. Ceridwen shocked her little sister by repaying in kind which made Trefor laugh. He never imagined Criddy had it in her to be so crude.

"Be careful you two," he said "if you get caught out there'll be a hiding for both of you. And you know what the grown-ups say about pulling faces."

"No," said Gwladys, "what do grown-ups say?"

"If the wind changes when you make a face it will stay like that," said Tref teasing his little sister by going cross-eyed and sticking out his tongue too. Dan laughed at his siblings enjoying the ride in the wagon pulled by Goliath. "Now be good girls like Mam said. We don't want to lose you overboard in this traffic."

They settled down to enjoy the remainder of the journey taking in the sights of the busy town centre before heading towards the river bridge. The wagon pulled up outside a tall four storey town house in a row of similar properties on the road leading north out of the town across the river.

"Welcome to my home. I am so glad you broke your journey home to visit us here," said Miah as he and Llew helped Elizabeth down from the wagon. An elderly upright woman in a neat black outfit, her faded fair hair pinned up attractively, opened the door on their arrival as if she had been waiting for them. "And may I introduce Mrs Kelly, my mother-in-law who has also been keeping house for me these past few years."

Mrs Kelly had put on a full meal for the family in the dining room at mid-day and it was as good as any they had eaten at the Metropole Hotel.

"At last I have the opportunity to repay the hospitality you have shown me over the years, Elizabeth," said Miah, "thanks of course to the culinary skills of Mrs Kelly." He nodded acknowledgement at the housekeeper who sat at the table with the rest of the family. "My mother-in-law has revolutionised this household almost single handed since she took on the responsibility of housekeeper. Now I cannot imagine being without her so efficient at running the house and kitchen as she is."

"It is not so difficult with you away on your travels or else shut in the study with your books and papers," replied Mrs Kelly. "But never knowing when you were likely to turn up or how long you would stay. That's been my biggest difficulty. Although you have no excuse not to keep me informed of your comings and goings now we have the telephone installed on the premises, if only you would use it for that purpose" she added.

"So, you also have the telephone installed in your home now," said Elizabeth. "If it is anything like our house you will get no peace again. My husband seems to think he is running a public service for the town. Making calls on other people's behalf and even letting Mr Braithwaite next door into his study to use the apparatus itself."

"It was a family emergency Elizabeth," said Walt "and I know you did not begrudge it under the circumstances."

"It just goes to show how useful speedy communication can be in a crisis as well in the office for conducting business. I realised that myself after Gwallt put the telephone to such good use during my... little indisposition shall we call it?" said Miah. "But you are no doubt curious to meet the other household members. Where is Mary at present?" he asked his housekeeper.

"Mary gives her apologies but is not feeling strong enough to join us all yet. She is taking her meal with Robbie in the nursery and hopes to meet your guests later," replied the housekeeper. "It is wonderful to see the nursery being put to its proper use. It probably hasn't been used as such since your mother was a child," she looked at Miah to see his response and he smiled indulgently at her. "Lovely it is to have a child in the house and him my great grandson."

"Yes indeed, but sadly Mary is taking some time to recover from her ordeal. Her constitution is weak and, in that respect, she reminds me of my own late mother. The doctor, however, reassures me there is nothing specific to concern ourselves with. She needs rest, good food and hopefully time will restore her to full health." Elizabeth nodded in sympathy but said nothing in front of the children.

"But how can I best entertain you over the next few days?" asked Miah. "Is there anything in particular you would like to do while you are here in Brecon or are you eager to see the usual sites of the town, the market, the barracks, the castle. We do not want to be house bound during this exceptional spell of fine weather. You seem to have picked the best week of the summer so far for your travels," he said to Walt.

"I have a request if you will indulge me," said Walt. "It is many years now since I last visited my grandmother's village... Llanfrynach. It is just a few miles outside the town. My father took me there many times as a boy to visit her. We came by train from Bargod to Brecon... and walked the country lanes out to the village. He often took me fishing in the river as a lad... Now, that takes me back."

"Your father's family are from this area then. You are familiar with the estates and other enterprises run by the de Winton family? They owned the Brecon bank and I have done a great deal of business with them in the past," said Miah.

"Indeed, my grandmother worked as a dairy maid on their estate in her youth. She lived on as a pensioner in an estate cottage in the village... and reached the grand age of 102. Mind you... most of the other estate cottages in the village were empty by then. Many of the following generation like my father moved to work in the industries south of here... in Tredegar and the Ebbw Valley," said Walt.

"Well, we must take a trip down memory lane with you, old friend. It is an opportunity to introduce the next generation of Lewis' to their family heritage. Would you like that?" Miah asked the children. Over awed by their surroundings in Miah's grand but intimate dining room the girls were silent so Trefor spoke up for his siblings. "Indeed, sir. It sounds like the best idea to me," he said and smiled at his father.

"There is a shop in town that sells fishing paraphernalia. Not that I know much about it although I could still tickle a trout I'm sure. We shall investigate and tomorrow take the horse and cart out to Llanfrynach... and a picnic. Could you manage a picnic for us Mrs Kelly?" asked Miah full of enthusiasm for the expedition. "If this heat wave keeps up it would be pleasant to spend the day by the river in some remote and shady spot. So, some fishing it will be then Gwallt."

Miah and Walt took themselves off to walk into town to investigate fishing tackle despite the heat of the afternoon. The boys, Tref and Dan went with them. Trefor had never seen his father quite so excited at the prospect of going shopping, or was it the idea of fishing and going back to his childhood haunts? It was good to see his father so relaxed and obviously enjoying himself.

The family holiday at Builth had been a success in many ways. Their first full day was a Sunday which they spent very much as they did at home, attending the services at the local Welsh Baptist chapel and then a well-attended Gamanfa Ganu in the evening. The town as a tourist attraction had developed since the arrival of the railway in the 1860s and there was a great deal to entertain the visitor. Street entertainments included everything from professional entertainers to the local brass bands. Amateur music, arts and drama societies put on bazaars and performances to raise funds from the visitors and vied successfully alongside professional travelling entertainers. Music festivals, eisteddfodau, concerts, recitals, lectures and book readings all peppered the calendar throughout the summer. Athletic sports meetings, bicycle races and cricket matches every weekend brought in the day trippers. Pony races, shearing matches, sheep dog trials, flower and vegetable shows, 'fur and feather' shows, horse fairs, jumping and trotting matches had also made the town a centre for agricultural pursuits which culminated in the local agricultural show in late August. The visitor was bombarded with a choice of entertainment throughout the summer.

The Lewis family had never witnessed entertainments quite on this scale before. The children saw a troupe of professional Pierrot entertainers who sang and danced on the street to drum up custom for their concert party. They went to a Japanese street fair organised by the Builth Wells and District Harmonic Society. They heard the Llanidloes Brass Band give a concert in the Park and watched the Town XI v Breconshire Gents annual cricket fixture; and all that on one day, the Bank Holiday Monday. The trains had brought in many day trippers to swell the number of tourists which had given the town a crowded, carnival atmosphere. Elizabeth was quite overwhelmed by it all when they retired to the hotel for afternoon tea.

Walt took the children out every morning after an early breakfast to visit some site of historic or architectural interest in the town. This allowed Elizabeth to sit in the hotel lounge, write postcards and make the acquaintance of the other families in residence. Their father bought the children a toy boat to sail on the lake and a hoop and stick for the girls. After lunch at the hotel Walt and Elizabeth strolled the parks and grounds, visited the springs and mingled with the great and good engaged in the same leisurely pursuits. It surprised Walt how many faces he recognised among the other visitors either through his work, the chapel or his many other varied interests. He was also recognised in turn and the couple frequently stopped to exchange the time of day with their many acquaintances come to take the waters that had made Builth Wells such a popular attraction.

The children were allowed to go off to play in the park, around the lake and indulge in ice cream and other sweet treats for which their father provided money. They had made several friends in the hotel by the second day, as children do, and the Lewis' brood were often accompanied by one or other of their newfound friends. There was one young girl in particular called Olwen, the only daughter of a solicitor and his wife from Abergavenny who they had met at chapel that Sunday and were staying at the same hotel.

She had captivated the attention of Ceridwen and Gwladys and was happy to play endless imaginary games with the girls. She was pretty too with exquisite manners and dainty ways. As an only child, she enjoyed their company and her parents allowed her to accompany the Lewis' children after both sets of parents had introduced themselves in the hotel lounge.

In the evening Walt and Elizabeth went to concerts at the town hall or assembly rooms, although Elizabeth had little taste for some of the classical repertoire of the various orchestral societies, music she was not overly familiar with from chapel. Walt took Tref along with him one afternoon to a talk on Llewelyn, the last Prince of Wales, organised by the local Cymrodorian society while Elizabeth and the children enjoyed the company of their newfound friends, Olwen and her parents. The weather remained glorious during their stay and the time passed very quickly.

It was true that Dan did not like the public rooms in the hotel. He remained sullen and withdrawn at meal times and uncharacteristically refused to eat. Several times his mother had to have food sent to the room for him. But most of the hotel staff were very understanding and accommodating of his needs. Dan was fascinated by the bellboys and the uniforms they wore with their rows of brass buttons and braided collars. He was afraid of the hotel lift and nothing could persuade him to enter it; not even the cheerful bellboys. He preferred to climb the several flights of stairs to their family rooms near the top of the hotel whereas the other children would have ridden the lift up and down all day given the chance. As always Dan preferred being outside and his parents were grateful for the good weather during their stay.

The highlight of the visit for the children had been the historical pageant involving over 600 performers from

211

the people of the town. They depicted scenes of local history from the ancient Druids and Roman occupation through to the coming of Christianity. Philip de Braose and the Norman Conquest were represented and all in elaborate costumes. The girls particularly liked the marriage festival in the days of good queen Bess. Every scene had musical accompaniment from a chorus of 150 singers and was quite epic in scale to anything the family had seen before.

All too soon it seemed the holiday was over. Their luggage was packed and they were transported in style to the railway station, all part of the service of the Metropole Hotel. Having their holiday extended by a visit to Miah's home kept the children in high spirits. Walt confessed that, in all the years he had known him, this was the first time he had an opportunity to see how Miah lived and find out more about his background and was looking forward to their stay in Brecon. There was also the not insignificant matter of finding out how Mary's story would end after the sad business of just a few short weeks ago culminating in the suicide of Hugh Brown.

Back at Miah's house the girls were outside in the garden playing quietly in the shade of a tree. An imaginary tea party for the dolls was in full swing using leaves and twigs as crockery and cutlery. The long narrow garden led down to the river and boasted several large fruit trees and a weeping willow. A sturdy if rustic wooden fence bordered the garden from the river. The water level was low given the recent lack of rainfall but the fence served to protect the unwary from the fast flowing water of the river Usk in full spate.

Elizabeth had persuaded Mrs Kelly to show her the kitchen and was now happily engaged in helping prepare a batch of scones for the oven and chatting away to the housekeeper like old friends.

"Staying in a hotel was a novelty for me but I have missed my own kitchen," said Elizabeth. "Baking has never been a chore but a pleasure. So, tell me, when did you take on the role of housekeeper in this lovely old house may I ask?"

"Miah was kind to offer me this position four, nearly five years ago now. It was not long after Mary disappeared from home. Mary had been my responsibility you see. She lived on the farm with me and my son's family when I took her in as a new born after my daughter sadly died in childbirth. It seemed the sensible solution with Miah grieving so and then busy with the Baptist church. He has never blamed me for her running off, but you know Miah and what a forgiving and tolerant nature he has. He always treats me as family, never as a servant. It was a good time to leave the farm tenancy to my son and I had no hesitation in accepting the post."

"It's a beautiful old house," said Elizabeth. "Has it been in the family long?"

"Miah's grandfather bought it but not from new. Mind you, the house was not so lovely when I first arrived. Things were going downhill after the long neglect of a widower's residence for many years. His previous domestic help did not live in and, with his frequent absences, let standards slip; although they took his money readily enough. I have some help in the house too," Mrs Kelly explained. "A young girl from the town comes in each morning to help with the fires and heavy cleaning and lifting. I did train up a lass from the orphanage for domestic duties. She lived in and was company for me but she has since moved on. We have a handy man cum gardener who you know, Llewellyn the wagon driver. He is most useful around the place even though Miah often takes him abroad visiting some of the more isolated communities in mid Wales when he travels by horse and carriage."

Elizabeth was so eager to hear about Miah's hitherto mysterious domestic arrangements that she was surprised when the door to the back stairs opened quietly. A petite young woman entered the kitchen leading a little boy by the hand. It was Mary, Miah's daughter who was startled to find Elizabeth's floury bulk where she expected to see the familiar sight of her grandmother now sat in the chair and watching her enter the room leading little Robbie by the hand.

"Come in Mary and meet Mrs Walter Lewis. Your father's house guests have arrived and, as you can see, are making themselves at home," said Mrs Kelly. She spoke quietly almost as if afraid she might frighten the girl. "This is my grand-daughter who you are eager to meet, Mary and this little angel her boy Robbie."

Elizabeth took in the frail, pale features of the young woman and could see the family likeness between the two women regardless of their difference in age. Both had thick, wavy hair but Mary's was a vibrant auburn compared to her grandmother's greying blonde. They had the same delicate features and upright bearing despite their diminutive stature but unusually Mary's eyes were much darker than her grandmother's blue-green gaze. Perhaps it was the deep shadows under her eyes that accentuated their hazel colour as Mary took in Elizabeth's presence in the kitchen.

"Well, come in child. It must be unusual to find a stranger baking in your grandmother's kitchen. What a beautiful little boy you have, Miah's grandson." She smiled

214

encouragement at them both. "Your father is so pleased to have you both back home safe, you cannot believe," said Elizabeth. "Now, let me get these in the oven and clear up here and we can go and meet my girls in the garden. Gwladys is not much older than your little boy. I am sure they will get along very well together…"

When the men and boys returned armed with a new fishing rod, reel and other accoutrements they found everyone in the kitchen preparing a high tea. Mrs Kelly's influence gave the ambience a farmhouse feel accentuated by the rich dairy products to accompany the bread, scones, biscuits and tea.

"My son has built up a large dairy herd and supplies his produce to many in the town," said Mrs Kelly. "We get a weekly delivery of butter, milk, cheese and cream straight to the door fresh from the dairy so are never short. Eat up children" she said spreading thick butter on the bread for the younger ones.

"I hope you do not mind us eating in the kitchen. But I have spent a most pleasant afternoon here with Mrs Kelly and it is so homely with all of us around the kitchen table," said Elizabeth lamely to Miah.

"What a gathering and what a feast to tempt us. How could I object, Elizabeth? Make room for your grandpa," said Miah lifting Robbie to sit on his lap as he slid onto the long bench crowded with children. "Let us give thanks to the Lord for the blessings heaped upon us today. Praise the name of Him who provides such bounty. Let us pray…" He clasped his large hands over Robbie's little ones in front of them both to say the blessing before the family descended on the spread before them.

"Another cup of tea Mrs Lewis?" asked the housekeeper poised with the large teapot ready to pour.

"Not another drop, my dear. Your hospitality and generosity knows no bounds," Elizabeth said in reply. "I cannot remember seeing these boys each so much in one sitting."

"It's good to see growing boys with such an appetite," said Mrs Kelly smiling at Dan in particular. "Now if we are all finished here I have things to get on with if you still want that picnic for your day out tomorrow. I will show you to the drawing room where you can spend the evening together."

"I will help you in the kitchen if our guests have no objection," said Mary quickly excusing herself from accompanying the others upstairs. Elizabeth had noticed how quiet Mary had been throughout the meal, helping to feed her son, eating only a few morsels and drawing little attention to herself. Unsurprisingly, what conversation there had been over tea had made no reference to the strange events which had brought the family to this house at Miah's invitation. Eager though Elizabeth was to find out if there had been a connection between Miah's assault and the dreadful suicide Walt had discovered on Gelligaer Common she would have to wait for a more appropriate time to be enlightened as she ushered the girls upstairs to find her sewing box.

Chapter 24

Elizabeth and the children sat in the drawing room which was on the first floor at the rear of the house. The large windows from floor to ceiling opened onto a small wrought iron balcony and looked out over the river towards the town. They provided a pleasant and peaceful view. The windows were open to catch some breeze on this late sunny afternoon but the lace curtains remained stubbornly still in the unmoving air.

Elizabeth settled at a table by the light from the window with her embroidery. It was another grand room, not overly large but well-proportioned with the high windows and ceiling. Elizabeth noted the quality of the old but well-polished furniture. The ornaments, though few, were tastefully arranged. Mrs Kelly's touch was evident in the room's homely feel just as it was in the kitchen. Miah was fortunate to have found such a dedicated and expert housekeeper in his mother-in-law. She suspected, however, that this room was rarely used by the 'master' of the house. Perhaps it would see more use now that Mary was at last in residence, thought Elizabeth.

Mary had seemed very withdrawn during the meal they had shared in the kitchen and eager to excuse herself from their company. Elizabeth suspected the girl was not well and suffered acutely from nerves. The prospect of being the object of curiosity to her father's guests would explain her reserve. Elizabeth resolved to make every effort to put the girl more at ease during their visit.

The presence of the children showed what a delightful family room it could be as they made themselves comfortable on the sofa and on cushions on the floor. Trefor sat and read aloud from a book he had selected from

Miah's library with frequent interruptions from his inquisitive sisters.

He had been given permission to browse the shelves in Miah's study to find something suitable to read to the younger ones. Among the black bound tomes on theology and volumes of sermons he found a section of children's classics. Each one had a book plate in a childish hand written by a young Nehemiah Thomas and a dedication in everyone commemorating a birthday, Christmas or other family occasion. They were dated and inscribed '*To my happy little boy... love Mama*'. Trefor felt he was prying into some secret past of Miah's as he read the inscriptions. He quickly chose the copy of Walter Scott's Ivanhoe which he now read from to his siblings, given on the occasion of Miah's 9th birthday.

Miah had taken Walt off to the privacy of his study on the ground floor. He sat at his writing desk while Walt took his ease in an armchair near the unlit fireplace. It was another white marble edifice in beautiful proportion to the rest of the room. "This is a fine old house you have here... Georgian I believe? And this... do they call it an Adam fireplace?" he asked reaching out to touch the smooth stone surface.

"Yes, at least in the style of Adam. It was my grandparent's home. My mother was raised in this house and I inherited the property with the rest of my grandfather's estate," said Miah putting down his pen. "It was held in trust until I turned 25."

"You really are a man of means," said Walt interrupting. "And all the time I have known you... I thought rumours of your wealth an exaggeration... no more than idle gossip."

"What rumours?" asked Miah amused knowing full well what was said about him in Baptist circles.

"That you were a man of property and great fortune... although you never boast of it. Perhaps I never associated the Miah Thomas I know with the tales of wealth and privilege," replied Walt.

"The first at least is true but it is inherited wealth. I was brought up in much humbler circumstances. There is a story in there and a sad one, almost worthy of Mr Charles Dickens..." said Miah as he pointed to a shelf behind Walt holding the great author's complete works bound in royal blue leather, "but one for another time perhaps. I have found my fortune at long last. I have my daughter returned and a young grandson to provide for; a family of my own and an heir to raise in the ways of the Lord."

"It must have been an anxious time... after we failed to find them at the cottage in Club Row," said Walt. "The attack your daughter suffered at the hands of Hugh Brown... and the consequences."

"Yes, you must tell me how you were led to discover the body of Hugh Brown so quickly and out on the common. It has quite mystified me," said Miah.

"Many would say it was a series of coincidences... but God works in mysterious way his wonders to perform. Our boy Dan saw the sketch of Hugh Brown... accidently in my study at home... He recognised him as a man he had seen living rough up the mountain," said Walt and proceeded to tell him how he had convinced the police to set out, with young Jack William's assistance, to apprehend Mary's assailant and the subsequent inquest into his death. "The local police thought they would bring him in for questioning... We had no inkling we would find the man killed by his own hand," said Walt in conclusion.

"A man with a troubled conscience and wracked by guilt to have placed his soul into such peril," said Miah. "'*He giveth and He taketh away*' Job 12 I recollect." Walt sighed and shook his head at the memory of the body in the stream and the blood, the biblical reference intended to remind him that suicide was regarded as a sin by many. "But '*everyone who calls on the name of the Lord shall be saved*' Romans 10, verse 13," added Miah. "There is always hope for those who truly repent."

"Amen," added Walt and both men set in silent contemplation of Hugh Brown's fate in the eyes of the Baptist church.

Miah cleared his throat. "Mary has helped to clarify some of the events that so perplexed us at the time," he said changing the subject. "I have explained to her the assistance you and Elizabeth so readily gave me and have her permission to share her tale of events with you. It will spare her the ordeal of recounting the details herself. She is still not as strong as I would hope," said Miah with a sigh. Walt leant forward in his chair eager to listen.

"You remember me telling of my assignation at the standing stone with Mary?" Walt nodded to encourage Miah in the telling. "It was the last thing I remembered clearly of that Monday. She left the lodgings bringing Robbie with her to meet with me that fateful morning thinking Hugh was asleep upstairs. He worked the night shift as ostler in the colliery, as the neighbour told us, and Mary hoped he would not notice their absence from the house that morning. She discovered later that he heard her leave and followed. He kept out of sight during our meeting, overhearing much of the conversation, no doubt. Although there are no witnesses, it puts him in the vicinity of the monolith when I met with my so-called accident. We are probably correct to deduce he was my assailant."

"There can be no other possible explanation for your injury," said Walt. "But ignore my interruption... Please continue."

"Hugh Brown did not return to the house. Mary thought him still abed on her return and carried out her usual chores - that is until she went to rouse him later that afternoon for his shift. His unexplained absence puzzled and alarmed her when he did not return for his meal. He had his routine which never varied, staying close to the house when not in work and keeping her without money. As the evening drew on she became increasingly more agitated. If something had happened to him she and the boy would be homeless and destitute. She had decided in that moment to put her trust in me after I offered to provide a home and protection for her and the child should she ever need it. It seems my offer was preferable to the workhouse at least." Miah laughed disparagingly. It always amazed Walt that Miah could make a light-hearted remark even about the direst situation but he let it pass. Miah was a good story teller and had him on the edge of his seat keen to find out what happened next. "Do carry on... what happened next?"

"Mary hastily gathered a few possessions together and hoped the little money I had given her would be sufficient for the train fare to Brecon. Remember, she was still not aware that Hugh had witnessed our assignation that morning. Or, indeed, that I was left lying helpless near the spot where we met on the hillside." Miah cleared his throat before continuing.

"But Mary and the little one did not get the chance to leave before he returned to the lodgings. She could not deny her intentions having been caught red-handed as they say. She tried to excuse her actions saying his absence during the day had alarmed her. But he was not fooled. Could not a man spend such a fine day roaming the common, he asked, and that she would be surprised by what he had seen up there. And where did she have to go unless she had some reason to think her father could ever forgive her for abandoning her family home. Only then did she realise that he must have witnessed our meeting on the common.

"Hugh threatened that she would only be leaving over his dead body. She tried to disguise her fear and diffuse his anger by carrying out the chore of preparing his food and putting the child to bed. But all the time he was watching her, making her increasingly wary of his mood as he brooded in silence. When it got dark and Mary usually retired for bed, she asked him why he had not left for his night shift as usual. He would be late and could lose his job if he was not careful. This seemed to rouse his latent anger. He could no longer trust her to be left alone. He knew I had given her money and demanded she hand it over to him saying she would never see her father again. She refused and tried to resist him but you have seen how frail she is and he was a powerfully built man. Her resistance only fuelled his anger. Thus began the most dreadful ordeal of her short life. She thought he would kill her and he very nearly succeeded when she passed out on the flagstone floor."

"The poor young woman," said Walt before Miah continued. "Perhaps fearing the noise had already alerted the neighbours he fled the scene into the night. We know what happened next thanks to the testament of Rachel Jones who informed us of the aftermath of the attack. And, of course, you solved the final part of the story with the discovery of his body just a few days later."

"Well, well... he must have thought he had two murders on his conscience," said Walt. "That would explain a great deal... Yes, all the different pieces of the story now seem to fit into place. But why did Mary make for Brecon having heard that you might have also perished at his hand? Why did she not alert the police to your possible fate when she had the chance?" he asked.

At that point there was a knock on the study door. Mrs Kelly told them she was making supper for the young visitors and asked if they might like some tea or a bite to eat. Miah looked at his guest enquiringly. "Some tea would be welcome," said Walt. "But... speaking for myself I could not eat another morsel... thank you."

"Yes, I am parched with all this talking. Tea would be most welcome. We will take it in here," added Miah. When Mrs Kelly left Miah continued his narrative without prompting.

"You must remember, dear Gwallt, Mary was in complete ignorance of my predicament. Hugh Brown did not confess to any attack on me but only made it clear from his remarks that he had witnessed our meeting on the common. When he said she would never see her father again she would not have realised that I might have come to any harm. No, you are wrong to assume otherwise. Mary was afraid he might return and was justly in fear of him. She knew she could not stay in those lodgings and continue to impose on the goodwill of her neighbours for all their care and consideration.

"After a night of much needed rest she found her opportunity to slip away with the child the following day.

Battered and bruised as she was and with only the few shillings I had pressed on her, she set off on foot with Robbie. She used the money for food and walked all the way. It took her several days, sleeping out at night and carrying the boy on her back. She even lost her way on the journey until some farm labourers set her back on the right track. When she eventually arrived at the farm where she had been raised, Mary was in a desperately weakened state and had to take to bed. Her uncle now has the tenancy, Mrs Kelly's son by her first marriage and my late wife's brother. He sent a message to me directly although it was several more days before the doctor advised we could move her here.

"She is still not settled in her nerves. Not surprising with all that has transpired; relief and joy at finding safe refuge with her family and even sorrow and remorse at Hugh Brown ending his life at his own hand. Again, her grandmother has been a great help and comfort to her and a tower of strength during this troubled time. I cannot think how we would cope without her calm efficiency."

As if on cue the woman herself appeared with a tray of tea and biscuits.

"I will leave you to serve yourselves while I help Mrs Lewis put the children to bed. Don't stay up too late. I think we will all be abed soon. The children are weary from the sun and excitement of the day and I must be up early about my chores," she said as she left the room closing the door behind her.

Miah opened the drawer of his desk and put on his reading glasses. "Now I want you to accept this for the expense you went to on my behalf in our search for Mary." He put a large white bank note on the desk and pushed it over towards his friend.

"There is no need... I cannot expect payment for what I did out of concern for an old friend. Your invitation here is enough reward..." said Walt.

"Regard it as expenses man. I am sure the sum is no more than you spent in hiring vehicles, telephone calls and the rest. You have gone to a great deal of trouble to help and, after all, am I not a man of means?" asked Miah smiling. "I have settled my bill with Dr Dan Thomas and paid some of the reward I was willing to offer for the apprehension of Hugh Brown to the police fund at Bargod. The rest went on paying for the burial of the body so there was no financial burden on the local parish." He leaned back in his chair.

"The only debt remaining is owed to my rescuers on the common. The Police Sergeant at Bargod station tells me the labourers who rescued me were Seth and Lewis Lewis. Another coincidence as they are brothers to Rachel Jones of Bedlinog. I really owe that family a great deal as you tell me now that without the husband's likeness of Hugh Brown we might still not have found out his fate."

"Someone would have found the body in the stream sooner or later," said Walt "although it would have been nigh on impossible for the police to identify him... There was nothing in his possession or about his person to indicate who he might be. There are still many young men on the tramp looking for work in the pits... especially this time of year... it is no great hardship to sleep out rough in this weather. But to think of young Mary and her boy out for days alone... that is quite another matter."

"Indeed, she seemed oblivious of the danger she placed herself in never mind the poor state of her health. Desperation drove her to take that action and I can only thank the Lord that she found her way back to my protection and the safekeeping of her grandmother," said Miah. "My prayers were answered, Praise the Lord."

"Indeed, Praise His name... from whom we gain our strength.   One last question on the matter... did the police find any next of kin for Hugh Brown? I know they are duty bound to try."

"He was an orphan, raised in the workhouse. As a young boy he was taken on and trained as a stable lad by a local land agent working for the estate. He was good with the horses by all accounts and his job as ostler in the pit was the first work he had found that offered any permanence. Mary tells me he hoped to settle in Club Row as he enjoyed working with the animals even underground."

Walt nodded.   "Some men have a true gift with animals... but I have never had much liking for horses... especially underground. Hauliers have the worst of it when it comes to accidents with horse drawn drams... I have witnessed it first hand... far too often."

"Yes, it takes a special skill. My family's wealth was based on haulage, horses and related trades," said Miah. "All this talk of these events has reminded me. I must write to Rachel Jones and her family to thank them for their help in the matter. They may not realise just how significant their contribution has been between them all. Her husband's accurate likeness of Hugh Brown, her brothers' concern over a stranger left helpless on the common and, not least, her kind consideration of Mary's wellbeing."

"And the good news that she is now safe with her family... and recovering from her ordeal. They will have probably already read of the inquest... it was reported briefly in the newspapers... but will not know the fate of Mary and her son," said Walt. "It never became a police matter and you must be relieved for your position in the church that nothing was reported in the newspapers."

"Thanks to you, old friend. You have a lot to tell Elizabeth. Please do so with my blessing. We must not be too late retiring tonight if we are to go on our fishing expedition tomorrow. And I hope I have satisfied your curiosity for the time being," said Miah.

Walt smiled at Miah's last remark. The conversation over tea passed onto church matters on which Miah was, as always, so very well informed.

Chapter 25

The following morning dawned bright and sunny. There was no sign of the good weather breaking yet awhile. It was early but the excited children had taken their places in the farm wagon pulled by Goliath and driven by the able Llewellyn with their father and Uncle Miah sat up front with the driver. Mrs Kelly's picnic basket was stowed safely with them along with stone bottles of pop, feedbags for the horse and Walt's new fishing rod and tackle.

Elizabeth had decided to spend the day closer to the comforts of the house. She intended to take full advantage of Miah's hospitality and the company of Mrs Kelly. She had seen no sign of Mary that morning. Robbie was deemed too young to go with the fishing party so mother and child were probably up in the nursery, no doubt keeping out of the way.

Elizabeth's excuse not to accompany her husband and children was that the weather was too hot and a fishing trip was not to her liking. More than that, she dreaded trying to get in and out of that wagon again in her stays and nothing would induce her to remove them in company, even in this heat. She kept that snippet of information to herself; it was hardly a topic for polite conversation and she would be too embarrassed even to mention it to her husband.

"Try and keep the children out of mischief and out of the river," said Elizabeth as she and Mrs Kelly waved them off at the front door of the house.

Elizabeth was far more at ease leaving little Gwladys in her husband's charge after their sojourn in Builth Wells. Now that the girls were getting older and more aware of the dangers of wandering off she had no qualms about letting them accompany the men on their fishing trip. Criddy also set a good example for her little sister; she had always caused far less trouble to her mother at the same age.

Trefor would also look out for the girls and keep Dan close. He really had been a great help to his parents over this holiday, shepherding his siblings most afternoons and giving Elizabeth time to enjoy with her husband. He was quite a different boy the last few weeks; ever since that dreadful incident when he had exchanged blows with some local louts. Reluctantly she had to admit that he was growing up and he most definitely looked the part of the young man in his fashionable new outfit. His mother definitely welcomed the change in him that summer.

Elizabeth followed Mrs Kelly back into the house towards the delightful little parlour at the back of the ground floor with a door out onto the garden which she had only just discovered. She would enjoy a leisurely cup of tea before her visit to the town. Mrs Kelly conversation was proving most enlightening on those aspects of Miah's life she could only have imagined before this unexpected invitation to his home. She looked forward to hearing more.

The wagon carrying the fishing party was soon out of the town and turning down the lane towards the village of Llanfrynach. They went at a steady walking pace, horses like Goliath were bred for strength and endurance not speed and agility. The height of the wagon gave the occupants a good view over the hedgerows and across the fields towards the mountains that surrounded them. It was only a few miles to the village and the road took them over the Brecon Monmouth canal. Llew stopped the wagon on the bridge for the children to view the canal, eager to spot any barges. But there was little, if any, traffic on the waterway since the railways had put so many watermen out of work. It was beginning to look quite neglected.

"I can show you where your great grandmother lived... and where your grandfather was born, children. There is a family gravestone in the village churchyard... if I can remember exactly where," said Walt as they recommenced their short journey. "And then we can find a nice spot on the river to have our picnic... and I can indulge in a bit of fishing and try out this new rod and line."

"I know the perfect spot, Mr Lewis," said Llew. "We'll be able to drive the wagon across the field to the river bank. I used to fish there as a boy myself years ago and there are a few pools created by the rocks and the meander of the river. The young ladies can dip their toes in the water and Goliath will appreciate the shade of the trees along the bank; it is going to be another hot day."

"I think we will all appreciate some shade by mid-day," said Miah.

When they reached the village of Llanfrynach, Walt pointed out the cottage where his grandmother had lived in later life and where he had visited as a boy with his father. It was in the centre of the village main street, opposite the church and just a few doors down from The Swan Inn. They drew up outside the churchyard where everyone except Llew and Dan got down from the wagon and walked into the graveyard in search of their only surviving family connection to the area in the form of a headstone. Dan liked Llew and the feeling was mutual; Llew had taken Dan under his wing given the boy's fascination for the horse, Goliath.

"Do any of the de Winton family still live at the house... Ty Mawr?" Walt asked Miah.

"Not for many years. They built a large house in the Gothic style they call a castle at Maesllwch over towards Radnorshire. Ty Mawr is let out, usually in the

230

past to officers based at the barrack and their family. But the De Winton's still own the estate. An agent runs it for them, a good man. I have had dealings with him over the years," replied Miah.

"Another lovely Georgian place Ty Mawr... and now I remember... they have their castle... Now, let's see if we can find this gravestone... It is definitely near here... somewhere over there I believe. Let's take a row each... We are looking for Walter and Ann Lewis born about 1790... and their children," said Walt.

Within a few minutes Tref hailed his father as he stooped forward to read the inscription in more detail. He brushed away some of the encrusted lichen on the stone. "Over here, I have found it," he shouted and stood up as Walt and Miah headed towards him along the row respectfully trying not to tread on the graves of the departed.

"Yes, indeed... this is the resting place of my grandparents. I was named for my grandfather Walter... my sister was named Ann for her grandmother," said Walt. "They are family names... like Dan and Will were named for their grandfathers also." Gwladys and Ceridwen came over to the spot where they were gathered around the grave carrying a straggly bunch of wild flowers, mainly buttercups, campions and dog daisies they had picked in the unkempt grass bordering the graveyard. Gwladys solemnly placed them by the headstone turning to smile up at her Dadda to make sure she had done the right thing. He smiled and laid his hand approvingly on her head.

"I see your grandfather Walter died aged 45 or is that a 3?" asked Miah.

"43," said Walt. "He died a few months before my father was born... I have no stories of him from my father's childhood... Although as you can see... his wife... my grandmother lived on to a grand age... She was over 100 years old when she died. I have vivid recollections of my visits to the village here to see her... both as a boy and as a young man. But her mind was confused at the end... she could not recognise me or my father when I last visited her. In fact, she thought my father was her long dead husband and me... she mistook me for my own father as a young man. But she was content in her own way."

"Look father, they also had a son called Walter," said Tref reading from the inscription after brushing off more moss from the bottom of the stone. "He died aged 22 and there are two infants also buried here. But why is the inscription all in English? Your parents were both Welsh speaking and I cannot ever remember them speaking much English at all."

"English was the language of the church here," said Miah. "The landowners, the de Winton family, became very prosperous. They married into English society, all heiresses who no doubt helped to swell the family fortune. The family name had been plain Wilkins or Watkins, I cannot remember which, but they chose to revive an old Norman name when they became so very well to do. See the large monuments over there near the church? They all belong to the de Winton family and there are several Walter de Wintons. It was the name of the eldest son and heir to the estate. The family even brought English speaking servants to work indoors at the big house. And then, when the barracks came to Brecon about a hundred years ago, there were even more English people in the area with the soldiers and officers."

"Yes indeed... My father's sister... another Ann... she met and married a sergeant from an English regiment stationed in Brecon," said Walt. "...it was around the time of the Crimean war. She even went on campaign with him... they were stationed on the island of Malta... that's in the Mediterranean sea... an important naval base supplying the campaign. She travelled the world with her husband as an army wife... the Caribbean, Asia... Eventually the regiment ended up based in Yorkshire... and there they stayed. Their son Arthur married my sister, your Auntie Annie children...and they still live up in Yorkshire... with your cousins Lily and Grace. They will all be coming down to visit us later in the month... as they do every year.

"Shall we go and look in the church before we take a turn around the village on foot? There was a delightful village shop... if I remember... that sold homemade sweets... I wonder if they still do?" he said taking Gwladys by the hand. He now had her undivided attention at the mention of the prospect of sweets.

By mid-morning the party were down on the banks of the Usk where Walt could not wait to try out his fishing rod for the first time. The children were commandeered to find some earthworms for bait. Miah took charge and off they went to the edge of a nearby copse where the soil protected from the heat was cool and moist and more likely to yield up some worms. Failing that, Llew suggested they could try some bread or meat out of the picnic basket as bait. He was eager to show Mr Lewis how to use his posh new rod and line to best effect.

*

Mrs Kelly had shown Elizabeth around the shops and stalls of the market hall in Brecon town where she had delighted in the range of fresh farm produce available including soft fruit. "I will make a summer berry pudding with these," said Mrs Kelly serving herself to raspberries, strawberries and blackcurrants at the stall, "A treat for the children."

"It is too early for berries our way. These are cultivated?" asked Elizabeth. "The children often pick blackberries and wimberries in the autumn from the hedgerow and heath at home. But there are few wild strawberries now, unless you know where to look. The village where Walt and I first set up our own home was called Cwmsyfiog, vale of the strawberry although few flourish there now."

Back in the kitchen at Miah's townhouse the women settled down to their mid-morning cup of tea or elevenses as Elizabeth liked to call it. The girl, Elsie who came in daily had done the bedrooms and swept through the house. With the fine weather, no coal had to be carried upstairs or fires laid. Mrs Kelly had set her the task of giving the dining room a thorough cleaning including the silver and glassware to keep her occupied.

Mary sat to take tea with them while Robbie played with his wooden picture blocks on the floor. He preferred to make a tall tower from the blocks and then knock it down than trying to recreate the pictures pasted in paper on each face of the block. He chuckled contentedly at his handiwork before knocking his tower over again.

"He is a fine boy," said Elizabeth "and such beautiful fair colouring. I cannot but admire the colour of your hair also Mary."

"My father was a redhead too," said Mrs Kelly "it runs in the family. Irish blood you know, or was it Scottish? Anyway, his ancestor came to this area to work on the canal. Navvies they called them, the men who built the old canal. But my grandfather settled here having met and married a local Welsh girl. He took on a farm tenancy and did well enough. Horses were his passion and he started breeding them to supply the army at the local barracks. That is how I came into the farm, a country girl to the core. Just like Mary here…"

Mary interrupted politely. "If you are going to reminisce with Mrs Lewis do you mind if I take father's letters to the post box? I will take Robbie and we can for a little walk along the river or through the park. We will not go far and I can be back in plenty of time to help you prepare food. I have heard your family stories often enough as a child," she smiled weakly to her grandmother.

It was also a good excuse to escape Mrs Lewis' continuing scrutiny. Mary was finding the presence of strangers in the house, albeit longstanding friends of her father, quite unsettling. She felt an object of curiosity since, as kindly as Mrs Lewis spoke to her, Mary was aware she knew a great deal too much about her recent circumstances and would like to know more. Mary's conscience made her prefer the anonymity of strangers to the presence of such an upstanding woman as Mrs Lewis undoubtedly thought she was.

"Off you go and get some fresh air. You do not need to be inside on a beautiful day like today. It will help bring the roses back to your cheeks. I have time enough to prepare our tea with the rest of the household away for the entire day. But don't tire yourself too much. The sun can do that you know. In fact, there is an old parasol in the upstairs closet. I shall fetch it," said Mrs Kelly. "It will keep the sun off your head."

"No really, grandmother, sit there and enjoy the company of father's guest. You concern yourself too much. I will wear my bonnet with the wide brim," said Mary who had never carried a parasol in her life. She kissed her grandmother affectionately on the cheek before offering her hand to young Robbie. "Come along, let us take a walk to see the ducklings on the river. Would you like that? Let's put your blocks away in the box nice and tidy before we go."

Chapter 26

Mrs Kelly's picnic had been demolished by the hungry children in the shade of the trees along the river bank. Miah and Walt had long since discarded their jackets and Walt looked as if he might indulge in a spot of forty winks sitting propped up against the trunk of the tree. Dan was fast asleep on the picnic blanket with little Criddy snuggled against him back to back, both overcome with drowsiness in the heat after eating too much and playing hide and seek most of the morning.

"Would you like to hear a story, children?" asked Miah. "Your father reminded me of it with his telling of the Crimea and fatherless children this morning."

"I love stories," replied Criddy "what is it about? Is it about soldiers and the wars? Does your story have a moral at the end?"

"All stories have a moral if we but look for it. Now, my story is about a little boy, a happy little boy who lived in a pretty little house with his dear and kind mamma. Although this little boy never knew his father he did not miss what he'd never known. His mamma would tell him stories about the handsome brave soldier his papa had been. She kept that image of his father alive in his imagination but preserved in a time before he had been born.

"The little boy's father had been a junior officer in the old Queen's army and wore his red uniform and rode on a big chestnut horse with gleaming harness and carried a sword. But, when the regiment was sent away to defend a remote part of our Empire, he had to travel far from his wife and home. A soldier's duty is to obey and follow orders. He had no choice but to go with the regiment even though his pretty young wife was not able to travel with him. But sadly, that handsome brave soldier never came home again, dying in the service of Queen and country."

"That is very sad," said Ceridwen "but you said the little boy was a happy even though his papa was gone to heaven."

"Yes, the little boy never knew his father. He was born after he had left on campaign but he grew up knowing him to have been a brave and dutiful officer. And he still had his mama who loved him dearly and made a very happy home for him growing up. He wanted for nothing and attended a good school. Every Sunday she took him to chapel where he learned to read the Bible and to understand the word of God. And he had his father's family, his grandparents, aunts and uncles living nearby in the town to indulge him also. They ran a successful seed and corn merchants with a shop in the high street and he would often run errands for them after school."

"Like Dan runs errands down the road for Mam?" asked Criddy.

"Yes, just like Dan runs errands in the town for your mother. But, to continue my story.

"Our little boy's dear mama had never been strong and, one day, she took to her bed. Over the next few months the poor lady wasted away despite the best doctors and care money could buy. She died peacefully in her sleep..."

"Oh dear, the happy little boy must have been very sad then. He is an orphan now without a father or mother," said Criddy "and he will have to go to the workhouse."

"Not all orphans need end up in the workhouse my dear. He had family and his grandparents on his father's side took him to live with them. He was not such a little boy anymore; he was growing up just like Trefor. But it did make him very sad losing his dear mama and their happy home together. There was no more money to keep him in school so he would never be able to go to the university and study the Bible as his mother had wished and which had also been his dearest wish.

"His grandfather decided to make good use of the boy's education and he was trained in book keeping and accounts. He also helped in the shop when it was busy and he still ran the errands for his grandfather and uncles who ran the business. The good Lord had shown him he must make the most of what he had and not regret what he could not have."

"Amen to that," said Walt who was not asleep, only resting his eyes while listening to Miah's story.

"So now our little boy, who was not so little anymore, settled into his new life and many good things happened to him, and a few sad things too, but such is the path our Lord has set out for us. He continued to study the Bible with the minister and good men of his chapel every week and grew up to be a happy young man. Then, when he was 25 years old, a very strange and unexpected thing happened. He was visited by two gentlemen who told him were trustees to an estate of which he was the sole benefactor."

"What does that mean?" asked Criddy.

"It means that suddenly he was a very wealthy young man. His mother had been an only child leaving him the sole heir to her father's fortune, the same wealth that had paid for their little house and his education when she had been alive. So, can you guess what he did with all his inherited money?"

"He went to the university to study the Bible?" asked Criddy.

"Indeed, that is just what he did child. And from there he trained to become a minister of the church and went on to help many other young men, not as fortunate or as wealthy as him, to go to college and study the Bible."

"Sir, may I ask if by any chance you are the happy little boy of the story?" asked Trefor.

"Very perceptive of you, Trefor," said his father sitting up. "I also think Miah has just given us a delightful account of his early life... before he became a minister and found himself in Argoed... where our paths first crossed. Are we correct old friend?"

"I am found out," said Miah laughing. "What part of the story gave me away, Trefor?"

"Oh, nothing you said, sir, but it reminded me of the books, all the children's books in your study. You let me look through them and I am reading 'Ivanhoe' to the others. The all say they were from your dear mama with a dedication at the front which always starts with 'to my happy little boy'."

"Yes, I had quite forgotten that. She was a kind and loving mother; no doubt the reason for my happy childhood. And when did you realise Gwallt?"

"Not until the end... when your young man inherited his maternal grandfather's wealth aged 25. I had no idea until then," replied Walt. "So what might be the moral to that story, Ceridwen... can you find one?"

"Yes, sort of... I think it means that if you are happy, and study the Bible, then God will make all your dreams come true," she replied looking to see if her answer had pleased her father.

"Well, that might be one way of putting it... but do not forget the power of prayer. God listens to our prayers... He does not fulfil our dreams and wishes. We must do that through our own hard work. I doubt very much if Uncle Miah ever prayed as a young boy to become a wealthy man... But it was God's plan for him... knowing he would use his money wisely to help others and further the work of the church..." Walt could not suppress a yawn and a stretch. The afternoon heat was wearying.

"Now, I am going to rouse myself and try to hook a few fish. So far we have nothing to show for our trip to this delightful spot on the river... we cannot go back to your mother and Mrs Kelly empty handed... there will be nothing to put on the table for supper. And I believe I am getting to grips with this fishing rod... with the help and expert tuition of Llewelyn here."

"Trefor, let us see if we can tickle the trout in the pool over there. I have not tried to do it since I was a child but I am sure the skill has not been lost. When he is a little older I hope I will have many opportunities to show my grandson Robbie the mysterious art of trout tickling," said Miah.

"Be careful you are not too successful... the landowner might think you a poacher after his game fish," said Walt.

"But Mr Lewis, he is the landowner of this stretch of the river," said Llew.

*

After preparing her summer berry pudding and baking a savoury pie, Mrs Kelly and Elizabeth retired to the pleasant back parlour of the house with their various sewing and mending tasks. Robbie had been put down in the nursery for his afternoon nap and Mary had disappeared upstairs with him. Elizabeth had learned more from the housekeeper about Miah's domestic routine but, understandably, Mrs Kelly knew little of his business interests. When he was not travelling he spent several hours each morning at an office in town from which his various businesses were managed and all his business meetings conducted away from the house. It was from here he managed his properties and holdings. He employed several clerks who carried out book keeping and auditing, mostly on behalf of the Baptist church.

Most afternoons and evenings were spent dealing with church correspondence and writing in the study at home. He dealt with a great deal of correspondence but invited few visitors to the house. It was rare for anyone to stay overnight and Mrs Kelly often felt quite alone when Miah took off on his travels for several days at a time.

"If it were not for Elsie, who comes in every morning I might not speak to a soul. You would not believe the change it has made having Mary and Robbie here. It is not just their company. The child has changed the whole atmosphere of the house which was like a mausoleum before their coming," said Mrs Kelly.

"And what of Mary's future? Will she stay here with her father?" asked Elizabeth.

"Oh yes, we have discussed it together and, when Robbie goes to school in the town, she hopes to take over the role as her father's housekeeper. It was her own suggestion. Miah will provide me with a home for life whatever my role in the household. He is such a generous man and I will persuade him to get some more help in the house. Mary cannot be expected to do everything in future with just a few hours of help from a daily maid and her with a young child to look after."

"I am glad to hear that you have thought about the future. It seems Mary's place here is secure after all the concern she has been to you both," said Elizabeth. "She is a most fortunate young woman. Her father has a more forgiving nature than many I can think of. Did you know this man, Hugh Brown? My husband tells me he had no other family, or at least none that could be traced. I believe Miah himself paid to have the man buried not to be a burden on the parish."

"Yes, I knew Hugh Brown by sight and his circumstances were common knowledge locally where we lived. But there were two boys, he had a brother. Their mother turned up to the workhouse gate when they were small children. She was sick, abandoned and totally destitute. She died a few days later of the consumption and the boys raised in the orphan school." Elizabeth nodded knowing the fate of many abandoned women often ended in hardship and tragedy.

"When they were about 8 and 9 years of age they were both taken on to work at the local estate. And let me tell you, two boys less alike for brothers you will rarely see. Hugh was very dark in colouring and was taken for being mute and a bit simple. But he grew into a tall and powerful young man after moving to the estate and working in the stables. His brother was Dennis, if I remember rightly, but was called Denny by all. He was fairer, much slighter and shorter than his brother. And he and had a real gift of the gab. Total opposites they were. He was a good-looking boy that Denny; they both were in their different ways. Denny was taken on as a house servant by the estate manager and we often saw him around the locality delivering messages and carrying out errands for his master." She put down her mending to better concentrate on her story.

"Those two boys had always been close and spent their free time together. I now know that Hugh had a fault with his speech, a severe stammer. He could talk but rarely did so in front of strangers but he was far from being stupid as most of the locals thought. Denny was also a very clever boy in his way. He would often call in at our farmhouse on some pretext or other. Lots of the young lads did, hoping to see the maids in the dairy and stop them in conversation during an idle moment. Oh, he was full of big ideas that boy and quite the charmer. He had ambitions above his station and dreamed of going to America to seek his fortune. The Lord only knows where he got his ideas from but I saw no harm in him then, little could I foresee what would happen."

"So, what did happen? What were the circumstances of Mary's disappearance and flight from the family home?"

"Well, when Mary disappeared around her sixteenth birthday at first I thought she had come to serious harm. You cannot imagine the distress it caused."

"You must have been beside yourself with worry. Did she leave no indication that she had simply ran off? It would have been kinder than causing you and your family to fear for her safety."

"No, if Mary had planned this there was no sign of it. She took nothing with her in the way of clothing or food... nothing to say she had run off of her own free will. Perhaps it was on the spur of the moment she chose to leave. All it took was one moment of weakness. The young are always looking for adventure, that sense the grass is always greener… Who can tell? I have not had the heart to press her on the matter since her return. Her nerves are not good you know. She has been through a lot." Mrs Kelly blew her noses on her lace handkerchief and look at Elizabeth as if pleading for her understanding. Elizabeth smiled in encouragement.

"When nightfall came and still no sign of her, my son organised a search party. They scoured the countryside for miles around over the next few days. But there was no news or evidence of an accident. Miah was away on church business at the time and it was several days before he returned when we could alert him to the news of Mary's disappearance. The police were told, but with no evidence of foul play there was little they could do. After weeks of fruitless enquiry Miah feared the worse.

"The police were not encouraging believing the best we could hope for in time was finding her body hidden away in the undergrowth. I could not believe something so dreadful could happen to my dear girl. It was almost the undoing of me. Miah was very understanding and apportioned no blame. In fact, he blamed himself for neglecting her education and not providing for her future."

"Yes, Miah has made me aware of how he feels about the whole affair. That he takes on himself a large burden of guilt for Mary's actions," said Elizabeth.

"At the time, my family were so involved in our own tragedy that we did not hear the news that Hugh and Denny had given notice and left their employment on the estate. After hearing this there always lingered the possibility in my mind that she might have run away in the company of those boys. And it would have been Denny that was behind it if you want my opinion. That boy with his silly dreams of America and silver-tongued promises, I am sure of it."

"So, she had run off with both of them when she disappeared," said Elizabeth.

"I always feared it. When I came here as housekeeper I confided my suspicion with Miah. Although he dismissed it I know it gave him hope that one day he might find his girl safe and well. As you now know, it turned out I was right to think she had her head turned by that boy. But, as for safe and well? She has suffered for her sins but, if her father can forgive her, then I am more than happy to follow his example."

245

"So, what happened then to this brother, Denny? Where is he now?" asked Elizabeth.

"Who knows, Mrs Lewis? Perhaps he did make it to America after all..."

Chapter 27

The Lewis family rose early the following morning. Not only was it their habit but necessary if they were to catch an early train from Brecon to Bargoed. It was Saturday and today their holiday was over; it was back home to Ty Gwent and Walt would undoubtedly want to spend some time in the Fed offices later in the day catching up on events during his absence.

The house was a bustle of activity preparing for their departure. It had been quite a panic getting everyone up, dressed and fed simply because there was a train to catch. Trefor helped Llew load the luggage into the wagon while Elizabeth checked the upstairs rooms to make sure she had packed all their belongings leaving nothing behind. She sailed down the elegant staircase, much less steep than theirs at home, hoping she could ascend into the wagon as gracefully as she could descend the stairs. She had deliberately not tightened her stays as much as usual in anticipation of the feat she was required to perform getting into that wagon. She was determined to do it with as much decorum as she could muster. The girls were waiting patiently in the hallway but there was no sign of Dan or Walter.

"Where is Dan? We are ready to go and do not want to miss this train," she said.

Mrs Kelley emerged from the doorway down to the kitchen with Dan behind her carrying a large package wrapped in waxed paper.

"A little something for the journey," said the housekeeper "just some fruit, bread and cheese."

"Really, you should not have taken the trouble; you are too kind and our journey is not a long one," said Elizabeth knowing full well she would have done the same for any visitor departing her home. "Well, it is high time for us to leave so that you can get back to your normal routine. We have enjoyed the generous hospitality of this household. You keep a tidy house, Mrs Kelly, one to be proud of and I have enjoyed your company these past few days. But we really must be going if we are to catch this train. Where can my husband be?"

"Farewell Mrs Lewis," said Mary descending the stairs holding Robbie by the hand. "I am glad to have met you and your family and had the opportunity to thank you for everything you have done for my father. He has found true friends in you and Mr Lewis. Goodbye children, I hope we may meet again one day, God willing."

"Farewell to you too child and I pray the good Lord's grace will be upon you. You have been blessed with a son; take care of him. Both of you are fortunate to be welcomed back into this family and make it complete. I know it was Miah's fervent desire to have you returned safely to his care. Be good to your father, help your grandmother and may the Lord bless you all."

Her parting speech was more magnanimous towards Mary than she felt. The girl had proved reserved in her manner and far less garrulous than her grandmother. She rarely stayed in the same room as her father's visitors long enough to be polite, the house providing too many rooms where she could hide away. Perhaps she was judging the girl unfairly given the unusual circumstances and, uncharacteristically, Elizabeth embraced Mary in farewell and turned to do likewise to her grandmother with more genuine warmth of feeling.

Walt and Miah emerged from the study into the crowded hall way. Walt tucked a white envelope into his inside jacket pocket before shaking hands with Miah in farewell.

He took his tin watch from his waistcoat pocket and glanced down at it in his hand, a sure sign it was time to leave. More fond farewells were exchanged with Miah and the rest of the family. Miah insisted Trefor take his copy of Walter Scott's 'Ivanhoe' to finish reading to the others at home and he shook Trefor by the hand as the children ran outside eager to get into the wagon for the ride to the station. Miah had always been a good sort in Tref's opinion and he returned his handshake enthusiastically.

Tref followed the children outside to give Dan and the girls a hand up into the back before hauling himself in after them while Llew did the same for their parents in the front. Walt got in first to help his wife while Llew gave her his strong arm to lean on. Elizabeth put her foot on the step while Walt grasped her hands to pull her up towards him. When she pushed herself forward and upward there was a brief moment she thought she might overbalance and was not going to make it. A firm shove on her backside propelled her upwards. She sat down heavily on the seat hoping that no one had witnessed Llew's timely intervention which had involuntarily caused her to blush crimson.

"Safe journey," called Miah as Goliath the horse strained in the harness and the cart began to move away from the door.

"God's speed," they heard as the children waved from the back of the cart at Uncle Miah and his family, stood together in the doorway of his lovely Georgian home waving while the cart joined the traffic over the river towards the town.

The train was not busy and the family found enough seats together for each child to sit at a window so there were no arguments. They could all look back at the mountain views as the train sped through the Breconshire countryside towards the industrial valleys just a few miles to the south and home. It was a direct train to Bargoed so they could sit back and enjoy the ride.

"Well... my dear... our first holiday away as a family... has it been a success?" asked Walt.

"It certainly has been an experience," replied his wife, "and a most enjoyable and enlightening one. But I am eager to be home and in my own bed tonight for all the comforts of the hotel and the care of Mrs Kelly. There is a lot of washing to be done on Monday or the girls will have nothing clean to wear."

"Yes, back to the daily grind of housework and laundry... shopping and cooking... It is true a woman's work is never done... That is if we have a house to get home to... and Esau has not blown up the gas geyser."

Elizabeth looked at him in alarm until she saw the broad smile on his face. "Why do the men in this family think that teasing a poor woman is some sort of sport?" she asked. "I should be used to it by now but I can never be quite sure when you are pulling my leg. You are pulling my leg Walter?"

"Of course, my dear... but you fall for it every time... you are too gullible," he said and opened out the copy of Y Genedl, the newspaper Miah had given him to read on the train. Sitting hidden behind a newspaper, and with the gentle rhythmic rolling of the carriage, Walt found train journeys a wonderful opportunity to think and reflect; there was a great deal to mull over after the family's visit to Miah's home.

What a grand house Miah had inherited from his maternal grandfather; far too big for a widowed man who rarely used most of the rooms, of course, but now it would make an excellent family home. He was fortunate to have found such a conscientious housekeeper in his mother-in-law and now he welcomed the prospect of raising his grandson as the heir to the family wealth.

It seemed inevitable that Mary would gradually take on more of her grandmother's responsibilities for the day-to-day running of that house as her health improved. But Walt could not see Mrs Kelly herself totally relinquishing her role; one she took so much pride in too.

Yes, this whole sorry saga had a most satisfactory outcome for Miah and his little family. Miah had an understanding of children and they responded well to him. Look at the way he entertained them with stories, thought Walt. Circumstances had conspired against him, depriving him of the joys of fatherhood. He had known only the heartache and guilt. But he would no doubt make an excellent grandfather.

The previous evening, after another of Mrs Kelly's excellent meals including a fish course, the men had spent some time together with the women and children in the drawing room sharing stories of the adventures of their holiday and the day's fishing trip before the younger children retired to bed. Ceridwen had even recounted her own version of Miah's story of the happy little boy, with embellishments of course and a moral to complete the tale. Dan, meanwhile, had gone with Llew and was outside watching him go about his daily routine in the stables and outhouses a short walk from the house.

When the party dispersed to their different chores in readiness for bed, Walt and Miah had the room to themselves. Miah had to admit that Ceridwen's version of his early life had been more entertaining than his own but, of course, he had withheld some salient facts from the story. He proceeded to enlighten Walt more fully with his childhood circumstances beginning with his mother's estrangement from her wealthy parents. It shed little light on current events but did explain Miah's willingness to forgive his daughter for her behaviour and the misery she had caused her family.

Miah told how his mother had met her handsome soldier at a local society dance in Brecon town to which the officers from the regiment stationed at the barracks were also invited. Her parents were scandalised by their daughter's association with the young lieutenant she had danced several times with that evening and forbade them to meet never mind conduct a formal courtship. Her parents had aspirations for their only daughter as the heiress to the family wealth. They intention was for a better match for her despite her grandfather's own lowly origins as the son of a local carter and his wife, the local blacksmith's girl.

Miah's maternal grandfather had worked hard all his life building up his haulage company, diversifying into many related trades and, after several fortuitous investments in land and railways, had accumulate his wealth. He and his wife had been married many years and had suffered several losses in childbirth until their only surviving daughter had been born in their later years. She had been raised to be a young lady befitting the family's new status in the area.

The parental ban on the match only resulted in subterfuge on the part of the lovers. Their behaviour seemed inevitable and oft repeated under similar circumstances. The young couple found ways to communicate and occasionally meet and romance blossomed. Miah did not know who instigated the idea but his parents decided the only course of action available to them was to elope together and throw themselves on the mercy of their parents after they were married. However, they had underestimated the intransigent nature of her mother who would not receive her daughter after her scandalous behaviour. She was disowned and forbidden the family home. Her father was given no choice but to comply with his wife's wishes despite his fondness for his only child.

Luckily her new in-laws, with fewer pretensions, welcomed the young lady into their home in a neighbouring town. There she stayed when her husband left the country with his regiment never to return. After Miah was born news reached his wealthy grandfather that his daughter was now widowed with a young child. The old man arranged an annuity to be paid during his daughter's lifetime to provide her and the child with a modest but comfortable home and which covered the school fees for Miah growing up.

All this was done in a business-like manner; there could not be any direct communication as her mother would not forgive her transgressions and was unaware of her husband's generous consideration towards their errant daughter. This annuity provided her with her a source of income after the death of her husband on campaign and some independence. Sadly, her handsome soldier had not fallen a hero in battle, as she encouraged her son to believe, but succumbed to a tropical fever; illness and disease being the most common cause of death among army personnel serving abroad.

Miah explained how his mother had honoured her husband's memory and remained faithful to him throughout her widowhood. To her he would always be a hero and the one true love of her life. She had not been wanton but a romantic and unworldly spirit in Miah's opinion. She also proved to be a kind-hearted and loving mother who raised her son in a good Christian home. It was not surprising, therefore, that Miah could not condemn his own daughter for her behaviour after it had been discovered she had run off with her young man.   Young love ran like a thread throughout both stories. In Mary's case, her lover may only have been an orphaned servant, but Mary had been raised in humbler circumstances and without her father's guiding influence; something for which Miah could not forgive himself.

Miah explained that, on the death of his wife, his grandfather put all his wealth and property in trust for Miah to inherit on his 25th birthday.   The old man died within months of his embittered wife, very wealthy but estranged from one another while living under the same roof.   His grandfather had not foreseen the early death of his daughter although her health had never been robust.   On her demise, the annuity stopped.

There was no provision made in the will for the orphaned boy until he reached the age of majority stipulated in the old man's will.   Miah was taken in by his paternal grandparents still ignorant of the source of his mother's income.   On coming into his inheritance after being widowed so young, it provided opportunities Miah could not have hoped for. He used his business skills and managed his wealth for the benefit of the church now that he had achieved his ambition to study the bible and become a minister.

With the full, un-expunged version of the story Miah had told the children, Walt had to agree it was indeed a story worthy of Mr Dickens, or at least the penny potboilers so popular with working families, especially the women. He smiled to himself and felt his inside pocket where the envelope Miah had pressed on him this morning laid unopened. He sincerely hoped his old friend had not sealed any more banknotes inside. The hospitality and frankness of their host during the past few days had more than settled any imagined debt between them. Walt had been happy to help his old friend in need. While he may not approve of Mary's past behaviour, her father had forgiven her and he hoped she sought the Lord's forgiveness in her prayers.

*

"I have the kettle on and there's tea in the pot. Welcome home," said Esau as the family trooped into the house.

"How wonderful to be back in my own kitchen. I feel as if we've been away for months," said Elizabeth removing her hat pins and sitting at the familiar table in her favourite chair. She released a sigh as she took of the hat and placed it on the table.

"Has everything been well in our absence?" Walt asked his brother-in-law. "Not in work this morning, Esau?"

"I just called in with a few groceries, courtesy of Peglars of course. You were lucky to catch me before I return to the shop. There's nothing amiss to report although you will be sad to hear Old John down the street has had the doctor to him. Given his age there's been talk amongst the neighbours of him on his deathbed," said Esau.

"Dear Lord in Heaven, let us pray the neighbours exaggerate," said Elizabeth.

"I will call in on the family later today... find out their situation and see what I can do to help," said Walt.

"Not before you have a cup of tea and something to eat after that journey. You cannot spend the rest of the day in the office on an empty stomach. Let us see what Mrs Kelly has made up for us, we don't want to waste her good food," said Elizabeth as the kettle started to boil on the gas stove in the scullery. "Now where's Dan got to? He hasn't wandered off already surely? "

Chapter 28

"Mam, you have a letter in the post. It came this morning after you left," said Edie. Her parents had just that minute returned home from Treharris and Rae was tired after spending the morning helping Mr Beynon serve his customers in the bakery. His young niece and Saturday help, normally very reliable, had not turned up to work. Ill with vomiting and diarrhoea her mother had sent her youngest with a message to the shop.

"Mam said it might be some meat she ate gone off in the heat and you won't want her here in the shop the state she is in. I am to fetch the doctor as she cannot keep anything down," said the young lad loudly in front of the shop full of customers. "Get on quick with you then bachgen," Mr Beynon had replied. "We can manage here. Can you give me a hand serving out front Rae?"

Under the circumstances she could not refuse but it had been a very busy day spent constantly on her feet and with her aching back.

"Pour me a cup and give the letter here," said Rae. "I need to take the weight off my feet after the morning I had helping Mr Beynon behind the counter. Now who is writing to me? This is very high quality this stationery. Feel the thickness of the paper. But I don't recognise the hand. Pass me a sharp knife to open this fancy envelope Edie."

"As long as it is not a demand for money," said Sam in jest.

"Quite the opposite it seems," she replied unfolding the letter inside to reveal a crisp white banknote folded in the page. "Someone is sending us money."

She passed the banknote to Sam as the entire family waited, eager to find out who was sending them money in the post.

Rae scanned down to the signature at the bottom. "It is from Nehemiah Thomas. Remember I told you about him? He is Mary's father who came here seeking news of her after she left with little Robbie. Now give me a minute to read what he has to say."

She took rather longer to read the untidy scrawl before passing the letter to Sam.

"You'll need your glasses to read the man's writing. He is sending us all money as a reward for our help girls. Mary and Robbie have turned up safe and well, returned to her family after all her troubles here. I knew that must be where she would go. He says he has recently learned that it was your father's sketch that helped the police identify the body of Hugh Brown and even the brothers are owed their share. Something about helping him in trouble up on the mountain track. I am surprised they did not mention it at the time. But there was a lot going on here."

"What a turn up for the books," said Sam after reading the letter himself. "Probably the one and only time any of my drawings will earn me money. Mary Brown's father must be well off to be so generous. It is good to hear news of her. She is safe and well where she belongs. We must share the news with the neighbours. Perhaps that will put an end to the gossip. Her story has a happy ending and there's an end to it. I cannot remember an event causing such a stir in the village. Not even the court case between our neighbours Maggie Prosser and Lydia Waters. Remember that? But I think we would be wise not to mention the reward money. Let's keep that within these four walls for now."

"It just goes to show girls. The Lord rewards those who keep his commandments," said Rae before taking a sip of tea. They looked at their mother puzzled. "Love thy neighbour…"

"But make sure you chose the ones with a wealthy family." Sam burst into laughter as he waved the banknote in the air. "We'll exchange this for some gold sovereigns when the bank opens on Monday Rae."

*

Later that evening Walt could be found in his study in Ty Gwent as usual. The children had been sent to bed and even Dan had disappeared upstairs with his siblings. Elizabeth was in the kitchen sorting through the unwashed laundry and creating two separate piles, one for the Hop Woo including linen shirts and cottons and another for her to see to on Monday which was wash day up and down the valley. While busy with her task she entertained Esau with stories of what they had seen and done during their stay at the hotel in Builth Wells.

Walt had spent the past hour in private while reading through the minutes of the lodge meeting last Monday, making notes for action, updating his personal diary and checking through a week's worth of post and sorting it according to priority. It was only when he finished his task that he remembered the envelope Miah had pressed on him that morning.

"Read it when you have a quiet moment," Miah had said. No time like the present, thought Walt. He fetched it from his jacket pocket in the hall and used his paper knife to break the seal. He removed a several sheets of paper covered both sides in Miah's untidy scrawl. Walt could only wonder what his friend might still have left unsaid in this whole sorry saga which must have taken him half the night to write.

My dear friend, Gwallt

 You have proved a true and trusted friend and mentor over the many years I have known you. I have witnessed first-hand your generosity and willingness to give help to those in need over recent weeks. You have always been a practical Christian putting into actions the teachings of our Lord. I was relieved that you and Elizabeth accepted my invitation to visit my home and meet my daughter and grandson. It was an act of forgiveness for which I will remain grateful.

 You will not be surprised to learn that I am in the process of applying to become my grandson's legal guardian and drawing up my will in his favour. Should anything untoward happen to me, or to dear Mary his mother, I do not want to leave either of them unprovided for. Thus, I hope I am preparing for his future more appropriately than my grandfather was able to do for me under the circumstances of the time.

 I regret that I never met the old man, my maternal grandfather, and daily thank the Lord for this unexpected gift in the form of my own grandson. I pray the good Lord will spare me long enough to prepare the boy for his future responsibilities and give him the best education and instruction in the Bible. It is one way I can atone for my neglect of his mother in pursuit of my own ambitions, no matter how worthy I deemed them to be at the time. Mary has paid dearly for my complacent neglect in not better providing for her future when she was a child. I should never have left the responsibility entirely to her grandmother.

I hope you will indulge me further by reading the remaining in confidence. Mary has made many errors of judgement in her brief life for want of better guidance from her parent. She has suffered greatly in consequence and not least from the shame of confession to those who care most for her, especially her grandmother whose love for her remains no less than that of any mother. I rashly agreed with my daughter that I would withhold certain facts not relevant to her immediate plight during your visit. It has laid heavily on my conscience and, now that you are safely home, I feel I can confide the full events that lead to her predicament and the suicide of Hugh Brown. You went to a great deal of time and trouble over the matter and your help proved invaluable in putting the matter to rest. I cannot leave you only partly informed of the circumstances leading up to these events and the resulting repercussions.

Hugh Brown is not the father of Mary's child and neither were they married. You, a man of the world, are no doubt shocked to hear it but this was a pretence they maintained for the sake of propriety. Hugh had a brother, Dennis, and it was he who courted Mary and was responsible for encouraging her to leave her home and family. He had dreams of seeking his fortune, first in the industrial towns where he hoped they could earn enough to add to their modest savings to afford a passage abroad to a new life and new opportunities.

Wherever Dennis went so went his brother Hugh and all three left their familiar surroundings towards an unknown future. The two young men found it difficult to find steady work and they lived an itinerant lifestyle for many months. They had to draw on their limited savings to survive when work was scarce. Dennis grew impatient trying to earn a legitimate living. He frequented inns and places of ill repute, took to gambling and other illicit *activities. Mary became disillusioned with her situation and disappointed in him. It led to many arguments between the couple and she made clear her wish to return to the security of home if he did not change his ways.*

One evening Dennis returned the worse for drink to find Mary alone in their meagre lodgings. A bitter argument ensued during which Dennis fell and cracked his head on the brass fender. He must have broken his skull and died instantly. When his brother, Hugh, returned from a shift labouring, he found Mary weeping over the body. Rather than inform the authorities and face a police enquiry, Hugh decided they should dispose of the body and move on. During the night Mary helped him move the body using a hand cart and they cast it down an old mine shaft. They were staying in Dowlais and the mountainside abounded with long disused shafts. It was not unheard of for the unwary to fall to their death down one of these. They did not return to the lodging house but fled the area the same night.

Mary tells me that Hugh forever blamed her for his brother's death although it was an accident. Dennis was very drunk and unsteady on his feet. He fell backwards when trying to rise from his seat. There were no other witnesses to the incident. She knew what they had done with his body was wrong but it was only later that she realised it was a criminal offence punishable with a prison sentence.

Mary already feared she was carrying Dennis child but had never revealed her suspicion to him being too naive to be certain. Ashamed of her condition, she could not return home to her grandmother. Robbie was born in Aberdare several months later. She had a difficult birth and both mother and child might have perished if not for the assistance of an elderly neighbour who was an experienced midwife.

Hugh was a different character to his brother and was prepared to work hard to provide for Mary and the baby. He found it difficult to find steady employment because of a speech impediment but he was a strong young man used to manual labour although the work was often short term. They left Aberdare when the neighbours became too interested in the welfare of the mother and child.

Strangers, as I have said, assumed Hugh and Mary to be husband and wife. Their relationship however was based on mutual guilt, the welfare of the child, need on Mary's part and suspicion on his.

He feared Mary would eventually find the courage or opportunity to leave taking Robbie with her and confessing to the crime they had committed. And we both know what happened when that opportunity arose.

Hugh Brown's death at his own hand was as much his fear of being sent to prison as remorse over his assault of Mary or myself. It is my belief a man as young and strong as he would have had little difficulty dispatching either of us if that had been his true intent.

So now you know the full truth of Mary's story and her many sins laid bare before you. I do not ask you to find it within you to forgive her. I am her father, however, and believe I share part of the guilt for the impetuous and foolish actions of her youth. She is full of remorse at the distress she caused by the thoughtless manner of her disappearance. Becoming a mother has changed her and I believe she is truly repentant.

Mary has never asked anything for herself only for her innocent child. I am more than willing to provide her with a home and a respectable position even though she regards herself as no longer worthy to be recognised as my daughter. My grandson, no matter the circumstances of his birth, is innocent of the sins of his parents and his very existence has already brought me great joy and hope for the future.

Your concern in this has always been for me as a long-standing friend and for my reputation and standing in the church. You need not fear on my account. I have been to the police regarding the circumstances surrounding the death of Dennis Brown. Mary has recounted the events to the most senior County police officers and, with little chance of recovering a body, they have chosen not to investigate further. Even if they could locate the particular shaft into which the body was cast, the cost of recovering his remains given the depth of many of the shafts and that it could also be flooded is prohibitive. It had been Hugh Brown's idea to conceal his brother's body using Mary as an accomplice. Without his knowledge of the whereabouts of the mine shaft the police are unwilling to proceed with the matter further other than keeping the report on record. Mary has been fined for failing to register the birth of her child and I have had to obtain a birth certificate retrospectively. Illegitimacy has no bearing on his eventually inheriting my wealth as the estate is not entailed. My grandfather earned his wealth through his own hard work and investments and, like him, I have no illusion of grandeur or aspirations to be part of the gentry. I am able to leave my capitol to whomever I choose and who better an heir than my own grandson?

Throughout all of Mary's revelations I have prayed for strength and guidance with fellow trusted members of the church as indeed we have prayed together for a satisfactory outcome to these distressing events. It has been many years since I have held the responsibility of a pastoral role within the church. It is my skill as a financial advisor and student of the scriptures that God has called upon to further His work. I believe that, in these respects at least, I can continue to serve both Him and our church.

I have never had any intention to keep these matters secret but I trust your discretion how much you chose to confide with Elizabeth. Mary has felt uncomfortable under Elizabeth's scrutiny these last few days. Be it guilt or feminine intuition, she believes Elizabeth suspects there is more to her story than she was willing to confess. For the present my conscience is clear. Let us pray I will not live to regret these decisions. I have taken action to put right my negligence and Mary's foolish actions. Throughout I have sort guidance in prayer and the legal expertise of lawyers and the police. Shaming Mary to confess the full extent of her sins in public after all she has suffered seems unnecessarily cruel and heartless, although you may disagree and see it as part of the process of seeking forgiveness. We will have to agree to differ on this point, a situation you must oft experience in your negotiations with the colliery management.

Mary will live forever with the guilt of her part in both those untimely deaths.

'Be ye kind one to another, tender hearted, forgiving one another, even as God for Christ's sake hath forgiven you' - Ephesians 4:32

I hope to remain your loyal friend

Walt read over the letter and sat for several minutes in quiet contemplation. He folded the pages and placed them carefully at the bottom of the desk drawer. Its content was not a suitable topic for tomorrow, the Sabbath day, and he needed time to decide whether revealing all to Elizabeth would indeed be a wise decision.

THE END

GLOSSARY of terms: including Welsh words and local English vernacular

Chapter 1
- Noddfa - Welsh word for nest/refuge and a popular name for Welsh Baptist chapels
- Gwallt - Welsh form of Walter
- Bach - Welsh word for small; often used as a familiar address to children and younger people
- Ty Gwent - Gwent House named after one of the Welsh kingdoms encompassing much of the old county of Monmouthshire
- Chopsing – v to chops - locally a common term for idle talking; modern usage is to be cheeky or confrontational
- Bara brith – a currant/fruit loaf; literally 'mottled bread'. Traditional Welsh recipes involve soaking the fruit in tea overnight
- Fed - South Wales Miners Federation (SWMF) was the miners' union for the S Wales coalfield

Chapter 2
- Dwt – Welsh word meaning a very little person
- Cwtsh – Welsh word for hug. Can also mean a small space or to huddle as incwtch down. Often anglicised to cwtch
- Bachgen - Welsh for boy and used locally as a term of endearment for a little boy

Chapter 3
- Mabon - the bardic name of William Abraham (1842 -1922) MP for Aberdare and President of the SWMF

Chapter 4
- Heisht - local term meaning hush, be quiet or shut up depending how it is said
- This popular welsh nursery rhyme translates as 'Gee up little horse carrying us two, over the mountain to hunt nuts, water in the river and the stones are slippery, we both fall, well that's the trick'

Chapter 6
- Twti - local term meaning to kneel down
- Bat and catti - local term for a game of rounders

Chapter 7
- Gamanfa Ganu - singing festival of sacred hymns in chapel
- Eisteddfod - festival of literature, arts and music where participants compete for prizes, usually cash
- Cwm Rhondda: John Hughes 1905 called the original tune "Rhondda" but it was renamed "Cwm Rhondda" to avoid confusion with another tune of the same name. Often referred to as "Bread of Heaven"
- Gwahoddiad – Invitation. Written in 1872 by the American minister Lewis Hartsough and known originally by its first line "I hear your welcome voice". After translating into Welsh it went 'viral' and is a favourite still in the repertoire of traditional male voice choirs. *Lord, here I am at thy call, Wash my spirit in the blood which flowed on Calvary*
- Dafydd y Garreg Wen - traditional welsh song   *David of the White Rock*
- Clychau Aberdyfi - traditional welsh song   *Bells of Aberdovey*
- Ar Hyd y Nos - traditional welsh song *All through the night*

Chapter 13
- Ych-a-fi - Welsh expression of disgust similar to 'yuck'
- Cariad - Welsh word for darling; term of endearment
- Ty bach - Welsh literally 'little house'; euphemism for the lavatory
- Butty or butti - slang for friend
- Tamping - local word for angry

Chapter 16
- Twp – local word for silly or stupid

Chapter 17
- Sam Siop – Sam shop. Nicknames were common at the time and often used to distinguish between people who shared popular forenames. Many were based on occupations, towns of origin, distinguishing features etc.

Chapter 18
- Band of Hope - Popular temperance group aimed at children held in churches and chapels throughout the UK
- Black pats – local word for cockroaches

Chapter 19
- To clec - to tell tales; from the Welsh verb clecan -to gossip

Chapter 20
- Rechabites - A friendly society founded in 1835 along temperance grounds and still active as a financial institution

Chapter 23
- Ty mawr - Welsh for big house and commonly used for the local manor house

Chapter 24
- Y Genedl – The Nation, was a weekly Welsh language newspaper containing general news and information

About the author

Cari Glyn is the pen name of Jen Pritchard. Jen was born in Bargoed and has many happy childhood memories growing up in the local community before the pit finally closed. After completing A levels in Heolddu Comprehensive School, she left home to study at University College, Cardiff and went on to complete a Ph.D. in Zoology.

After a 30-year career in education, Jen recently retired and returned to live in south Wales. She has used her research into local and family history online and the local newspaper archives to write this first novel based in the Rhymney Valley.

'Give Me Strength' is also available to download as a digital e-book from Amazon.

If you have enjoyed reading this book, please consider leaving a review on the Amazon website. Every author welcomes feedback from their readers.

You can also contact and follow the author via Facebook @cariglynauthor for news of current and possible future projects.

Published by
www.publishandprint.co.uk

Printed in Great Britain
by Amazon